Right and Left Grand

A Darla King Novel

By Rosalee Richland

Right and Left Grand

A Darla King Novel
By Rosalee Richland

Published by Wordsmiths4u
P.O. Box 3864
Bryan, TX 77805-3864

ISBN-10: 0985012927
ISBN-13: 978-0985012922

Published: October 2012
Revised: October 2014

The eBook version of *Right and Left Grand* is available online from most booksellers. Discover other titles by Rosalee Richland at: http://rosaleerichland.blogspot.com/ or find Rosalee Richland on Facebook®.

Dedication

This book is dedicated to the warm and welcoming community of square dancers worldwide.

Acknowledgments

Thanks to so many people who have encouraged the writing, completion, and publication of this book. Special thanks to folks in the Sam Houston Square and Round Dance Association, Circle Squares Dance Club, and Brazos Writers. And, of course, to friends and family, who make it both easier and all worthwhile.

Author's Note

While Houston, Dallas, and other cities in Texas are certainly real, Clearton and Isquith and other locations in Right and Left Grand are completely fictional. So are the characters and the plot. Square dancers are a warm and welcoming bunch, just like they are portrayed in this book. But the individual characters are totally the figments of author imagination.

Hopefully you enjoy meeting Darla King and her friends. This story is the first of Darla's chronicles, so look for upcoming books to let you keep up with the crew. Load the Boat continues the saga. The third in the series is Follow Your Neighbor.

NOTE: October 7, 2014 edition

Chapter 1

I'd gone over the dance movement a half a dozen times but four people still hadn't caught on. Each time, twenty-four people moved smoothly and quickly through the dance. Eight stumbled and stopped.

"Okay, let's try it this way," I said patiently. "Reach out there and shake hands with the person across from you. Then pull yourself on past them and to the other side. When you get there, do the Courtesy Turn we learned last week. A Right and Left Thru movement is a combination move. Pull thru then turn. We've already learned Right and Left Grand. This is different. With Right and Left Grand you continue moving forward. With Right and Left Thru, you stop after one pull thru and then turn."

The music started up and I went over it a few more times until I figured the repetition was driving everyone more than a little crazy. In square dancing, each square is made up of four sets of partners for eight dancers total. This night we had four squares dancing for a total of thirty-two dancers. One of the students was frustrated with the other new dancers in his square, including his wife. Unfortunately he was not very subtle or quiet about it. It was a given that some new dancers take a little longer to learn the steps than others. Unfortunately, it was also a given that some think they have it all figured out. Often they are wrong.

Square dancers come in all shapes and sizes, all ages, and with varying capacities for patience. Tonight one of the better dancers, Doug, wasn't here. With his patience and mild manners, he would have been a great help with the newbies. Tonight anything would have been a help.

Lord knows I'd taught a Right and Left Thru to dozens of dancers in the past few years. Tonight I tried all my tricks and jokes to no avail. Some of them just weren't going to learn it this session. They all seemed to get the Right and Left Grand

and the Courtesy Turn okay, but somehow there were still a few who just weren't hearing the difference between 'Grand' and 'Thru.' Rather than frustrate all of us, I decided not to push it. There was always next time.

I reviewed moves they had already learned and changed up the combinations to challenge them a little without trying their patience or mine. It was important for us all to remember that square dancing was just supposed to be fun. The remainder of the night went better. All in all, I felt pretty positive by the time we let out at ten o'clock.

I ended by calling a full-circle Right and Left Grand. All the dancers formed a big circle, and good-nights were shared as the ladies moved clockwise to take the right hand of one man and the left of the next, while the men moved counterclockwise doing the same. The large open space of the Clearton Presbyterian Church fellowship hall, where the Clearton Square Dance Club met on a regular basis, provided lots of space. Dancers didn't feel cramped even though the circle expanded almost to the walls. Several dancers dodged folding chairs as they progressed around the circle.

My name is Darla King and I'm a square dance caller. The caller is the person who directs the dance and provides the choreography so that all dancers are more or less doing the same thing at the same time. I also teach square dancing. Not too many women have thrown their hats into the caller ring, so I find I don't get stereotyped often. No one knows what to expect of a square dance caller, much less a female one. I like it that way. I was never one to fit into a mold. I became a caller after getting burned out investigating the dark side of life as a criminal investigator for the Florida State Attorney's Office. I hadn't fit into that mold either. But at least square dancing put me in contact with friendly, social people just having good clean fun. It is low on excitement, but high on positive feelings. Besides, dancing is good exercise! The occasional dancer might be rude or inconsiderate, or even sometimes outright inappropriately dressed, but generally square dancing is a positive experience.

"Darla, you did a great job tonight," offered Carlotta, as she walked up to me. The twinkle in Carlotta's hazel eyes told me she recognized the tough time some of the students had, as well as my frustration. Carlotta Morris is my best friend. She's a little bitty thing, not more than five foot tall. She's been dancing quite a few years. Tonight she wore her red hair, apparently natural, fairly short. It stuck out in free form tufts all over her head. I never could really decide whether she intentionally arranged it that way or whether she had just given up on it and let it have free rein. Either way, I envied her. My chin-length highlighted bob never looked the way I wanted, no matter what I did or didn't do to it. I call it ash blond, but the ash is leaning more toward gray every day. I also call it straight, but it frequently contradicts me with uncontrollable contrary waves.

Carlotta wasn't one of the new dancers. She was here as what dancers call an 'angel.' She was here to help the student dancers catch on to dance moves. Carlotta was dressed in the traditional square dance garb. She sported a short full skirt, crinoline petticoats, and peasant blouse. True to form, everything was color coordinated down to the pettipants underneath. With her petite frame and curvy figure, the traditional garb fit her to a tee.

At one time, all square dancers wore the same style, but more and more the dress has become individualized. This change creates some conflicts and disagreements among dancers, particularly among the more traditionalist dancers and callers. Those who prefer the old-style petticoats and matching skirts and shirts don't see eye to eye with the more easy-going dancers who prefer a version of street clothes. Tonight I wore jeans and a western-style shirt. I find this to be more casual and comfortable than traditional outfits. I also like that pants de-emphasize the ample hips on my 40-plus figure. My sedentary lifestyle of late wasn't helping me keep my weight down any. Although square dancing is great exercise, calling certainly isn't. I probably need to join a health club, take up kick-boxing, yoga, or something else, but somehow I've just never gotten around to it.

"Thanks, Carlotta," I said in response to her comment. "It'll all work out. Sometimes, things just don't click the first time. So far, I've managed to get everyone through classes in the past!" I smiled to reassure myself as much as her. Relatively new to the caller and teacher role, 'so far' actually amounted to only three sets of classes. I didn't have a long history, but a history, and each class had several squares of new dancers.

"Course it will work out, Darla Darlin'," added Sam Conners. A rancher and square dancer for some 20-plus years, Sam walked up soon after Carlotta. A single widower, he and Carlotta often danced together. During lessons they split up and danced with students.

"You've gotten us through every class yet. You'll do it this time too," Sam continued. "I was surprised Doug wasn't here tonight, though. Carlotta, do you know if anybody heard from him?"

"No, at least I didn't. And that's strange. He'll usually call somebody in the club if he's not coming to lessons. He knows we count on him," Carlotta responded. Doug was another solo club member and, like Sam, a widower. Because most of the club came in couples, when I had first started calling for Clearton Squares I had dubbed those three friends – Sam, Carlotta, and Doug – the three musketeers. I'd known Doug the longest, but we'd all become good friends. Oftentimes now I was their fourth musketeer. I was surprised, and a little disappointed, that Doug hadn't been here tonight.

"I've got my cell phone right over there on the bench. I'll give him a whistle and let you know what I find out," Sam said. He walked toward the bench that was almost hidden by jackets, purses, umbrellas, and miscellaneous belongings. In the meantime, I set about packing up my CDs, CD player, laptop computer, speakers, and microphone. These days most callers use electronic music and so the equipment is lighter and less bulky than the vinyl records used in the past. Still, there are multiple pieces that need to be packed up and carted to the car, since I haven't graduated to technology newer than CDs.

A few dancers came up and asked me questions or said goodbye. Others, including most of the beginners, gathered their things and headed home. Several of the club members hung around to visit with each other, but the room cleared quickly. Carlotta helped clean up the leftover snacks and empty the ice water containers that were almost always present anywhere dances took place. In Clearton, the square dance club rented the church's fellowship hall every Tuesday night, so napkins, cups, paper plates, and water jugs got stored until the next week. Although I could have used the storage space for my equipment, I call for multiple clubs in different locations. I like to pack everything up and carry it with me so I can use it wherever I go.

Everything followed the usual routine at the end of a dance night. I closed the last case when I looked up to see Sam. He held his phone tightly to his ear, turned quickly and headed toward the door. When he saw me watching, he waved for me to follow him. I looked over to Carlotta. She'd seen the signal as well and we both headed for the door.

"…and are they still there?"

I heard the tail end of Sam's sentence as Carlotta and I entered the hallway. After a short pause, Sam continued, "Well, hell, man, you've had some excitement out there tonight. Want some company for a while? We're finished here and about to go home, but your place would be a lot more interesting. Okay, I'll be out in a little while and I'll see who else wants to come."

He snapped the phone shut. His pale blue eyes sparkled under the shock of white hair that fell across his forehead. Sam was mid-60s and had the wiry body that years of outdoor work gives ranchers. He was over 6 foot, and his slim build made him look even taller. Sam was one of those guys who knew everybody and was liked by all he knew. He was active, alert, and positive. His wit was as dry as his weathered skin and his mind was always searching for something to explore. His hair and appearance may have aged with him, but his spirit was definitely young. I only saw Sam mad once and that was in relation to someone who had abused an animal. He was usually calm and hard to rile.

"Doug's had a big night. When he started out to come into town for the dance, his headlights picked up something just off the road. He thought it might be one of his cows down, so he stopped to take care of it. Turned out it was a man. Out cold, but not dead. Just lying there in the ditch as far as I could understand. He did what he could for the man and called for the paramedics. So far he's had just about all the local emergency workers and law around his place. Apparently they're not thinking this was an accident but he couldn't tell me much as yet," Sam explained in a rush. His eyes held a twinkle. It was pretty obvious he was energized by the excitement.

"This is the most excitement we've had in Clearton since that judge got caught dipping his hand in the till. Or maybe when the mayor got caught with his administrator at that hotel," he laughed. "And both of those were nigh on to 20 years ago." He poked his head into the main room from the hallway and took a final look around. "Looks like everything is under control here, so let me give you a hand with that gear, Darla. We'll head out to Doug's place for some coffee. I can't wait to hear the whole story." He looked at Carlotta and me. "You both in?"

"Is Doug okay?" I asked, concerned.

"Sure," Carlotta answered at the same time.

Sam nodded an answer to my question and the three of us walked into the dance area. As he reached for one of my cases, his excitement was radiating and contagious. Carlotta grabbed her stuff and we all went out to the parking lot. Sam helped me load equipment into my car. Then he and Carlotta got into his car. Within minutes we left the empty parking lot behind and were caravanning toward Doug's ranch.

The drive out to Doug's ranch seemed even longer than its twenty-five miles of county road. Normally I might have taken the time to enjoy the peace and quiet, but tonight my mind reeled with unanswered questions. Somebody injured and on Doug's property? What was Doug's connection? Why were the police still there? If it wasn't an accident, what had happened? I remembered reading in the paper this morning about the curator of a museum who was killed in a burglary. I sighed as I reflected on how much violence there was in the world these days.

Doug was probably the last person I imagined being involved in anything violent. His background was in military intelligence and he was trained in military tactics. Neither of those was obvious in his current life. Now, as a civilian and rancher, he was a gentle and kind man. More than that, he was a highly ethical man who wouldn't hurt anyone or anything if he could help it.

My investigative training kicked my curiosity into high gear. My experience with the criminal element exaggerated all the negative possibilities in my mind. With little prompting, my imagination could concoct all sorts of malicious scenarios. My curiosity and I have a running battle, and admittedly my curiosity usually wins.

Doug's ranch wasn't far off the main road, but it wasn't exactly located on a main thoroughfare either. Doug's folks had died not long after he retired from the Air Force. About then Doug took over his family ranch. His family bred horses on the ranch for years. After one of his mares had to be put down, Doug sold many of the horses. He still had a number of them, but now he boarded other people's horses and helped train them. He also offered riding lessons to kids, and he ran a few cattle on one part of his land. He talked about getting involved with equine therapy in conjunction with one of the rehabilitation hospitals. This was a man who was warm and caring. He certainly wasn't someone I'd connect with acts of violence. It had to have been an accident.

Doug was in his mid-40s, same as me. He had that rugged, solid build of the stereotypical cowboy I found tough to resist. He wasn't exceptionally good looking, but he was definitely an attractive man. Doug's wife passed away before I met him. We'd met before I started calling, but over the past year we'd gotten closer and begun an off-and-on thing. Even in the off periods we kept in contact in my role as the club caller. We were pretty quiet about our relationship, such as it was. That was mostly because at least one of us, that would be me, wasn't sure where it was going or if it would amount to more than an occasional outing that didn't involve square dancing. I just wasn't ready for the pressure a spotlight on a public relationship would bring.

We'd gone to Houston to the rodeo and livestock show, gotten together for dinner, that sort of thing. It was hard to tell if this was going to develop into something romantic or what, especially with me so wishy-washy about any romance. So far, our dates had been few in number. Every time Doug tried to up the intensity, I withdrew in panic. Lately his kisses had lingered and the heat was definitely on the rise. Panic was just at the edge of my mind whenever we were alone together.

On the drive out to his place now, my impending panic was of a different sort. I cared a lot for him and I didn't want to think about the possibilities my imagination had conjured up on the ride. What if the intended victim of foul play was really Doug? Was he in danger? Did I know him as well as I thought?

I felt simultaneously relieved and apprehensive to see the 'Weathers Ranch' sign and the open gate marking our arrival. I turned in by the famous and quite distinctive patch of prickly pear that marked Doug's lane. Everyone in the county knew that looming bunch of cactus. It surrounded the gate and grew along the fence posts on either side.

Doug's ranch was small by Texas standards, only a couple of hundred acres. The main house was visible from the road, as were the remaining emergency vehicles and sheriff's car. Sam and Carlotta had dropped back, so I was in the lead. As I drove past the gate and down the drive, the lights from Sam's car were no longer visible behind me. I was struck by how dark the night had become. It suddenly didn't resonate with peacefulness anymore. I was glad when Sam's car turned down the drive behind me and provided a little more light. Backlit by the porch lights, a sheriff's deputy waved me over to the side fence as I approached the house.

"Ma'am, you can't be coming up here right now. We've had a little trouble here, and we're not letting anyone in," a very young officer remarked as he leaned into my open window. His attitude did not brook any argument, but I made an attempt anyway. Maybe I could talk him into it.

"Yes sir, officer, I heard about the trouble. But I'm here at the request of Doug Weathers, owner of this ranch. He called and asked us to come up," I explained, indicating Sam and Carlotta. I realized Doug hadn't actually called us. We'd called him but close enough. Innocent and necessary fabrication, I rationalized. Carlotta and Sam caught up with me by this time and walked up to my car. I noticed Carlotta had taken off her petticoats somewhere between the hall and here, but she still wore her dance dress. The ruffles made her look a little like Bo-Peep. The officer straightened up, faced Sam and Carlotta, and spoke loudly enough we could all hear him.

"Sorry, folks, I have my orders…" the deputy continued.

Sam stepped over to the deputy and extended his hand. Despite his good nature, Sam looked tough and gruff at first glance. Grumpy accompanied by Bo Peep, I thought, and smiled despite the situation. Come to think of it, I didn't look very impressive myself. I'm a dowdy forty-something with graying hair, a few extra pounds, and faded jeans. We were quite a crew.

"Officer, the lady explained why we're here. Can't you just check with whoever is in charge? I think they know we were coming," Sam started, with authority and insistence that more than matched the deputy's.

Before the officer could answer, Sam changed tactics and exchanged gruff for good-ole-boy charm without skipping a breath. "Well, now, aren't you one of Bob Reardon's boys? I'm Sam Conners. I've been knowing your dad quite a while. See what you can do for us, won't you, son? Mr. Weathers sure wanted us to come over." Somehow, along with the charm, Sam's Texas drawl and manner of speech slipped in there too.

Deputy Reardon knew when he'd been bested. He nodded, shrugged his shoulders, and turned toward the front door. He wasn't moving in any great hurry. I thought it was to make a point he wasn't kowtowing to us but no one made a big deal of it. He disappeared through the door and left us in silence.

I got out of the car and stood with Carlotta and Sam. It had been cool and rained earlier in the day but now the warm, muggy air felt more like summer than middle of September. I insisted on thinking of September as fall and expected cooler temperatures. This belief hadn't changed, despite the fact that I had lived in the south, first Florida and now Texas, for most of my adult life.

"Darla, this looks serious. Why do you think they're still here? Why won't they let us in? This doesn't look good!" Carlotta's face was serious and her eyes were wide. Both she and Sam seemed to expect me to know what was going on. I wondered whether if it was because they remembered my stint with the State Attorney's office. I'm generally a private person and I don't often talk much about that chapter in my life. It hadn't ended on an up note.

"Sometimes police assume the worst. Sam said Doug gave him the impression that they didn't seem to think this was an accident. It's hard to tell what they might be thinking. We really don't know what happened yet," I responded. I heard myself slip into an official tone of voice out of habit.

I knew all too well that some police officers were quick to jump to conclusions and always seemed to think, and from my experience hope for, the worst. The idea again occurred to me that Doug may have been the intended target and not whoever it was who had been injured. I remembered him telling me that he had gotten into some arguments with some of the locals who were against a camp he wanted to open for kids with disabilities. He wanted to start equine therapy at the camp, and the kids could ride his horses as part of the program. He had been one of the staunch supporters and the arguments at the town council meeting had apparently gotten heated. Surely not to the point of violence though, I thought.

Carlotta had been silent as long as she could. She runs on fast and faster, and now her staccato questions interrupted my thoughts. "Sam, did Doug mention anything about who the person was? How badly hurt they were? Hey, did he really want us to come out or did you invite yourself? Doug's a friend and all, but what can we do to help in this situation? We might just be in the way and make things more difficult for the authorities." She looked from me to Sam and back again. I don't know what she expected us to say, since she had as much information as we did – or as I did, anyway.

The same questions had occurred to me, although as far as I knew I was closer friends with Doug than either Carlotta or Sam realized. It certainly didn't look like we were just here for some coffee and dessert. Why did Doug want us to come out here, if it was his idea? Like Carlotta, I was beginning to wonder if Sam had overplayed his hand.

"I've known Doug a long time," Sam hedged. "He's been in the square dance club for about ten years. He and Lou both used to be regulars. They were officers for a while. Doug and I have been through a lot together. Lou and my wife passed about the same time. With everything he went through with his wife's illness and death, he's kinda kept to himself. Except for dancing, which I'm glad he's kept up with. I guess I may be one of his closest friends. Can't hurt to have a friend by your side if there's trouble, that's my way of thinking. I can't say for honest that he specifically asked you two to come out, but definitely me. I figured maybe he'd need a little support – and laughs for that matter." His face crinkled at the corners and he looked around. "I counted on these guys being long gone before we got here. I can't imagine why they are still here. Uh…we may not have to wonder much longer, here comes that Reardon boy again."

"Okay, folks, I talked to Sheriff Lorys, and he said you're to come on up to the house. He has some questions for you," Deputy Reardon explained, sounding a bit reluctant to me.

Deputy Reardon firmly took my elbow and guided me toward the house with a look to Carlotta and Sam that told them they'd better follow along. I'd been in Doug's house before and under other circumstances would have felt comfortable here. Now, I just tried to ignore the tension as I walked past, or more accurately, was propelled past, two more officers in the foyer and into the main living area. There Doug and two other men, one I recognized as Sheriff Lorys, stood or sat. Sheriff Lorys had made a special appearance to welcome dancers to one of the anniversary dances last year, or I wouldn't have known who he was. Well, maybe I would have, given he was in uniform. Even if I hadn't recognized him, I would have been able to figure out what his job was. I didn't know the other man at all. With Carlotta and Sam in the room, the officers from the foyer joined us. None of them looked particularly warm or friendly, but then I guessed that wasn't in their job descriptions.

This was looking more serious all the time. It was no longer a 'come in and have some coffee and cake' invitation. We had now been 'invited' to participate in the investigation, or, it seemed to me, it was like we were suspects in some unknown incident. And we didn't even know what was being investigated. Or why we would be asked questions.

As I looked around the room, my mind set off on one of its fanciful side trips. One of these days, my imagination and curiosity are sure to be my downfall. My mind took flight and I noticed that if you counted the official uniforms as club dance outfits, there were more than enough 'dancers' to stand in for the men in a dance square. Being short of men is often a problem at a square dance, but not with these uniforms surrounding us. With only Carlotta and me, we'd be short of women in this square. Some of these macho men might have to dance the 'ladies' part. I caught myself smiling at that absurd picture, straightened my facial expression, and refocused my attention on the reason we were here.

As we joined the group, Doug moved closer to me and took my hand. He extracted me from the deputy's grasp in the process and I rubbed at my elbow. He caught my eye but I couldn't tell what he was trying to communicate. I realized our budding relationship wasn't going to be secret much longer, if it ever was. I noticed Doug's face become less strained as Carlotta and Sam joined the group. I guess we really were welcome as a support group of sorts.

Both Sheriff Lorys and the other man continued to question Doug and wrote down Doug's responses to their questions as we entered the room. Sheriff Lorys was a hefty man. He was about six foot and carried about 20 extra pounds. He sported an old-fashioned sheriff's badge reminiscent of old Texas westerns. He wore khaki head to toe, except for his black boots and ivory felt hat. He definitely had a case of 'hat hair' with the ghost of a rim in his white hair when he tipped his hat to Carlotta and me.

The other man who asked the questions was dressed in a suit. He wasn't wearing a badge or holster, or at least not one I could see. I couldn't readily determine who he was connected with or what his role was. He reminded me of the type in the movies who looked important and only talked to those with a 'need to know.' He was a little shorter than Sheriff Lorys, much better dressed, and obviously worked out regularly. I imagined he turned a lot of ladies' heads. I wasn't looking, but if I was, I would certainly consider him attractive. I visualized his six-pack abs even though he was probably in his 40s. He was tanned, so he must spend time outside, I thought. He had sandy brown hair and blue eyes that seemed ominously deep.

It occurred to me that he probably broke a heart for every head he turned. His manner struck me as stiff, abrupt, and unbending, not romantic or approachable, or well, southern. His aloof manner and aura of dark mystery put me off some. At the same time it added to his allure and piqued my curiosity. It was kinda sexy. He didn't smile and seemed to bark his questions at Doug. Some were the same questions Sheriff Lorys asked, but he was obviously not pleased with some of Doug's "I don't know" answers. For that matter, regardless of the questions, he wasn't satisfied with the answers that he got.

He gave the impression that people should give him what he wanted. Definitely could use an attitude adjustment.

Showing more southernly manners, the sheriff stood when he realized we were in the living room. The suited man was already standing, and he hardly spared a glance at us. Although not exactly short at 5 foot 8 inches, I felt very small next to all of these men. They were of an average height of over 6 foot with the girth to match. Carlotta was positively dwarfed by them. Introductions were made all around. The suited notetaker turned out to be named Paul Harbinville, but nobody offered any identifying information about him. I guessed we didn't have a need to know.

As I smiled in polite response to introductions, it occurred to me that this was definitely not a simple matter. I began to wonder seriously about the status of the person Doug had found. Was it someone famous? Someone important? We didn't even know if he was still alive. Did they suspect Doug of something? Or, as I imagined earlier, did they suspect Doug was the intended target? I obviously had more questions than answers.

"Folks, we've been talking to Doug about this situation here," Sheriff Lorys began. "I gather you know that Doug found someone down off the side of the road. That person was taken to the hospital but we haven't got much information on him. We're still waiting on an ID. He didn't have a wallet on him. Doug said he didn't know who he was." The sheriff's tone implied he didn't know whether to believe Doug or not, but he continued without saying it. "He seems to think he might have seen this man before, maybe at some dance. He's tried to explain the costumes you dancers wear. Apparently this man was wearing one that indicated he was from Fort Worth." This last comment came with some degree of dismissal and a puzzled look at Carlotta's Bo-Peep dress. "Anyway, he said you folks go to dances all over the state and beyond, so that if this man was a square dancer, then one of you might be able to help us out."

"Doug, did the man have on a club shirt? What club?" The same question was on my lips but Sam stepped in before I had a chance to ask.

"Looked like a Stepping Square's shirt to me," Doug said. "Remember when we were in Dallas at the dance last February? I danced a few squares with folks from the Fort Worth Stepping Squares. I'm pretty sure the club shirt had a pair of boots embroidered on the yoke. I didn't think about it 'til after they took the guy off in the ambulance, so I didn't get a good look at it. I think maybe that's what he was wearing. Darla?"

Every face in the room, except for Paul Harbinville's, looked my way. Harbinville was preoccupied with his notes. I had no idea whether he knew I called dances all around the state and was familiar with a lot of the clubs and club dress choices. Each club has its own distinctive club dress that the members wear on special occasions. The 'costumes' the sheriff referred to were nothing more than coordinated dresses and shirts that identify the home club of a dancer. Even with different styles, short skirts or prairie skirts for the women, for example, or bolo ties or ascots for the men, the fabric pattern would be the same. In some ways, club costumes or outfits were sort of like gang colors, but without the negative connotation. I thought about the Fort Worth clubs and pictured their chosen styles.

"That's right," I answered Doug. "The Stepping Squares club outfit is blue and green. The women's blouses and men's shirts both have an embroidered pair of boots near the collar." I started out talking to Doug but now I turned my attention to Lorys to explain. He was looking understandably skeptical of the whole club outfit ID scheme, but he listened.

"It looks a lot like the Bayou Belles and Beaus in Houston, though, so even if it is a club shirt we'll need to make sure. The Belles and Beaus wear similar colors and the emblem is the same size, but it's a pair of dancers instead of boots." As I added this I could tell that neither Harbinville nor Lorys were particularly impressed, but they were at least being polite.

"Well, it's not much but right now it's about all we have to go on," muttered Lorys. "If you can give us some contacts in the Fort Worth and Houston groups we'll check it out." He turned to Doug. "Anything else you want to add, Mr. Weathers?"

Talked out, Doug just shook his head. After a manly ritual of shaking hands with everyone, Lorys, Harbinville, and the rest of the officers left the house. We could hear them continuing to talk and look around outside. I figured they'd be out there looking around for some time to come.

While I felt a bit apprehensive about the situation, Carlotta's petite frame fairly vibrated with repressed curiosity. Her normally high energy level was barely contained and her spiked red hair seemed to be shooting sparks off the top of her head. Sam wasn't much better, but he hid it pretty well behind a wry grin. Carlotta beat him to the punch. She barely waited until the men were out of earshot before she started in on Doug.

"So, tell all, tell all! What happened? How did you find him? Who do you think it is? Who did it?" she asked all in a rush.

Still standing, Doug took a deep breath and put up his hand. He reverted to his role of host and offered us drinks. We gratefully accepted after our exertion at the dance and our pent-up anxiety. Sam took a beer and the rest of us settled for ice water. When Doug returned from the kitchen, he handed out the drinks and only then took a seat on the couch next to me.

As Doug went through the story, it was apparent he'd told it several times before. He was leaving for the dance and driving down the lane. He noticed something on the left side and was concerned that one of the cows might have wandered from the pasture. He explained he had some recent trouble with fences being down, probably from the storm the other night. Thinking the form might be a cow, he had stopped, gotten out, and found a man instead. He had tried to roust the man, but couldn't. Doug could tell he had obviously been beaten up pretty good. He didn't want to move him, not being sure of his injuries. So he called 9-1-1 and reported the injured man.

Paramedics, fire department, and the sheriff's department had shown up. He explained that the ambulance took the man away and the fire department left, but then Harbinville showed up. A scowl passed his face when he mentioned Harbinville and it was obvious they had not hit it off. Both too used to being in charge, I figured, but it might be something else. Doug went on to say they asked questions and wanted to check out his cars, fences, and just about everything else. They wanted to know if Doug had any enemies, any valuables on site. He had no clue what the man was doing on his property, who he was, or how he got there. He kept telling them that, but he felt they didn't believe him. At least not at first, or the next ten times they asked.

He sighed again and his fatigue was obvious. I felt an urge to put my arms around him, but I wasn't sure how he'd respond. He didn't make any moves other than to take my hand, so I just gave his hand a little squeeze. Funny how when you think someone might be in danger of some sort, you realize how much you actually do care about them. My conflicted feelings aside, we all got down to the topic at hand and talked until long after the searchers outside called it quits.

When we'd covered the same verbal ground for the umpteenth time, we called it a night. Doug looked tired, but a little less tense than when we'd arrived. I gave him a hug as we all moved toward the cars to head out. It felt good to be in his arms and I hoped he wasn't in any danger. There were actually hugs all around, but his hug lingered somewhat. Perhaps his embrace would have lasted longer if Sam and Carlotta weren't part of the equation.

In my car outside Doug's place I reached for my phone to call home. I caught myself after I punched speed dial and remembered there was no longer a need to call. I snapped the phone shut before it made the connection. My daughter, Heather, wasn't home. I was conditioned to checking in with her to tell her my plans. It was still hard to remember that she'd been away at college for about a month in her second year at The University of Texas. Even if she had been home, she probably wouldn't have noticed if I didn't call. She's much more carefree than I am. I hadn't broken the habit of thinking I needed to let her know if I wasn't coming home on time. I was usually home before she was. I tucked the phone in my purse.

Carlotta got out of Sam's car and ran up to my driver's side window.

"Hey, Darla, it occurred to me that it's really late. You want to stay at my place tonight instead of driving back to Isquith? If so, Sam can go on to his house, but we'll need to swing by to pick up my car on the way to my place," she offered.

It sounded good, and I took her up on it. She waved off Sam, who waved his hand out the window as he headed down the drive. He turned right at the main road, and we turned left to head back to the church to pick up her car. Then I would follow her to her house.

I live about two and a half hours east of Clearton in a little town called Isquith. Most times I drive back and forth on dance night. It's a long drive, but calling was my only job these days. I didn't even have to be a full-time mom. I could sleep late in the morning and the traffic was generally pretty light that late at night. Usually I would be home by this time, but when we left Doug's place it was late enough that I was grateful for Carlotta's offer.

I was tired and felt drained. I'd wanted to get a chance to talk to Doug alone, but it hadn't worked out. Although we've dated, more often we meet at a dance somewhere, like Austin or Houston. As a couple, we haven't progressed much past the initial stages. Something always seemed to come up for one of us. I didn't ask to stay over at his place, and he hadn't suggested it either. Probably a good thing. What with my concern for him, my decision-making on matters of intimacy might not have been the best.

Once we got to town, it didn't take long to run by the church and then to Carlotta's. She lived alone in a one-bedroom townhouse in a newer section of Clearton. It was decorated in bright colors that I found a little loud, but they reflected her effervescent personality. It was located in the more recently developed section of Clearton rather than the rural section where Doug lived. Carlotta's townhouse was small and her living room doubled as a guest room. I opened the couch into a bed while Carlotta went to get sheets. There was no chance that Carlotta's tiny clothes would fit me, but she managed to find an oversized tee-shirt for me to sleep in.

"So, Darla, had any good dates lately?" she asked as she handed me the tee.

"Not any good ones, or any bad ones either, for that matter." I responded casually, trying to be noncommittal through humor.

"Come on Darla! I saw the way you and Doug acted. And holding hands?" she teased.

"Well, we've been out a few times, but … oh, you never can tell. I am worried about him though." To change the direction of the conversation, I asked, "How about you? You have a dance partner lined up for the Dallas Hoedown coming up?"

"Nope," she said. "No dance partner, and before you ask, no dates either. I'm dancing solo this year. Karen's feeling better so Rick doesn't need a partner." Karen and Rick were long-time members of Clearton Squares. Karen hadn't been dancing since she had surgery a few weeks ago, so Rick had been available as a dance partner for solo dancers like Carlotta or me.

In square dancing, 'solo' doesn't always mean unmarried. Square dance is an acquired taste, and sometimes only one spouse acquires it. In other cases, one member of a couple may experience health problems that keep him or her from dancing, as with Karen. Or one may travel extensively for work and not be able to make the dances. For whatever reason, some solo dancers are not single people just single dancers. Now that

Karen was on the floor again, Rick couldn't be considered a solo dancer anymore.

"Well, you never end up sitting out many dances when you go solo," I reassured her. "I imagine you won't sit many out this time either."

"I hope not! Sam will probably be available once in a while. On the other hand, he's in high demand by all the solo ladies. Hopefully Doug will be there, and who knows who else." Although Carlotta danced a lot with Sam, she and he were not a couple. At regional or state dances, he was quite the popular partner and considered quite a catch.

Square dance clubs struggle with the demographics of today's population. For many years, clubs were made up of couples only. In fact, single dancers presented a logistic and social quandary. In some communities, clubs formed specifically for solo dancers who felt shut out from couples clubs. Solo women dancers seemed to out-number solo men. This is especially true at a dance venue where the callers tend to be men and their wives or girlfriends become solo dancers while their husbands call the dance. Unless they've arranged for a partner for an entire event, solo dancers have to secure partners for each dance tip. Dance planners don't always factor in solo dancers or give them time to line up dancing partners between dances.

It's a balancing act, and solo dancers are still finding their way in the square dance community, with some clubs more receptive than others. Some solo dancers wear badges or tags identifying themselves as solo. The tag helps dancers identify who to ask to dance without getting someone's wife (or husband, I suppose) irritated. At a time when so many different opportunities for entertainment are available, square dance club memberships are dwindling in some communities. An increasing percentage of single adults in the population means that dance clubs can't afford to limit membership, so most clubs welcome both couples and solo dancers. Only the most conservative clubs continue to enforce the 'married and both dancing' restrictions these days. Luckily for square dancing, the current generation of teen dancers seems to embrace the pastime.

"You'll do fine," I said.

"You're right," she responded with a smile. "Dates or not, it's the dancing I enjoy. I generally manage to dance nearly every tip so I imagine I'll get my fill at the Hoedown. And don't think you're getting off the hook so easy. I want to hear all about you and Doug!" We chatted a while, but not a lot longer. My relationship with Doug hadn't progressed much, so there really wasn't much to talk about. Besides, we were both pretty well exhausted. Eventually we couldn't fight off the sandman any longer.

When I woke up the next morning, I brushed my teeth with a washcloth. One of these days, I would get around to packing an emergency overnight case for times like this. Luckily I carried a change of clothes with me when I traveled out of town, so I could put on clean underwear and a fresh shirt. I didn't bother with clean jeans but just pulled on the ones I'd worn the night before. They weren't that dirty.

Carlotta rose early, talked a lot about the night before, and then left me to my own devices when she went to work. I wondered just where Carlotta found all her energy. I surely wouldn't have been able to get up and go to work that cheerfully with just a few hours of sleep. Although I considered her my best friend and we tended to hang out together at square dances, I had only known her a couple of years and really didn't know much about her personal life. She had on occasion lamented the shortage of males in the small population of Clearton. Doug and Sam were about the only two around as far as I could tell. While they were all good friends, it was clear that she didn't have a romantic interest in either of them. Once she made reference to an ex-husband, but she hadn't elaborated and I hadn't pursued the matter. Her bubbly demeanor had slipped and it was obvious she didn't want to share. We always seemed to have better things to talk about.

Besides, I'm the club caller, not the resident matchmaker. Although by nature I'm curious, I usually tried to keep it at a level below busybody. Even though I was curious to the point of being nosy on puzzling events like the attack at Doug's ranch, I tended to shy away from asking questions about people's personal lives. It wasn't any of my business and if I wanted to keep my personal life private, I couldn't expect otherwise from anybody else.

Chapter 2

I pushed in the doorknob lock on Carlotta's townhouse behind me, checked to make sure it caught, and was on my way. The morning sun glared on the windshield as I drove to the sheriff's office. I'd been calling in Clearton for about a year now, and it was a small enough town that I didn't have any trouble finding my way. With about 15,000 people, there were enough services for the town to sustain itself, but no major mall. Most of the people who live in Clearton either worked in the local small businesses, the medical center, the school district, or commuted to Austin about 50 miles to the west.

As Austin continued to grow and spill over to the outlying areas, Clearton was growing at a slow but steady pace. Although Austin wasn't exactly a short commute, Clearton's sense of community, lower prices, and lower crime rate seemed to make the hour or so in the car worth it for more and more folks these days. The newer part of town where Carlotta lived had modern townhouses and large ranch-style homes. The houses there were too close together for the more traditional ranchers, but it was perfect for those who wanted to get out of the city. This newer part of town was connected to sprawling old large ranches like Doug's by the main street, which turned into rural road not far from the center of town.

As I made the short drive from Carlotta's townhome to the sheriff's office, I noticed that some of the trees showed hints of changing color. This was a reminder that fall really was a season, even in Texas. The touch of gold amidst the green was striking. As is the case in so many small towns in Texas, the growth of the community hadn't completely compromised the natural beauty of the landscape. Even on the main thoroughfare, there was a green strip down the middle of the road with crepe myrtles already past bloom, petals speckling the stripe of green grass. The presence of the occasional tree and greenway gave at least the illusion of open space. Open space was something I valued with my tendency to be a little claustrophobic. The old main street still retained the stereotypical 'western' look with some of the original building storefronts in the downtown area. The sheriff's office was one of these.

Because I knew most of the dance clubs in the area Doug, Carlotta, and Sam had decided I was the logical person to check whether the victim was wearing a club shirt. If so I would give Lorys all the contact information I kept on dance groups. It helped that I was also the one who didn't have a day job or animals to feed. Given my natural curiosity, it didn't take much to get me to agree. I had promised to let them know anything I found out. I pulled up to the sheriff's office and headed inside.

"Good morning, ma'am. Can I help you?" The deputy at the desk wasn't any older than the Reardon deputy from last night, and was so fresh-faced and fit I felt old immediately.

"Sheriff Lorys asked me to stop by to look at some clothes and drop off information on the man you found last night," I replied.

"Oh, yes ma'am. You must be from that square dance group. The sheriff said to go ahead and take your statement when you came by, but I don't think we'll need it anymore," he added.

"What do you mean? Did the man wake up?" I asked. I avoided thinking the opposite, that he wouldn't be waking up ever again.

"Well, no, he hasn't yet. Leastwise, as far as I know. But we found what we think is his vehicle up the road a ways. We've had a couple of car-jackings in the county lately, so we get notified about any stolen or abandoned cars in the area. One was involved in a collision last night and it looks like it might belong to the victim," the deputy explained.

"How do you know?" I asked.

The young man smiled, but he didn't answer my question. "Well, ma'am, we'll find out more later on. But right now I'd better get back to what you came for. You wanted to leave some information for us?"

"Yes, but I will have to look at the victim's shirt first." I saw a glimmer of resistance on the deputy's face. I realized I'd phrased my words poorly, more like the state investigator persona of my past than a simple citizen and lowly square dance caller. My curiosity was aroused and I didn't want to miss this opportunity so I softened my tone. "That is, Sheriff Lorys asked me to look at it. Even if you know the victim's identification, it may be a while before he regains consciousness, if at all. This way the sheriff thought you could go ahead with the investigation without waiting." Again a little fabrication or elaboration, another thing left over from my prior life.

I saw the gears turn behind his eyes and then he nodded as he gave in to the logic of what I'd said. I followed him to a cabinet at the rear of the room and he pulled out a bag of a laundry in a hospital pillowcase. He dumped it on the counter. Not the best of forensic procedures, but then I was used to the rigorous requirements of state law offices.

"What do you need to see?" he asked.

"Probably just the shirt, but I'm not sure." I pawed gingerly through the clothes, pulled out the blue and green shirt, and held it up by the shoulders. Doug was right. The emblem on the yoke belonged to the Stepping Squares. I put the shirt aside and rooted through the remaining clothes. When I saw the briefs, I wished that I'd asked for latex gloves before I handled the clothes. Oh well, it was a little too late to worry now. I avoided the briefs and tugged on a small towel in the pile. It came out attached to the belt loop of the jeans and had square dancers embossed on it. It was rumpled, but clean.

"This man's a square dancer all right," I told the deputy. "The shirt has the emblem we discussed with the sheriff, and this towel hooked to his pants is a sort of dancer's sweat band, so to speak. It's clean, so he must have been on his way to a dance rather than coming from one. The shirt shows he's part of a group in Fort Worth. I can give you the contact information for the club."

While I gave him the information I had looked up on Carlotta's computer and brought with me, I tried to pull more out of him about the car they'd found, but with no luck. He'd obviously told me as much as he thought he should. I figured Lorys might be willing to tell me more, so I asked when the sheriff would be back. When the deputy told me it would likely be after lunch, I considered coming back to see if I could find out more. I left the office and moved the car down a few blocks to Clearton's town café. I didn't want to leave it parked in front of the sheriff's office while I went in for a cup of coffee.

I needed to get home, but felt I was leaving something unfinished. I had no reason to be involved in the situation any longer. I had identified the club from the shirt. But now that I'd been drawn in I wanted to find out at least a little more. Like a dog with a scent, I just couldn't leave it alone.

The minute I went inside, I was reminded again why I like small town cafés so much. I breathed in the homey aroma of bacon, biscuits and gravy, coffee, and donuts. The familiarity of the Norman Rockwell groupings around well-worn tables gave me a sense of refuge in a changing world. I figured the tantalizing smell of bacon probably raised my cholesterol without even having to eat it. Mostly older men, retired or maybe farmers and ranchers, with a few women and children thrown into the mix, chatted leisurely. One waitress circled the room with a pot of coffee and another wiped up a spill on the cashier stand.

I didn't know many folks in Clearton other than members of the dance group and I didn't see any of them here. Conversation hiccupped when I walked in and every face turned in my direction. When they realized they didn't know me, most people turned away again and took up where they'd left off. A few looks lingered a little longer, maybe trying to figure out if they should know me or decide why a stranger was stopping in. The waitress at the cashier stand welcomed me.

"Mornin', honey. Be right with you." Her name tag identified her as Sadie. She was middle-aged, round on her edges, probably the result of the donuts and bacon, and friendly enough.

I told her I'd be right back and, thinking about the clothes I'd just handled, headed for the ladies' room hoping I'd find soap there. When I returned, she had finished cleaning up and exchanged the rag for a menu from under the countertop. Without a word she led me to a table next to the wall, and snagged a coffee pot on our way. She didn't ask if I wanted coffee, just poured it up to the top of the waiting cup.

"Be back in a minute for your order, honey. Get you anything else right now?"

I assured her I was fine and she took off. I doctored up the coffee with as much cream as the cup would hold and took a sip. Even with the cream, it was hot and strong enough to make an impression.

"So what brings you to Clearton? We don't see many strangers in here ya know," Sadie asked when she returned to my table. She balanced the coffee pot precariously and prepared to take my order.

"I'm the caller for the local square dance club. I stayed over last night rather than driving home," I offered.

"Oh, so you must know Sam? He is just the best man. He would do about anything for anybody. He keeps trying to get me and my husband to come learn to square dance, but Jeb just isn't interested, ya know what I mean? Sam and his wife used to come in here pretty regular before the dancing, but now… I guess Sam just goes straight to the dances," she rambled.

"Oh, yes, I know Sam. And yes, he is definitely someone very special. I don't usually pass through town when I come in, but I may have to make a point to stop here," I responded, gesturing around me and turning my attention to my coffee.

"So did you want any biscuits or such this morning, or just the coffee?" she asked.

"Just coffee for now, thanks Sadie," I answered.

As I sipped at the coffee, I tried to figure out what my next step should be. Should I call Carlotta, Sam, or Doug to let them know what I'd confirmed at the sheriff's office? Carlotta was advertising director at Clearton's weekly newspaper. She was enthusiastic and dedicated to her job. Some people would say she was a workaholic. I hated to disturb her at work, and I figured tonight would be plenty of time to catch her up. After all, I hadn't learned much. But I did want to talk to someone before I left town, if for no other reason than to get it out of my system.

If Doug wasn't out with the horses, I figured I could catch him on the phone. With what I knew of Sam, he might be over at Doug's and I could reach both of them with one phone call. Part of me was a little hesitant to call. I was afraid it assumed too much about our friendship or implied too much about our relationship to Doug. But I wanted to fulfill my promise to keep them updated. I also wanted to see what they knew about the car-jackings the deputy had mentioned. I pulled out my phone and dialed Doug's number.

"Weather's ranch." Doug's greeting sounded both business-like and tired.

"Hi, Doug. Darla, here. Any more excitement over there this morning?"

"Hey, Darla. Sam and I were wondering when we would hear from you. That Harbinville fella came by again, but his vocabulary seems limited to 'uh huh,' 'hmmm,' and asking questions we don't know the answers to. Not exactly an enlightening or helpful guy. Asked all sorts of questions. He even asked about you. And what about you? Did you see the sheriff?" Doug asked.

What had Harbinville asked about me, I wondered. Certainly he had no reason to think I had any part in the events of the night.

"I had a similarly enlightening talk with the deputy. But he let it slip that they found a car they think might have belonged to the guy. They seem to think it was a car-jacking. Mentioned something about a string of car-jackings – does that sound right? Either you or Sam know anything about that? It certainly hasn't lit up the news as far as I can tell."

Even as I said it, I realized that come to think of it, I didn't remember hearing of any car-jackings in the past couple of months. Granted, I lived a distance away, but I was down in Clearton every week and 'local' news usually covered the whole county. Not to mention that between tips square dancers generally chit-chatted and gossiped with the best of them. A car-jacking in Clearton would have been big news.

"Nah, I don't remember hearing about that. Sam is chomping at the bit to find out if you were able to ID the club shirt. Was it Stepping Squares or Belles and Beaus?"

"You were right, Doug. It was definitely a Stepping Squares club shirt. He had been wearing other square dance stuff, but no name badge. Wonder why he chose this week to come to Clearton? This was a 'lesson' night and not a 'club dance' night, so it seems a little odd," I added.

Most dance clubs hold a series of lessons once a year or more. On 'lesson' nights, the focus is on the teaching and most of the dancers are students. In Clearton, every other Tuesday is lesson night and the opposite Tuesday covers a combination of lessons and general club dancing. On 'club dance' nights, only the first part of the night is for lessons, and folks from other clubs come for the last two hours with a mix of dancing levels. Visitors from other clubs are always welcome, but don't usually show up at 'lesson' nights. They tend to find the repetition a little boring. I would have been surprised if someone from the Fort Worth area came as far as Clearton just for lesson night.

"Hey, Darla, how about you stop by here on your way out of town? Then the three of us can hash this out. In the meantime, Sam and I can do a little investigative work by going through the newspapers. I have them stacked here for recycling. If there's information on a car-jacking ring, it should be in there somewhere," was Doug's suggestion.

"Sounds like a plan, Doug. I'll finish up my coffee. Want me to grab some doughnuts or anything on my way out of town? I know Sam is always hungry!" I said with a laugh.

Doug chuckled. "Great minds must think alike! Sam suggested you stop at Krispy Kreme just at the same time you mentioned doughnuts! You know where it is, right?"

"Yup. I'll head over there and then be out to the ranch. Don't go running off on me!" I disconnected and finished my coffee. The waitress came back, as if on cue. "You want anything else, honey?"

"No, just the check please." As Sadie started to total the charge for the coffee, it occurred to me that she was probably a goldmine of local gossip. I added, "You hear anything about those car-jackings lately?"

"What car-jackings, honey? Clearton is a peaceful kind of place. We don't have no trouble around here. No car-jackers, no bank robbers. Might have been one over toward Austin earlier this year. Last crime I heard of in Clearton was when Thrifty Mart got robbed a couple months ago. You're not the only one asking, though. Hey, Jonna, when was it all those nice-dressed government types were in here? They asked about strangers and such? Was it June or July?"

"July, I think," was the response from the other waitress. "I don't really remember the month, but it was hot. I kept thinking that hunky one would melt or pass out in a wool suit! Hard to forget a nice-looking man like that even if I could tell he wasn't from Texas," she added with a laugh.

"Thanks a lot," I said. I paid the bill and walked out of the café. I immediately connected the man she described with the Harbinville dude at Doug's last night. Just because you thought he was good-looking, I chided myself. My mind churned as I got in my car and started toward the ranch. If there was a car-jacking in June or July, why was it kept so quiet? Why was the sheriff so quick to jump to a conclusion like car-jacking after more than 60 days? And why call in those 'government types' like Harbinville? And why were government types in Clearton, anyway? Once again, I had more questions than answers and my mind spun.

Assuming it was Harbinville, it was no wonder those waitresses remembered him. He had the looks of a model. I laughed at myself. Debonair is what I think my grandmother would have called him. Just thinking of him made my stomach flip flop and I wasn't sure I wouldn't drool if I ran into him again. The waitress's description of him entertained me and I started thinking of him as that Harbinville Hunk.

I pushed him out of my mind, but happily acknowledged to myself that my reaction was at least a sure sign I was still alive. I also reminded myself I was no longer a teenager. I needed to focus on the car-jacking itself, not the handsome man or sheriff or whoever said it was a car-jacking. For some reason, I didn't wonder why I kept wondering about it now that my role as officially closed.

As I puzzled on the situation, I remembered I had another mission. I needed to stop at the Krispy Kreme! Sam would never forgive me if I didn't stop and pick up the promised snack. A dozen doughnuts, I decided, all varieties. I realized I wasn't sure of Sam or Doug's preferences. Actually, I don't remember Doug ever ordering desserts when we ate out, so I think the desire for doughnuts was all Sam's.

Krispy Kreme out of the way, I continued on my way to the ranch. I smiled at the giant stand of cactus as I turned in at Doug's gate. As I drove up the drive, it seemed almost empty with all the official vehicles gone this morning. And this time, nobody stopped me as I got out of the car and made my way the front porch. Already, this visit felt better than the last.

"Hey, Darla, let me take that box for you!" Sam offered as he met me on the porch with a quick grin and sparkle in his eyes. "Doug's kitchen is pretty barren on the sweets and you know I have a sweet tooth, well, a whole mouth of them. Oh, boy, chocolate covered, powdered, almond crunch. You went all out. While I chow down, you can fill us both in and then we can tell you what little we found out. Want some more coffee with these sweet delicacies?"

"Sure thing, Sam," I answered as Doug joined us on the porch. Like a mind-reader, he already had coffee for all of us on a tray and set it down on the table to the right of the door. He greeted me with a hug and guided me to a seat.

His ranch house was one of those with the wrap-around veranda that went all around the perimeter of the house. Round wooden tables with chairs adorned either side in the front. The view of the countryside, mostly Weathers Ranch, was impressive and relaxing all at the same time. More importantly, it was still early enough in the day that there was a breeze, and we were in the shade. All in all, it was pleasant to be outside. We all sat down and dug in to the Krispy Kreme box.

"Well, first off, after we talked to you on the phone, I called over to the Medical Center and they still don't have a positive ID on the man. I also wormed it out of the nurse that he's still unconscious. So whatever his story is, he isn't telling us yet. I called up a friend at the police department and sweet-talked the car owner's name out of her, though," Sam offered between sips of coffee and chunks of sugary goodness. When he turned on the charm, Sam could just about sweet-talk anybody out of anything.

"And, I went through the newspapers. Only found one little clip. It's in the house. In July there was a car-jacking near Austin. Nothing that made it sound like this was a pattern, or one of many. It was over by Thorton, not here in Clearton," Doug added.

Thorton was the next town over to the northwest, closer to Austin, which was probably why Sadie or the other waitress hadn't remembered it. Unless it was purposely kept under wraps. Any place but Texas the next town might be close, but from the center of Thorton to the center of Clearton was about 60 miles.

Since becoming a caller, my sense of geography has reorganized itself based on the various clubs and where they are relative to my hometown in Isquith. Other than the major cities, my geography is usually limited to a circle about three to four hours from Isquith. Most of the folks in Thorton didn't know the folks in Clearton. There were a few folks from surrounding towns like Thorton, Wheeler, Hisfered, and Fort Gorda who came to the club dances in Clearton. The next closest square dance club to Clearton was in Austin. A little farther the other way was the Bayou Belles and Beaus outside Houston. For some reason, most of the Clearton Squares dancers tended to go to the Houston clubs instead of the closer clubs in Austin.

"I have to think that either the sheriff or this Harbinville guy is pulling at straws and looking for a quick solution," Sam said. "When he came by this morning, Harbinville had pictures of this guy Doug found, but nobody's recognized him. He sure isn't someone who came down to dance with us on a regular basis. And that car they found, my friend told me it was registered to a Nick Tricot. The name doesn't mean anything to me even if we jump to the same conclusion they are and assume the car belongs to the man Doug found. Name Nick Tricot mean anything to you, Darla?" Sam asked.

"Tricot? No, I don't recognize it. But then, I've only been guest caller at a couple of dances up in the Dallas-Fort Worth area. I'll be up there Saturday night for the Hoedown and maybe I'll ask some questions, especially if I see anyone from the Stepping Squares," I offered. "And, this is really weird, but one of the waitresses at the café said she remembered something in early summer. It might have been June or July. She described someone that sounded like Harbinville coming in and asking questions. Do you remember that?"

"The guy sure gets around, then. The darn man still hasn't told us who the heck he works for," Sam said.

Neither of them had heard about it and none of us knew what to ask next so the conversation drifted. My mind kept nagging at questions, though. As a result, I wasn't doing much to hold up my end of the conversation. It certainly seemed strange that some square dancer, one that none of us seemed to know, would end up unconscious on Doug's property. If it was a car-jacking, had the car been taken on Doug's property? Or had they driven onto the ranch just to drop the body? It was too much of a coincidence that Nick Tricot, if that's who he was, was dressed for a square dance. It wasn't like Doug was listed on the web as an officer or contact for the Clearton

Squares. Sam was listed, but not Doug. As far as I knew none of them listed home addresses. I made a mental note to check on that. And why was a federal agent, which I'd begun to think Harbinville was based on my experience, interested in the situation?

"Doug, is there any chance that whoever did this thought that man was you? That you were the intended target of the assault?" There, I had finally said it out loud.

"Hey girl, now that's a new twist I don't think these law enforcers have considered," Sam said as he suddenly came to attention. I doubted they hadn't thought of it, but I didn't dispute Sam. He continued, "What do you think, Doug? Can you think of anyone you've pissed off enough to come after you?"

"I can't think of anyone. If I got somebody that mad, I don't know about it or haven't given it as much weight as them. Did you have anything in mind, Darla?" Doug looked calm but maybe a little worried, as if he hadn't thought of this possibility.

"Well, Carlotta mentioned that there was a group in town who were really upset about that kid's camp you support. Were they sufficiently upset to take action like this? Maybe someone tried to buy some of your land and you refused? Or has anyone associated with the camp been threatened? I know that I'm pulling at straws, but I am just trying to come up with some reasonable explanation," I responded.

Doug shook his head and said, "No, I can't see those folks becoming violent because of a debate at a town council meeting. They were scared, afraid that if these kids came here to go to camp, their own kids would be affected somehow. Like disabilities could be contagious or something." I could hear the disdain in Doug's voice and wondered if he had someone with disabilities in his family. I realized I didn't know Doug as well as I should, given our time together. Odd, given my natural curiosity, that I hadn't dug out all sorts of background from him – or about him.

Sam nodded his agreement with Doug's take on the situation. "Now, Doug, you remember that we did have a very…well, you might say spirited…discussion at that town meeting in June," he said. "But I don't rightly recall any threats of violence that I heard or heard about. I guess it wouldn't hurt to make a few calls if you think it's a possibility."

"No, I don't want to stir up anything, Sam. The camp is on the agenda again for this month, so I'll feel it out then if it's still an issue," Doug responded. "As for the land, nobody has made any offers. I think it's all just a coincidence that it happened here, a fluke.

The phone rang and Doug went inside to answer it. Sam and I could hear him through the screen door and shamelessly eavesdropped.

"Hi Carlotta! Yeah, we're all here, eating doughnuts and drinking coffee. The powers that be seem to think it was a car-jacking gone bad….yeah, me neither. Of course Sam, Darla, and I have way too many questions to be satisfied, and nowhere near enough answers," he spoke into the phone.

After a slight pause, he continued, "No, he's still unconscious, but he's been tentatively identified as a Nick Tricot. Darla confirmed that he was wearing a Stepping Squares club shirt, so he probably calls the metroplex area home."

Another pause, then excitement crept into his voice. "You do? Someone named Nick at the state dance in August? We shoulda asked you first, shouldn't we? You meet all the single guys, don't you?" Doug teased. A longer bit of silence, while I was sure Carlotta was returning the teasing as good as she got. Doug laughed and then went on, "Well, I wonder if it's the same guy?"

There was barely a hesitation this time before he continued. Carlotta must be calling from work and making it a short conversation.

"Yeah, we'll keep you posted," he said. "When you get a chance, you might want to check with the sheriff and see if you recognize the guy. Talk to you later, Carlotta." Doug disconnected and came back out to the porch.

"Carlotta remembers meeting somebody named Nick at the dance in August. It could be a coincidence, or it could be the same guy. But why my ranch? I still don't get it. It's not easy to end up here from the highway." Doug shook his head and sat back down.

"Well, I don't think we'll ever know unless Nick wakes up and tells us. In the meantime, I better be hitting the road and heading home. I still have a long drive. Keep me posted and I guess I'll see you guys at the Hoedown." I got up, gave both men a hug and walked to my car. Doug walked with me to my car, put his arms around me, and kissed me. Sam was still on the porch, and the kiss lasted long enough, I was sure, that he realized Doug and I were more than just friends.

"Call me if you hear anything new," I told Doug when we parted. I waved to Sam, got in the car, and headed home. There didn't seem to be much point in going back to the sheriff's office. And the drive would give me time to mull over the information we'd gathered.

Chapter 3

The time during the drive didn't prove as productive as I'd hoped, but the traffic was light, and the pastures and farmland were pretty. By the time I got home I still didn't know which direction to head if I was going to help decipher our puzzle. After unloading all my gear, and taking another shower, I took care of basic stuff around the house, did some light grocery shopping, and made myself a salad. Somehow the salad would undo the damage from doughnuts that morning, I was sure.

I worked on some new singing calls. Most of the CDs had two tracks. One had someone else doing the singing call, usually the person who figured out the choreography. The other side just the music so I could call the moves using it as background. The challenge was to match my timing using the music-only side after listening to the choreographed side a few times. Being new at the caller business, I don't have a large repertoire and some of the songs, though tried and true for square dancing, are not my faves. I really wanted to get some more contemporary pop and country songs under my belt, and that took practice before I could try the song at a dance.

I worked for a while but my mind kept coming back to the man Doug had found and the possibility that it might have been Doug instead. Out there on his ranch alone, if Doug had an accident who would find him, and when? I had to remind myself that Doug wasn't my husband Clint. History didn't repeat itself. Doug didn't work in the justice system and come in contact with criminals all the time, criminals who might be out to get him. I often had to remind myself of these facts. My devastation when Clint was killed and fear of being hurt that badly again, were my biggest obstacles to pursuing any relationship. After five years, it should be easier but it still seemed like a betrayal to want to be with someone else.

Doug was a nice-looking man with brown eyes and graying brown hair. He wasn't exceptionally tall, about my height. He was rugged in a good way, well educated, intelligent. He was stable, had a nice ranch, no bad habits I was aware of.

I should try harder with him. He would be considered a real catch, but I was too skittish to get close to him – or any other man for now. Obviously, the distance between us didn't help, but in Texas, driving a few hours to get someplace is pretty common. Lots of folks carry on long-distance relationships, and I was on the road a lot with my calling commitments anyway, so that wasn't what was keeping me from a relationship. I was my own enemy on that front.

In the midst of my litany of his good qualities, I realized I had drifted into the personal arena and was trying to convince myself he was the one for me. I corralled my mind and refocused on the possible explanations for yesterday's attack. Doug's participation in the camp for disabled children and related equine therapy was really pretty far out there for the Doug I knew. Maybe there were other parts of his life I didn't know about that could relate to the current incident.

I had no real reason to keep going on the Clearton incident, but I'd given up thinking I would give up thinking about it. Between my musing and my work on calling, the afternoon sped by. The next time I checked the clock, I was surprised it was later than six o'clock. After another salad for dinner, and with a glass of wine in tow, I couldn't stop myself. I checked on the web and sure enough it was Sam's name and phone number listed for the Clearton Squares, not Doug's. No address for either one. And the blurb on the club website did clearly specify that the club dances were alternate weeks instead of every week in the fall. So how did Nick Tricot get Doug's name and address, and why was he on the way to our dance – if that's where he was going?

I suppose he could have been passing through town, just discovered the Clearton Squares danced on Tuesdays, and wanted to go to a square dance. Square dance clubs are usually a welcoming bunch and, especially as short as most clubs are of male dancers, he could have counted on being welcome on that front as well. But I didn't buy it. It isn't like anyone is likely to just happen to end up in Clearton.

I started poking around on the internet. Amazing what you can find there these days, especially if you have a little experience. My stint as an investigator in the Florida State Attorney's Office gave me more experience than many folks. And simply by being me, I already had the curiosity and need to solve puzzles. Although the ten-year stint as an investigator was not one of the more enjoyable periods of my life, it was one that provided me with lots of skills I've found useful since that time. It also left me with a healthy skepticism that serves me well.

As usual, it didn't take much to get me reflecting on my past, so I was glad for a distraction when my phone rang. Thankful that internet surfing no longer relied on telephone lines, I checked caller ID before answering the phone. "Hi Heather! What are you up to? Anything wrong?"

"No, mom. You apparently tried to call me last night. I left my cell phone in my office so I just got the 'missed call' information this afternoon. You didn't leave a message, though. What's up?" she asked.

"You know me, Heather. Creature of habit. I ended up staying in Clearton overnight and was calling to let you know so you wouldn't worry. I didn't leave a message when I remembered you were at school, not at home! So I guess I made you worry by wanting to not make you worry. There was some trouble here at one of the dancer's houses. It was late and I was on autopilot. I guess I still haven't gotten used to you not being here at home."

"Geez, mom, did you have too much caffeine today? Slow down. It's okay, no problem, but what happened? The dancer is alright, isn't he?" she asked.

"Yes. Do you remember Doug Weathers? A man was found on his ranch, but it wasn't Doug. The man is in the hospital, but so far nobody is quite sure what happened or who he is. The sheriff seems to think it may have been a car-jacking.

We still don't really know. It was just a very strange night, to say the least," I added.

"Yeah, I remember Doug. Glad he's okay." She paused for a few seconds and I started to ask her some questions about college, but she started up again. "Ya know, mom, I saw an infomercial just last week talking about increased rates of car theft, including an increase in the frequency of car-jacking. Ten or fifteen years ago, thieves would break into cars in parking lots and steal the cars by hot-wiring them. The new cars with the chips in the keys make it harder to steal them without keys. The person doing the infomercial said that increased security features on cars have resulted in thieves stealing cars more often these days when people are in them instead of parked. You know, at stop lights or such, so car-jacking is increasing. Professional car thieves could probably bypass those chips, but not the average thief. Interesting, huh?" I let her go on; just happy we were now on a comfortable basis with each other after several years of tension. I wondered what the infomercial had been selling.

"Sure is," I said. I couldn't help myself and started with the mom-questions. "So what's new with you? How're classes going? Are you learning as much in class as from infomercials?" My humor on the last retort went over her head – or more likely, she just chose to ignore it.

"You bet, in fact, I'm on my way to the library right now. Anyway, it was good talking to you, glad nothing was really wrong. Love ya, mom!" she answered.

"You too, see ya soon I hope." I replied and hung up the phone. Nostalgia swept over me and I realized I missed my daughter a lot. There was more I wanted to check on the internet, but Heather's call had made me sad, and I could always get online a little later. Besides, I was pretty tired from getting to bed so late last night. Sometimes sleeping on a problem helps me brainstorm possible solutions. Sometimes it just helps me avoid problems. Either way, I decided to sleep on this one. I was in a dilemma, though. My cell phone told me it was 8:15. Did I want to go to bed this early, or take a nap that might keep me from sleeping later? I opted for a nap, telling myself I'd just take a short one.

It was late when I woke up, and I realized I needed to finish up reviewing my list of music for calling at the Hoedown. I spent another few hours getting things in order for the dance and puttering around the house, just glad to be home with no immediate schedule to keep. It was a productive evening and I finally went to sleep for the night. I'd worried about nothing – I slept like the dead.

Thursday morning I woke up before the alarm sounded and returned to planning what I needed for the weekend Hoedown. Before I even changed out of my pajamas, I went through some of the CDs I had practiced yesterday and played around with mixing up the calls a little. I had gotten a couple of newer CDs with current music and suggested call patterns, so I explored them rather than the singing calls I had worked on already.

Using caller software, I tried out the music to get a feel for how the dance patterns would play out. Without actually having real dancers in front of me it wasn't reality but you could call it virtual reality. The animation was definitely helpful. For lesson nights, I could change the recommended calls to ones I had already taught if I needed to, if I made sure that the moves and beats of music were still synchronized. It boggled my mind that callers did this before computers were available to visualize the process.

One of the tasks I set for myself, in order to be able to call for differing groups, was to figure out call combinations for a lesson that included or excluded certain calls. Square dancing is taught and danced at different difficulty levels. First Basic, then Mainstream, then Plus, then various advanced levels. I had to be ready to call dances for whatever level of dancers showed up. That meant I had to be able to use the calls for a regular Mainstream tip, which was the standard fare, and to include Plus calls for a Plus tip. For lessons, I could only use calls the students had already learned. All in all, a brain teaser for sure.

Between coming up with various scenarios and combinations and three possible call sequences, prepping my calling took most of the morning. I stopped to take a couple of breaks, got dressed, did laundry, and cleaned up the house a little. I wasn't calling today and hadn't gotten much accomplished on the home front yesterday. As a result, I kept myself busy for the morning with little trouble.

By afternoon I wrapped up my chores and I couldn't resist resuming my internet surfing and the Clearton supposed car-jackings. My curiosity had kept nagging me all morning. By the time Doug called late in the afternoon, I already knew that if the man was Nick Tricot I'd identified his address, phone number, driver's license number, height and weight, and a dozen other personal facts. I could even see an aerial map showing where he lived, and a shot of his house and one car in the driveway. I didn't know when the satellite photo had been taken, though, or if that was the same car that was hijacked.

It's scary what you can find out about people online. Not that I discovered anything the sheriff's office hadn't. They had all the same tools at hand and knew how to use them. I was pretty sure they just didn't share their information with unauthorized curiosity seekers. When I thought about it, that was really what our little group had become. We told ourselves we had a right to know because the victim was found on Doug's ranch, but when you came right down to it, we had no more right than anybody else to whatever the cops' investigation revealed.

When Doug called me, I didn't let on how much I already found out. Not everyone felt that being able to access personal information on the web was such a wonderful thing, so I kept it to myself. Knowing Doug like I did, and given that he tended to the conservative side, I figured he might not look kindly on my snooping. I just let him tell me what he knew.

Doug said the man had regained consciousness and the sheriff had taken his statement. He was, after all, Nick Tricot and, according to the sheriff, it was a simple car-jacking, case closed. But it just didn't fit in our eyes. It didn't explain all the rest. The sheriff hadn't told Doug why the man said he was in town or at Doug's ranch. Doug and I discussed it and neither one of us was satisfied, but then again neither one of us had time or reason to chase it around if the officials called it closed. And, I reminded myself, I'd purposely gotten out of investigative work! Doug indicated that he tried to get to the hospital before the man was released, but he missed him.

Changing the subject, Doug assured me that he and Sam and Carlotta would all be at the Hoedown this weekend and that he'd see me there. Doug and I talked about the Hoedown and maybe finding some time together. With my calling gigs, that wasn't always easy, and finding time alone was particularly difficult. The personal part of the conversation was fairly short, and I found myself disappointed that we hadn't had more to talk about.

Nevertheless, when I hung up from talking to Doug, I wasn't able to stop myself, so I searched newspapers electronically and online crime databases. I found that there actually had been a number of car-jackings or car thefts in the greater Austin and Houston areas during the last year or so. Well, that should be the end of it all, right? Thank heavens. I moved on to other things and got my mind off the man who was attacked. And maybe, I thought, I'd be able to focus on Doug the man, and not Doug the intended target.

I tried to figure out which outfits to bring with me to Dallas when my mind again took off in its own direction and flashed a picture from that night at his house after the attack. The vision included that mysterious man in the suit or the Harbinville Hunk, as I'd started calling him. Irritated with myself, and feeling a little adolescent, I went back to the web and tried to find information about him. If anyone had asked, I surely would have said I tried to find out what his connection to car-jackings might be. What I thankfully didn't have to admit was that I wouldn't mind finding out some personal information as well.

Although it's usually pretty amazing what shows up when you enter the name of an individual, in this case "Paul

Harbinville" didn't generate much that looked useful. There was a Paul Harbinville who was a painter, and one who was a chef in New York, and someone trying to get information on Harbinvilles for a family tree, but nothing I could obviously connect to the Paul Harbinville at Doug's house. Okay, the usual approaches weren't working, and I convinced myself, it wasn't that I was interested in the hunk – I mean, man – but now I was just curious as a matter of principle.

So, I decided to try another approach. My investigative instincts told me he was with some federal agency, which was probably why he was able to keep his online information scarce. I did a search of the Federal Bureau of Investigation website. Interestingly enough, it turned out car-jacking would come under their jurisdiction if the car-jackers crossed state lines. That seemed to give some credence to that whole possible line of investigation, but I still didn't buy it. Finally, thinking of the camp Doug wanted to help open, I checked out news stories on openings of rehabilitation centers and citizen protests against group homes, against inclusion of people with disabilities, and anything related to that I could think of.

Other than news clips on 'heated debates,' petitions, and peaceful protests, I couldn't find anything of significance. Certainly there was nothing to indicate that attacking supporters of such endeavors would be a common occurrence or would warrant the attention of federal types. No protestors or agitation groups. Camps for Kids with Disabilities didn't show up as a big 'hate crime' target. There were actually a couple sites about camps for kids with disabilities, including some offering hippotherapy as well as general equine therapy. None of the sites were located in Texas though, so no direct link to Doug. The pictures and testimonials were impressive for the various camps and I could understand Doug's interest in using some of his land for such a noble purpose.

I checked some of the sites to see if there were any staunch or aggressive campaigners against this treatment approach. Other than a few negative comments or concerns about potential mistreatment of animals and the need to ensure appropriate care of the horses, I couldn't find anything there that would make Doug a target. As a rancher all his life, I had no doubts that Doug would be sure the animals were treated appropriately. I didn't have the names of the folks associated with the camp Doug supported, so I more or less reached a dead end, and reluctantly returned to packing.

I vacillated between outfits to wear or bring and contemplated shopping. Not quite packed, the phone rang.

"Hi Darla, it's me, Carlotta. How are you?"

"I'm fine. Staring at different combinations of prairie skirts and tops, trying to figure out what I need to take to the Hoedown this weekend. How about you? You're still coming, right?" I asked.

"I'm doing great! Yep, all three of the musketeers are heading to Dallas. I just wanted to check in and make sure Doug had called to let you know that it was Nick Tricot he found. Haven't heard anything else. Clearton is back to being a quiet place, and still a little short on men," she added with a chuckle.

"Yes, Doug called with that information, and I certainly haven't heard anything more about the incident. So when will you three get to Dallas, do you think?" I asked. The shindig started today with what was called a 'Trail In' dance. It was already evening, so I was pretty sure they weren't going up for that. The Thursday night dance wasn't on my calling schedule, so I wasn't headed that direction tonight either.

"We hope to leave here in time to be there for a bite to eat and the official start tomorrow night. I couldn't get off work today, and have to work half a day tomorrow. I don't have the freedom of those two guys, or you either for that matter. With both Doug and Sam at the Hoedown, you better be sure to bring a skirt or two!" she offered, knowing I preferred skirts to pants if I danced instead of called.

"Yeah, that was what I was trying to figure out. I need an alternative to my more comfortable jeans! I seem to always wear the same skirts though, and my options for tops to match are limited," I sighed. "Carlotta, you and I may have to find some time Saturday to check out the vendors and buy some new duds. I definitely need to look at some more dance shoes or boots I can dance in", I continued.

"Sounds like a plan to me! I love to shop and some of the better vendors for square dance apparel are at the Hoedown. I could use another outfit or two myself. The holidays will be coming up and with them a lot of special dances. We might want to find you some sexy duds too!" she teased. "Anyway, I just wanted to touch base. See ya tomorrow night, and drive careful!" ended Carlotta.

"Same advice from here! Don't let Sam do the driving. He can be a little wild behind the wheel," I added with a laugh and hung up. It felt good to have a friend I could joke around with once in a while. When it comes to close friendships, I still hadn't formed many in Isquith, and I had lost most of the friends I had in Florida after the turmoil before I left. Isquith was a quiet little township, and I was the newcomer. I had met my neighbors, and they were friendly enough, but we had little in common. It didn't help that most of my neighbors worked days while I worked nights, or that I was a single mom. To be honest, I just wasn't the social butterfly that Carlotta was.

As I packed, I mentally went through the schedule for the weekend. Friday night was the first official night of the Hoedown. Then there were workshops Saturday morning and afternoon and a 'Trail Out' dance on Sunday morning. With Doug and Sam coming to the Hoedown, I was pretty much guaranteed a partner for at least a few tips when I wasn't calling. I'd be one of four callers for the annual Dallas dance, each of us taking turns calling a tip. There were two dances, each going from 6 until 11.

Slim Greenville, one of the best callers around, was doing some of the workshops. His brother, Tom, was doing some too. Slim and Tom had been calling for some time and had a steady following. For those of us who were relatively new callers, things like the Hoedown are an opportunity to be seen and heard. That's how square dancers decide which dances to go to and which callers to dance to and hire for their club dances.

Not all that time would be square dancing though. In between, there would be cuers who would guide round dancers. Round dancing is ballroom or country dancing synchronized and directed by the cuers with all the couples going in a circle following the line of dance. Sometimes a waltz, sometimes a rumba, sometimes a two-step, but all the couples doing exactly the same thing, cued by the cuer, and moving in a big circle. Some dancers do both square and round dance, some do one or the other. I had never gotten involved in the round dancing or cuing so the round dancing provided me with a break. Sometimes, instead of round dancing, there might be a freeform waltz or a polka, and if I had a partner I could dance during the break.

Maybe I could even finagle a tip with someone from the Stepping Squares and, casually of course, ask if he knew Nick Tricot. There aren't many women callers, so you'd think I would be able to count on other callers as partners. But most of the callers are married and if they dance at all, they dance with their wives or with the 'extra' women who've paid to attend the dance. That meant I didn't get to dance a lot, but often did get to socialize. Anyway, what with breaks and the round dancing, I figured I'd have plenty of time to chat with the other callers and members of various clubs.

Just in case I decided to dance, I figured on a prairie skirt with matching vest and shirt in addition to my usual jeans. I included a second prairie skirt and two additional tops as well. I had just never gotten into the crinolines, pantaloons, and short skirt thing. They looked good on Carlotta, but my hips did just fine on their own and didn't need any added emphasis. I'd leave the more traditional garb to petite figures like Carlotta. Even with the longer skirt, though, I still wore pettipants – the shorts-like undergarments that prevent any indecent exposure during enthusiastic dancing. Square dancing can get pretty fast-paced and I didn't want to have to think about keeping my skirt under control when was twirled or was up on stage.

With my indecision on outfits to take, I ended up with way too many clothes. I tucked and folded and squished and squeezed until I had everything packed for the weekend. And I told myself again that the excitement was over. This weekend would be just for fun and perhaps a little romance if Doug and I could get off by ourselves at all. Well, and a little profit, of course, since I'd get paid for calling. As I thought about the romantic possibilities, and felt the panic rise, I scolded myself and turned in to get a good night's sleep.

Chapter 4

Friday morning I slept in until about nine o'clock. Actually, I woke up at seven but I rolled over for a few additional winks. Anticipating a hectic but enjoyable weekend I figured a little extra sleep could go a long way. About noon, I would head toward Dallas and the convention center where the Hoedown would be held. Dallas is the epitome of Texas for a large city, with something for everybody, including the many billionaires who have heralded from Dallas and left their own mark on the metroplex area. Dallas has its fair share of historical sites and monuments, including the museum dedicated to John F. Kennedy, numerous art museums and Pioneer Plaza, not to mention the Dallas Farmers Market.

This trip I didn't plan to take in any of these sights or to take advantage of Dallas glitz either. I would just stay at the convention center and adjoining hotel. On the way, I planned to stop at the Cracker Barrel on the outskirts of Dallas for a bite to eat. It was close enough to the convention center that I might even run into some square dancers or other callers, get a feel for how big the crowd was, and find out how the Trail In dance went last night.

I locked the deadbolt on my back door but then I heard the phone ring inside. I'd already loaded my sound equipment in the car, but I had a case of CDs in my hand and my purse over my shoulder as I juggled the keys. I was tempted to turn toward the car and let the machine pick up, but I couldn't overcome my curiosity. I flipped my wrist the opposite direction, swung the door open again, and stepped across the threshold. I set the case on the floor and jogged across the utility room with my purse bumping in time against my back. I got into the kitchen just in time to hear the beep of the recorder. Then a familiar voice came through the speaker. It was Heather. I had talked to her not too long ago, so I was surprised.

"Couldn't remember what time today you were leaving for the dance, Mom. Nothing important. Just had a couple of things…"

I reached the wall and grabbed the handset off the base. "Hi, honey! Don't hang up. I was just headed out the door. Glad I came back in to hear your wonderful voice. What's up?"

During Heather's first year in college there was some question whether she'd make it through the year without probation, but she managed to tone down her partying just enough to squeak by. This year seemed to be going more smoothly, but it was still early and I was holding my breath. I always loved hearing from her, and was glad I'd chosen to answer the phone rather than let the answering machine take the call. Still, I couldn't help worrying that something was wrong.

"Nothing, Mom. I just had a couple of things I wanted to talk to you about," she added.

I could tell by her voice the 'things' weren't serious, so the tension in my shoulders eased. I waited for her to go on.

"I'm doing a report in my English class and I need a book from my room. I was wondering if you could send it to me?" she asked. Well, this was do-able!

"Of course I can. What do you need? And when do you need it?" I answered.

"It's on the shelves in my room, I think. It might be in a box on my closet floor. Or maybe in the attic, but I don't think so," she explained.

Oh, great. A treasure hunt.

"Would it be easier for you to just buy another copy there in Austin, honey?" I asked.

"I can't, mom. It's a textbook and it's reserved for students taking one of the freshman classes. I've already checked all the bookstores in town and they are sold out and there isn't time to order it online and…" the laments continued.

I broke into her laundry list of excuses. "How about borrowing one? From a friend, maybe? Or the library?"

"Jees, mom! I'm a sophomore. I don't know any freshmen!" How could I have thought she would be so uncool as to know anyone a year younger and so much lower in the university pecking order? "...and I'm sure all the copies in the library are checked out. I didn't think it'd be any big deal, but if you don't have time to help me..."

"Hold on, Heather. I was just thinking it would be quicker for you to get it there. I'm happy to send it to you, you know that."

If I was going to go on a treasure hunt, maybe at least I could find out what I was hunting. "What's the book you need?"

"Mom, you're the best! It's called The Vampire Who Sucked the Life Out of English and it's sort of a dull blue..." she responded, obviously pleased that I would find and send it to her.

"Are you kidding me? What kind of title is that for a textbook? Surely I would remember it if you studied it last year," I said with some skepticism.

"Well...I didn't actually use it much last year..." was Heather's hesitant response.

Of course. That would explain the D in freshman English from my daughter who loved to read. At least she was studying this year. I'd better do all I could to encourage it.

"Don't worry, Heather. I'll find it. When do you need it?"

"Ummm....the paper's due on Wednesday." Great.

"Okay, it's too late today but I'll FedEx it to you on Monday. That's the best I can do. You said you wanted to talk to me about a couple of things. What's the other one?"

I heard her voice change tone when she answered. From cajoling to enthusiastic.

"Oh, mom! I've met a great guy! He's in my bio study group and..."

We spent the rest of the conversation talking about Micah. That is, she talked. I listened and made appropriate mother-noises about her new love interest. I had to walk a fine line. I knew from experience that if I showed too much interest she'd clam up, but if I didn't show enough she'd get mad and accuse me of not taking her seriously. Ah, life with a 19-year-old. When she finally wound down, I reassured her I'd send the Vampire book, told her I loved her, and hung up missing her. I grabbed a piece of paper, wrote a reminder on it, and stuck it on the fridge with a magnet. Then I picked up my CD case, purse, and keys, and dashed out the door again, on the way to the Hoedown.

It was a pretty smooth drive. There really was not too much traffic for a Friday. I hoped my timing was good and I could avoid the rush hour and stop-still traffic all the way. For most of the ride, I entertained myself by trying to figure out some way that all the pieces of Doug's puzzle would fit together. It was kind of like choreographing a square dance tip. I figured if I moved the 'dancers' around enough they would end up where they belonged and it would all make sense. Before I knew it I spotted the sign for Cracker Barrel and pulled off the highway and into the parking lot. It was late for lunch, early for dinner, so I probably had beat the crowds. Still, I saw square dance outfits scattered around the restaurant's veranda.

At first I thought there was a line. Then I realized it was just a small group of men, some of them smoking. That was why they were outside, not because of a wait. It occurred to me that it was kind of strange to have four men, all in square dance garb, and all smoking. Four single men would be a gold mine at a square dance. There were usually a lot more single women looking for dance partners than men, but then again maybe they were just waiting for their partners to finish shopping in the restaurant's country store. At a square dance, there isn't any alcohol, and, as in most public places these days, no smoking. That doesn't mean nobody smokes or drinks outside the dances. I just don't associate smoking or drinking with square dancing.

As I got closer, I looked for their club badges, the name tags that include the name of the club as well as the person. But they had obviously decided not to wear their name badges into the restaurant. I hadn't put on my name badge yet, either. I didn't recognize the matching yoke pattern of their shirts, so I wondered if they might be from out of state. Then again, it's not like I know all the club outfits or that dancers only wear the club dance. The dance tonight would likely be the one when dancers would be in club dress, not the dances during the day. Besides, often for big dances like this, folks come from all over the country. At dances in Dallas, it wouldn't be unusual at all to see people from Oklahoma, New Mexico, or Arkansas at the very least. I smiled and offered a generic 'How d'ya do' but they either didn't hear me or weren't particularly interested.

I walked into the restaurant and immediately heard someone yell my name. Turning around, I found myself facing my co-caller Tom Greenville and his wife, Stacey. Tom was in his mid-thirties, a nice-looking man who could fit in anywhere. He wasn't tall, but not short. He wasn't overly attractive but he wouldn't stand out in a crowd. He was personable, articulate, and a caller most dancers enjoyed. Most callers have a day job, and when Tom wasn't calling he worked as a photographer and artist.

Stacey was the other half of the set. She was perky, cute, and genuine. She had an accounting background and kept the books from their various business enterprises. This allowed her to travel with him, regardless of whether the travel was art-related or dance-related. They had come into town for the Hoedown yesterday. Tom had called the Trail-In dance and then a workshop or two today. They invited me to join them at their table. Glad of the company, I agreed.

"So anything exciting happening at the Hoedown so far?" I asked once we had been seated and our order taken.

"Nah, the same old same old. The workshops went well. I had the 'Dancing by Definition' group this morning and tried to do a 'Mainstream' group too. As usual, there weren't really enough folks for a Mainstream lesson. Most of the time, even when Stacey helped out, we had trouble making one square. Don't know why organizers keep trying to do so many workshops at these things, especially on Friday. One couple got pretty mad and complained to the organizers already." Tom shook his head and sighed.

When people organize these big dance events, they try to have an opportunity for dancers to get better at the various dance moves. For some reason, they include Mainstream, which is the beginning level. The problem is that most beginning dancers don't come to the big dances and the more advanced dancers don't want instruction at that level. They want it at the more advanced levels. So for the few Mainstream dancers who go to the workshops and the caller who is supposed to do the workshop, the whole thing can be pretty disappointing.

"Well, at least you got to do the Dancing by Definition in the morning," I said. Dancing by Definition or DBD is precise instruction, exactly by the book, regardless of 'men' or 'ladies' parts and with no fancy twirls or other things that dancers tend to add on. More than that, callers move the dancers into positions for calls that are not usual. This requires that the dancer truly know the movements involved in the call, and not just what the ladies' or men's part is supposed to be, or the shortcuts most dancers take to complete calls. Callers usually enjoy the challenge of calling DBD as much as experienced dancers enjoy dancing it.

"Is there a good turnout, do you think?" I asked.

Stacey chimed in, "Yes, other than Mainstream, most of the workshops were pretty well able to get three or four squares going. For the first day, and a work day for many folks besides, that's pretty good. It's hard to tell where folks came from though. For the day's activities, most people just wore casual clothes and not their club dress. Tonight, we may be able to get a better feel for which clubs are here. I think they will make some kind of announcement after the Hoedown officially is opened."

"I imagine that's true. Do either of you know any of the members of the Stepping Squares?" I asked. As Tom nodded, I continued, "One of their members was apparently going to the square dance in Clearton earlier this week. He landed in the hospital. Nick Tricot? Do you know him?" I tried to sound casual.

"Can't say that I know him by name, but I've been a guest caller for them a few times. So I might recognize him if I saw him. He alright?" Tom asked. I assured Tom that Nick seemed to be doing fine, hoping that was true, and Tom turned his attention to the approaching waitress. I figured Tom and Stacey assumed a car accident, and I didn't correct them.

"Here's our food and none too soon. We have to head back in time for the presentation of the colors and the dance demonstration by the cloggers," he said as he dug in to his meatloaf and baked potato.

We ate our food with little more conversation. As we ate, I kept glancing around, looking to see if I could spot anyone with the Stepping Squares emblem or badge.

"So who are you looking for Darla – prince charming?" Stacie teased.

Laughing, I answered, "Aren't we all? You're just lucky you found yours! No, not looking for anyone in particular. I'm just always a people watcher I guess. But we need to get going, so I'll hold off on people watching until after I eat!"

After a pleasant meal, I followed Stacey and Tom to the Hoedown. The parking lot at the convention center where the Hoedown was going on was already packed as I pulled in and parked. I grabbed my laptop and CDs for the tips I planned to call. I added some extra discs for good measure, in case someone else used a song before I got to it, and found my way in. One thing I like about square dances, especially big ones like the Hoedown, is all the bright colors and patterns of the clothes and friendly greetings of the square dancers and spectators alike. From southwestern patterns in yokes and skirts to paisleys or calicos, every color of the rainbow was scattered about. As I signed in and quickly scanned of the immediate area, I picked out the club dress of the Stepping Squares as well as the patterned outfits for the Clearton Squares.

"Darla, honey! What took you so long to get here?" Sam's booming voice broke through my concentration as he spotted me. He and Carlotta made their way toward me.

"Howdy Sam, Carlotta. I wasn't calling last night or today, so I figured now was as good a time as any to get here. When did you guys get here?" I bantered.

"As early as I could roust the carpool this morning!" laughed Sam. "Doug is looking around. He's hoping he'll see someone from Stepping Squares who he recognizes to casually start up a conversation, if you get my drift. Wait a minute, here he comes now, and he looks like the cat who caught that canary!"

Sam was a people-person in his element. He led us toward the main hall as Doug moved our way. We met up quickly despite the growing crowd. Let me tell you, it's not easy moving quickly through all those big skirts, but Sam played blocker well. Doug gave me a quick hug and rolled his eyes.

"You are not going to believe who is in there, just leaning against the wall, like he did this every day," he said. "Paul Harbinville! And he and Lorys want us to believe that they think this is a done deal, all part of some probably non-existent car-jacking ring! Right!" Doug laughed sarcastically. I felt myself wanting to go find this Paul Harbinville. I just wanted to ask him questions, of course, not to see if he was really as good-looking as I remembered or whether my imagination had embellished him as a result of my naming him the Harbinville Hunk. I caught my own thoughts and couldn't believe they were so adolescent. I sighed inwardly about my lack of control over my imagination, as well as my apparently alive and well hormones. Do we ever really grow up, I wondered.

The four of us didn't have much chance for conversation as all the dancers began to assemble around us for the Grand March that got the Hoedown officially started. For the Grand March, dancers first line up in sets of four dancers, or two couples across. At the front of the line, the first groups of dancers are officials from the national, state, or regional associations. This year, all the state and regional representatives wore color-blocked outfits in red-white-and-blue with an appliqué of the State of Texas in white overlapping the red and blue in the shirt and on the ladies' skirts. Each regional association had its own style of dress as well.

The regional reps would be followed by the clubs hosting the dance. In this case, several of the Dallas clubs. Everyone else would line up behind the Dallas clubs, generally with members of their own clubs. For dances like this, dancers usually wear their club dress to emphasize their club's presence at the dance. One way to think of it is like the colors associated with differing colleges or schools at football games. Anyway, there were lots of people sporting matching outfits, and many groups represented. Sam, Carlotta, Doug, and I stepped to the side and waited for the rest of the Clearton Square Dance Club to pass by so we could fold into the moving throng.

As the dancers marched into the hall in rows of four, the colors changed along with the association or club. From red-white-blue to yellow and black to gold and green to the blue and green of the Stepping Squares and so on. The right and left sides met each other, and formed lines of eight. The kaleidescoping of colors from the various club dresses continued as the lines of eight reached the front.

Jerry Barnette, the designated caller and master of ceremonies, announced that there were 20 squares in the hall. That meant that at least 160 square dancers had made it to the Hoedown for the Friday night dance. That didn't include the folks sitting and watching or the solos who hadn't found a partner in time to participate in the Grand March.

"Ladies and gentleman, welcome to the Hoedown. Those of you not already standing on the dance floor, please stand as you are able and remove head gear for the presentation of the colors," continued Jerry. Jerry was probably in his 60s and one of the officers of the Callers Association. His eyes crinkled when he smiled, and he smiled a lot. His boots, cowboy hat, and large belt buckle fit the stereotype of the Texas cowboy. "Colors are being presented by officers of the local Veterans of Foreign Wars in the Dallas-Fort Worth area. Fred Jemison, co-president of the Dallas Darlins, will lead us in the pledge followed by Mickey and DeeDee Charteen singing the national anthem."

These events were followed by cheering and then a moment of silence and the long awaited, "OK, folks, spread to the left and right, find some space, and let's square dance," announced by Jerry. He was scheduled to call the first tip in this, the main hall. I needed to find the other callers to make sure I was where I was supposed to be when I was supposed to be there. I had entered the hall as Doug's partner, and I hadn't had time, or remembered, before the march to let him know I'd have to skip out. Now we were already squared up, and I felt bad leaving the square short one dancer.

"Doug, do you have time to find a partner for this tip?" I asked. "I really need to locate someone to find out where and when I'll be calling."

"Okay," he agreed. He immediately began scanning the perimeter of the room to find a solo dancer waiting for a partner. "Sam, hold my place, I'll be right back," he said.

Doug hurried off to find a dance partner and I excused myself from the other dancers in our square, explaining that I'd see them later. Sam and Carlotta knew I was a caller, of course, but I took a minute to explain to the other four and then ducked out. Good thing, too, because I discovered I was helping call in a neighboring room. I better get the entire schedule soon, I thought, so I don't miss any of my commitments! Tom was right, I was cutting my arrival pretty tight.

It was about an hour and a half later, well after the break for exhibition dancers and opening ceremonies, that I spotted Harbinville. To his credit, he had traded in his suit for jeans, looking suspiciously new, and a western style shirt with bolo tie. With no pattern on the yoke or patterned tie, he was not trying to display a specific club affiliation, but didn't look too out of place. His nametag, a hand written one, simply said "Paul."

I had noticed him while I called, and now I watched him as I put away my things and got organized for my next session.

If he looked good dressed up, he looked even better dressed down. It had not been my imagination, and my stomach was doing those unfamiliar flip-flops again. A few of the solo ladies had approached him, but so far he hadn't danced. I doubted that he knew how. I realized that he had turned in my direction, and decided it would be best to just go over and say hello.

"I didn't realize you were a square dancer, Mr…., uh, Paul," I said looking at his name tag. "You didn't seem to be very interested when we met." I bit my tongue, but really wanted to add, "Do you expect to find many criminal types or car-jackers here at the Hoedown?"

"Hello. No, I don't square dance." Was it just my imagination again, or did I hear distaste on the last words? "We always try to follow up on all cases. I don't have to ask how you happen to be here. How long have you been doing this?" he asked with a wave of his hand to emphasize the "this."

"If you mean the calling part, just a few years. If you mean the dancing part, I've square danced recently for the past few years and quite a while a long time ago. I decided to try my hand at calling when I needed to make some changes in my life. I enjoy it. It gets me out," I explained.

I continued, "The people are nice and usually pretty predictable, which I find comfortable. But I guess last week wasn't so predictable."

"You explained about the shirts to Lorys. I see what you mean about the matching outfits. Point out some of the different clubs here by their clothes." Even when he was making conversation, it sounded more like he was giving orders.

Obviously, he wasn't going to give me any information, so I did my civic duty. I started with the Clearton Squares and their bluebonnet pattern on a background of tan. Then I directed his attention to the Stepping Squares and the other clubs. I pointed out the outfits of the national organization and the officers. I also pointed out that if the yoke of the man's shirt didn't have a pattern, you looked at his tie. Either the yoke, or the tie, or both, usually matched the dress or skirt of his partner.

This seemed minor to some, but to a caller who has to mix up four couples and then get the right man back to the right woman, it was helpful when partners' clothes matched. When the entire square matched, it was more of a challenge, but one most callers enjoyed. After a while, Harbinville's attention seemed to fade. He made some excuse to end our conversation and moved on. Good thing. I needed to cool myself down and go call a tip in the next hall.

The night continued, and other than one dance with Sam and one with Doug, I didn't have a chance to talk to anyone from Clearton or the Stepping Squares. I smiled and socialized with members of the Forsby Footstompers, another club I call for. I chatted with some of the other callers, too. All in all, I was pretty well beat when the dance ended.

I never saw Harbinville again. Maybe he really was just checking it out to make sure he hadn't missed anything. Maybe I had piqued his interest. Well, not me, but my discussion of club outfits anyway. I wasn't conceited enough to think I had caught his interest personally. As I reflected on my flights of fantasy whenever I thought of Harbinville, I decided I clearly had been single way too long. It was nice to know my hormones were still working, but I needed to find a more agreeable trigger for them. I hoped this awareness would spur me forward in my relationship with Doug, maybe even beginning this weekend.

I gathered up my gear and headed for the lobby with hopes of meeting up with the other 'musketeers.' We had tentatively agreed to go to a nearby late-night diner after the dance ended tonight. Sam had been pretty sure that Carlotta would have been able to charm information out of somebody from the Stepping Squares by that time. At any rate, we just needed to finish processing the happenings of the week before. Sure enough, they were waiting for me, and we all moved down the street, with Carlotta bursting to share everything she had learned.

"I talked to a couple of members of the Stepping Squares, and apparently Nick is a pretty quiet guy. But they knew him, all right. He's been a member for several years. He hadn't mentioned to anyone specifically about taking a road trip to Clearton. One of the guys said that he often goes out of town to visit various businesses he works with. He also said that Nick usually tries to catch a dance when he can. He's an insurance agent of some sort and it is not unusual for him to be on the road." Carlotta stopped talking long enough to catch her breath and Sam took the opportunity to get a word in.

"So it really is possible that he just happened to have marked Tuesdays as Clearton dance nights and not realized we were doing lessons," he said. "It really could be a car-jacking and being dumped at Doug's just a coincidence," Sam continued, almost disappointed.

"I guess," Doug chimed in, "but it just seems too easy. One of the Stepping Squares who was an officer for the state association last year said that Nick has been asking about the regional and state dances. He asked if there was a directory or dictionary of club dresses. Jack said he just laughed at that one. Clubs change their dress pattern too often for the state or national associations to even try to keep track. Jack suggested to Nick that he contact me Jack remembered I'd done some reading on the history of square dancing and written that bit for the state newsletter some years back. That makes it seem a little less like 'just coincidence' to me. I don't know. And Harbinville being here seems a little too much for this country boy. Why would he be here if it was cut-and-dried, case closed, already? I bet he doesn't know a Left Allemande from a Swing Thru!"

We all laughed, drank our coffee and, almost as if by agreement, changed topics. It certainly seemed like there was a reasonable explanation for Nick having been in Clearton, and possibly even having looked up Doug's address, in particular. Maybe it was a random thing, maybe Nick had questions. I still had to wonder though, if whoever had done this had realized it wasn't Doug they beat up.

Doug asked how Heather was doing at school, then Carlotta and Sam started telling Doug about my frustration teaching Right and Left Thru at lessons earlier in the week. I mentioned the four men I'd seen at Cracker Barrel and teased Carlotta about the possibility of four available solo men. She hadn't seen them but had managed to dance most of the tips.

It was getting late and we needed to get back to our hotel and get ready for the workshops tomorrow. I still had to locate a full schedule, but I knew I was scheduled to call for Mainstream in the morning and a Plus workshop with Tom in the afternoon.

Doug explained that he was going to visit with his late wife's family. They lived in the area, so he would miss the workshops during the day. He'd connect up with us in the evening for the Saturday night dance. Carlotta planned a day of shopping and sleeping, while Sam actually planned to attend the workshops.

Back at the hotel, we all split up and went our separate ways. After the other two walked away Doug murmured in my ear, "Tomorrow, maybe we can find some time for just the two of us." His gave me a goodnight kiss that lingered and I felt myself flushing as I agreed. I headed for my room, again feeling as ill at ease as a teenager.

#####

The Mainstream workshop Saturday morning went about as well as Tom had indicated for the day before. At best, we had two squares. Most times we had one and part of a second, which made it awkward for the dancers. I went through the laundry list of Mainstream calls, including Right and Left Grand and Right and Left Thru. I hoped that enough people would come in to get a second square for the singing call. In the meantime, I had couples rotate in and out of the square on a regular basis so I could accommodate everyone. By noon, I was ready for a much needed break. Tom, Stacey, and I caught lunch in the conference hall food court. We ordered at the counter and took a number to place on the table.

"So how did Dancing by Definition go this morning, Tom?" I asked after the immediate pleasantries. DBD was usually reserved for advanced callers like Tom, and so far I hadn't attempted a DBD workshop.

"As expected, by the book," he replied with a grin.

Stacey laughed at his joke and added, "Everyone is so serious about getting it right in DBD workshops. They seem to forget it's supposed to be fun! And Tom really gets them going by doing every move with men in the ladies' position and vice versa. So everyone breaks down at first. There were a couple of dancers who were looking pretty pissed."

"But they all got it by the time we were through, didn't they? I had most of them laughing in spite of themselves," he said. "And how did the Mainstream go this morning, Darla?"

I explained about my frustration of few dancers in the Mainstream session, and moved on to the business at hand. Tom and I would be co-calling the afternoon Plus workshop, and that would be fun. I was sure more people would be taking part. People who chose Plus workshops were already seasoned dancers, making it easier to teach. Calling with another person meant that we had to coordinate what music we wanted to do individually, as well as identify a few singing calls we could do as a duet.

"So what tips do you want to duet this afternoon?" I asked.

We went back and forth on potential songs and how to best approach the afternoon as the waitress brought our food and we ate. I had a little time and headed for my room to clean up before the 2 o'clock start time. I got in the elevator and just as the door was about to close, Paul Harbinville got in the elevator with me.

"Hello again… Paul. You still here?" was my surprised response to his appearance. He was dressed in the suit and tie again. He definitely wasn't going to be blending in now.

"Hello, Darla. You in this hotel, too? I assume you'll be calling again this evening," he said with minimal expression that conveyed feigned interest.

"This afternoon and this evening actually. You might want to take in one of the workshops and actually learn how to square dance if you're going to hang around at the dances," I teased. "You probably wouldn't have any trouble finding a partner, but I gotta tell you, you won't be blending in with a suit."

"Maybe next time, but I doubt it. I prefer my dancing up close and personal," was his response. The elevator dinged and stopped on the sixth floor. We both exited at the same time and I bumped into him. Now, how was that for coincidence, both of us on the same floor! He stepped back and said, "Ladies first, Ms. King." I couldn't tell if he was being chivalrous or sarcastic. Either way, we separated and went in opposite directions.

I realized I'd been holding my breath after his unexpected response about dancing up close and personal produced fleeting romantic thoughts about this mysterious man. Really, I told myself, you have to get a life! My stomach was doing flip flops but I credited it to a suspicion that he might be using his federal status to find out which floor I'd booked. Silly, I chided myself, why would he? I couldn't be a suspect. I'd been calling for lessons the night Nick Tricot was attacked. Shaking it off, I let myself into my room, changed my blouse, freshened up, and went back down to the hall to call with Tom.

The Plus workshop went well, and I had no more Paul Harbinville sightings to distract me. I managed to sneak off after the workshop. There was a very long break in the activities until the next dance and I was just plain tired of smiling! I decided some down time in my room was probably what I needed. I stripped down to the bare necessities, opened the curtains to give me a feeling of space, and fell into a restless sleep.

In my sleep-bound mind, Doug was dancing with me and we were having a great time. Not square dancing, but holding me in his arms as we circled the floor. Things were heating up and I actually wasn't putting up any barriers for a change. His hands felt good on my back as he massaged my shoulders and somehow slid his hands up the back of my shirt. All my worries were resolved, and any excuses I came up with, Doug had an answer to.

We waltzed around our very private dance floor and my feet barely touched the ground. I opened my eyes as the music ended and stared into his eyes. No wait, those weren't Doug's brown eyes, they were Paul's blue eyes! I awoke with a start and looked around. I half expected to find either Paul or Doug in the room with me. They weren't of course, but I discovered I was warmer than the air conditioning could account for. I don't think I'm old enough for hot flashes yet, but that was a more reassuring explanation than others I could come up with.

The phone rang, and I answered it with a groggy "yeah?"

"Hi Darla, Carlotta here. You sound like you were sleeping."

"Yeah, and I'm still not awake. What's up?" I asked. I decided I needed to shower and grab a quick bite when I looked at the clock and realized it was almost 6 o'clock. Another hour and the dancers would be lining up for tonight's Grand March. I hadn't heard from Doug yet, but I figured we'd just locate each other in the dancehall. That time together he wanted was slipping away.

"I got back to the hotel after shopping. You should see what I got. I was thinking about getting a salad here in the hotel before the dance. Want to join me?" said Carlotta.

"Yeah, but it will take me a few minutes… how about I meet you down there at 6:15? Will that work? But it will have to be quick," I said.

"I'll be there," she answered, and added, "I'll see if Sam and Doug are around in the meantime." With that she hung up, and I headed for the shower. I again donned a prairie skirt and peasant blouse. I added my basic black pettipants in case I had the opportunity to dance. As a caller, I was affiliated with more than one club, so I needed to make sure I wasn't dressing to match one club over another. This further complicated my deciding what colors to wear. Finally dressed, I opted for a light dinner before the dance.

Getting off the elevator, I immediately spotted Carlotta. She was dressed in a multicolored print, cobalt blue top with gold trim and gold crinolines. The colors made her eyes sparkle. Carlotta's clothes were always perfectly color coordinated. I would guess that her pettipants matched the cobalt blue but she could have gone with the gold instead. With her petite frame, the traditional garb suited her, but on me, they wouldn't quite look the same.

"Hi Darla, you're right on time. I couldn't find Sam or Doug, so it's just us girls for dinner," she greeted me.

"That's fine with me. I want to hear about all of the characters you've met up with. You do usually manage to find them! And what you found in the shops," I said.

Carlotta laughed, signaling to the hostess that we were two. Once seated, she commented, "Well, I checked out the singles social room, but I'm beginning to think that there is a serious shortage of men I could be interested in. Actually, I think there is a shortage of single men in general. Those four guys you saw must have wives you just didn't see. I have been able to find guys to dance with, though. Sam or Doug, of course, and Mainstream with several guys I've met at other dances. All in all, the dance promises to be fun tonight. My dance card is filled. Even with the shopping, I managed to fit in a workshop. A couple of squares broke down, but that's to be expected in a workshop. Everyone was nice about the breakdowns and the dancers and the caller recovered well. The caller, though obviously not as good as you, was pretty good," she ended with a smile. "He was one I hadn't heard call before." I always wondered where tiny Carlotta got all the breath needed for her mile-a-minute monologues.

"Well, I'm sure the rest of the callers are great! But thanks for the compliment. I'm glad you are getting to dance. It does seem like there are usually very few single men at these dances, and the best dancers are usually booked up," I said.

Carlotta nodded. "That reminds me. I don't know that he's single, and he's sure not a dancer, but did you see that Harbinville guy around here today?" she asked.

I related my encounter with him in the elevator in what I hoped was a nonchalant manner. I left out my thoughts and suspicions. I added, "I still find it hard to believe that he is just 'following up' if he really thinks Nick was the victim of a car-jacking. It just doesn't seem like you follow up by going to a square dance."

"Nope, but I guess we won't ever know what the real story is. He is nice to look at, at least, and I guess he isn't bothering anybody. Too bad he doesn't dance. I could use another solo partner! Anyway, let's finish up and catch the exhibition before the dance," Carlotta urged, bringing us back to the here and now of the Hoedown.

Saturday night went pretty much like Friday. Jerry started off the dance again in the main hall with a Grand March after an exhibition by the Denton Cloggers. Clogging is sort of like tap dance, square dance, Irish high-stepping, and river dancing all rolled into one. The shoes have double taps, and as they kick and step, the beat is tapped out in double-time. The Denton Cloggers were all fairly young, and it was not surprising that they were clogging to rap music. Most other clogging groups often used marching or patriotic music. The cloggers clearly had more energy than most of us older folks.

Clogging, Grand March, and national anthem out of the way, the rest of the dance was predictable. Tonight there were 35 squares, or 280 dancers, in the Grand March and the hall was about ready to burst. I didn't manage to find Doug for the Grand March, and didn't see much of Doug or Sam or Carlotta again until the end of the night. Tonight there was an official after party with country-western dancing. My calling went by in a blur, and the night was over in no time. I headed to the main hall for the after party.

"Darla darlin', you better come join us over here. We got ourselves a table and Doug could probably use a partner," Sam said with a wink. He never came right out and said anything about Doug and me. I wasn't sure if he had picked up on our relationship the other day at Doug's or if he was just playing innocent matchmaker. I don't see how he could have missed

Doug's kiss at the car when we were out at the ranch, but I wasn't about to ask.

"You bet, Sam. I guess Carlotta is joining us too? And all the new friends you've managed to make this trip, huh?" I teased. Sam was always a popular man at these dances, in part because there were fewer single males than females, but mostly because he was such a nice guy and a great dancer.

The band set up and was playing in no time at all. Tables were at the far end of the hall, the band at the front end, and room for dancing in between. Most of the crowd had opted to get some sleep, but probably about 80 dancers were still here and enjoyed some refreshments and the company of each other. As the band began the next song, a two-step, Doug tapped my arm and we went out to the dance floor. We danced that one, sat out a few, and then danced again. It felt good to be in his arms and if I closed my eyes I could almost forget about the rest of the couples dancing, and imagine the two of us alone.

He was warm and affectionate, and I enjoyed being with him. It felt good to have his arms guide me around the dance floor. Only once did I flash back to my startling dream from the afternoon. I must have jumped a little when I did, because Doug pulled back and asked if I was okay. I assured him I was. Fatigue eventually took over, and about midnight, I decided I had to call it quits and head for bed. As I pleaded fatigue, I thought Doug looked a little disappointed and perhaps a bit put off, but I just couldn't function any longer.

We said our goodbyes and exchanged hugs. Doug walked a little way out with me and gave me another of his lingering kisses, which surprised me and I felt my temperature rise. We would all be on the road and heading home first thing in the morning. Doug said he would be leaving early, and he would call me. His eyes had an imploring look and I half considered suggesting we not call it a night. I think he sensed that, because his eyes cleared and he said with a chuckle, "Darla, you're falling asleep standing up. Get some rest!"

One quick kiss and I headed for my own room, alone. I was not calling for the Trail Out dance the next day, and that meant I could hit the road whenever I wanted. Doug and I would see each other later this week, when lessons on Right and Left Thru would continue at the next Clearton Squares lesson night. Hopefully there would be less excitement this time and Doug would be there to help out.

Sunday came early, and the ride home was uneventful. My day wasn't over when I got home, though. I saw my note on the fridge and remembered I'd promised Heather I'd send her the English book Monday morning. I felt like an intruder when I went into her room, a holdover from years of working out the delicate balance of a teenager's need for privacy and a parent's need to be involved. From the time she was thirteen, Heather had been responsible for cleaning and keeping her own room. I'd been allowed in only as a visitor, though a frequent one, and never denied permission. It was her domain and it had become her sanctuary after her dad's death six years ago. Neither Heather nor I had handled grief very well after Clint's death, both of us retreating to our respective corners to nurse our wounds. We hadn't fought, but it wedged a space between us that we were finally working hard to bridge.

I rooted around in her closet and found the book. I curiously flipped through its pages to see how the vampire sucked the life out of English. The book proved to be a fairly standard English usage book, far less enticing in content than in title. I boxed it up, ready to carry it by the FedEx office first thing in the morning when they opened. Then I found my bed and to welcome rest.

Chapter 5

The Hoedown behind me, it was back to my regular routine. It was Monday, so tonight I was calling for the Forsby Footstompers for their regular dance in Forsby. Forsby was the other side of Houston, about an hour-plus from Isquith. Forsby was a quiet, well-established small town. Not a growing area like Clearton, but more of a settled community. Unlike the Clearton Squares, where I called every week, I called for the Footstompers alternate weeks only. The group was a well-established, older club. The current presidents, Hal and Lenore, had been square dancing since before I was born, and they weren't even the most senior of the members. As usual, they greeted me as I arrived.

"Howdy, Darla! It's good to see you. How are you doing tonight? Good drive from Isquith?" asked Hal. Hal had a receding hairline, and what hair he still had was white as snow. He was beginning to hobble a bit when he walked, but nonetheless could keep pace with anyone once he got on the dance floor.

"I am doing fine, didn't run into too much traffic and the weather seems to be holding out. Probably be raining when I head home later though," I responded with a smile as I carted in my equipment. "And how are you doing, Hal? And you, Lenore?" I asked.

It was Lenore who answered, "We are doing just fine. Enjoying the Fall, such as it is." Lenore was a strawberry blonde this month. Sometimes her hair was a little darker, sometimes a little lighter. She still moved pretty well, though she has put on some weight over the years and it seemed to make dancing painful some nights. Hal grabbed one of my bags and helped me get set up. Hugs exchanged, they moved to the door to greet members as they came in.

After the terrorist attacks on 9-11, the Footstompers had adopted a red-white-and-blue club dress and the practice of starting each night's dance with a singing call to a patriotic medley. The club dress had changed over the years, still maintaining the red-white-and-blue colors, and the starting patriotic dance remained. Not surprising. Most of the men and probably some of the women had served in the military. I had to find an appropriate CD to get started. I searched through my bag and came up with one. I chose "God Bless America." I checked the time, smiled at some dancers as they gathered nearby and got the dance started with a "Hey there, Footstompers, let's square up!"

Four squares formed with no problem. There were some folks sitting out, some playing dominoes in the back of the room. For some members who couldn't move as well anymore, coming to the dances was still the highlight of their social calendar. For others, this was a fun activity that kept up their cardiovascular system and got them out of the house. That's why when the club's original founders, a couple named Clifton, had donated money for the senior center, they had designated that this activity room be available for the Footstompers at no cost. They also had stipulated that the wooden floors be maintained and provided the funding for keeping the floors in excellent condition.

Although the Cliftons had passed on several years ago, the accounts were maintained in trust, and the Footstompers were set. So, although not all the members would qualify as 'seniors' and visitors were more than welcome, the Footstompers danced in an extension of the local senior center. And that meant that sometimes there were folks just sitting and watching the dance, or playing dominoes.

I looked around and figured it was time. "Bow to your partner, bow to your corner," and then the CD took over. I called them through the melody, but they all were singing along, they knew it so well. The red-white-and-blue and sense of patriotism always got to me. My eyes were moist when the CD ended and the dancers stopped. I was more or less on autopilot and in the zone. I wasn't teaching anything and just went right into the next CD. After it ended I told them, "OK, take a break

. I'm putting on a waltz for any of you who want to take advantage of the opportunity," as I headed for some more coffee.

"Hey Darla, I heard there was some excitement down in Clearton the other week. What's the story?" Flo asked. In her late sixties or maybe even seventies, petite and almost fragile looking, Flo was one of the mainstays of the Footstompers. She knew everything about everybody, kept the history of the club, and was always there whenever a member was sick or in the hospital. Sadly, with the older crowd, that was a frequent occurrence. Flo also had a unique sense of humor and spoke out when others would remain silent. Sometimes other dancers wished she didn't. In fact, sometimes what she came out with even made me blush.

"Now, Flo, how did that news make it all the way to you?" I returned with a laugh.

"I ran into Sam at the Hoedown… wouldn't you like to know what we were doing?" she added with a laugh. Flo was a pretty upbeat and energetic lady for a woman of any age. I smiled to imagine what she and Sam might have been up to. "He mentioned that poor man, a square dancer no less, and the car-jacking. Terrible world we live in these days. That wouldn't a'happened in years past. Just simple country folks helping each other out." Her eyes looked at the ceiling as her words drifted away.

Then she took a deep breath and wound up again. "Ooh, and then all the police and at that Doug Weathers house. In case you didn't notice, Doug is fine specimen of a man. A little too young and stuffy for me, but you know you know what I mean. You know you could do a lot worse than Doug Weathers, Darla," she added in almost a conspiratorial whisper.

Well, that wasn't where I expected the conversation to go. It took a lot of effort for me not to laugh or be disrespectful to Flo. Some of the older dancers felt like I was a 'youngster' that needed guidance or looking out for. I didn't resent that really, I was just surprised when it happened.

I opted for, "That's the truth, Flo." Then I changed the subject away from me and my love life by getting her onto one of her favorite subject, her grandchildren. "And how is the world treating you? The grandkids?" I responded as I drank my coffee and hoped for the best.

Flo proceeded to tell me about her grandchildren and now her first great-grandchild, as well as the comings and goings of the other Footstompers. She even threw in her take on local politics. Flo was a sweetheart, even if she was a little outspoken. As I listened and nodded and drank my coffee, I recalled that she had been a state and national square dance officer and that brought up some questions.

"Now Flo, you know everything," I interrupted. "Getting back to the excitement at Clearton, do you know this Nick Tricot who was hurt? Ever see him in your various travels and adventures?" I added.

"Sam asked me that too, Darla. I've been racking my brain and trying to jog my memory, but I gotta tell you, as I get older, it gets harder and harder to remember folks' names. I have been at dances with Stepping Squares dancers and even to one of their club dances way back, but the name just doesn't ring any bells. If I saw him, I might recognize his face. Especially if he has dimples – you know I always remember a man with dimples. Sorry," Flo answered with a smile. She abruptly turned and went over to the group playing dominoes, and I moved back to my gear. Time to call the next tip. "Let's square 'em up!"

I called two more tips with a waltz and two-step to break up the rhythm and to keep me on schedule. Although I really loved calling for the Footstompers, I missed the friends I had in the Clearton Squares. They were more my age and easier to relate to. It's a bit disconcerting to realize that in another 20 or 30 years, this will be me. After the third tip, I turned and almost knocked over Flo and a man I had not met before. I seriously hoped she wasn't trying to fix me up.

"Darla, oh, sorry! Darla this is Jonnie. He used to be a member of the Stepping Squares, but moved here to Forsby when he retired. What was that man's name again? I can't remember it, but Jonnie here may know that man!" rambled Flo. Her friend, Jonnie, looked to be about 65, probably newly retired. He had thin white hair that I was sure was thick and beautiful when he was younger. He wore it a little on the long side, pulled into a ponytail for dancing tonight, and had a beard. He had blue eyes and an easy smile, and sported a Texas A&M baseball cap that I'd noticed he left on when dancing. About average height for a man, he was taller than Flo but seemed almost overwhelmed by her. She tended to have that effect on folks, especially men. She'd been known to pat a few men's butts when dancing, and I'd heard from Sam that she wore a garter under the crinolines. I hadn't pursued how he knew that fact, nor had I had occasion to verify it.

"Hi Jonnie. Nice to meet you," I said with a typical square dancer's side-hug. "The man's name is Nick Tricot. I really don't know much about him. I do know that he was wearing a Stepping Squares shirt and was apparently coming to the dance in Clearton. The story is that he was the victim of a car-jacking ring," I added in explanation. "Do you recognize the name?"

"Nick Tricot? Humph. I do remember someone named Nick. Not sure of his last name. He seemed okay, a pretty good dancer. I don't know much else about him. I seem to remember he was on the reserved and quiet side. Flo was telling me he almost died. Good thing he was found in time. Doesn't make much sense, does it? I heard that there had been a bunch of kids in town here joyriding in 'borrowed' cars. The kids didn't seem to think what they were doing was all that serious. But I don't know of anything that was really car-jacking. Boy, were those kids surprised to find out they were criminals!" he rambled, his head nodding all the while.

We chatted for a few more minutes, discussed the Hoedown, and then I called the last two tips. As in Clearton, I had to pack up my gear, this time with Hal and Jonnie's help, and headed home. I thought I'd put the Clearton incident out of my mind, but after all the conversation tonight I was thinking about it again. Things just didn't add up. That it was kids and not professionals would make more sense, but it didn't compute. Hopefully, there would be some light shed on the matter when I called in Clearton the next night.

I was one of the few cars to leave the parking lot immediately after the dance. Most of the members stayed to socialize with the other seniors. As I left the parking lot, I continued to think about the Hoedown, Paul Harbinville's appearance, and the number of 'coincidences' that supposedly occurred in such a short span of time. I continued down the main street to get to the highway entrance, and noticed that the car behind me was following way too close. I hate when cars follow too closely, and I resisted the temptation to speed up to get them off my tail. I thought about pulling over, and then remembered the infomercial Heather had told me to watch. The speaker warned not to pull over if another car looked suspicious. I wasn't quite sure where the sheriff's office was, but I did notice a gas station ahead with a couple of cars at the pumps. I pulled in there and let the car behind me get ahead of me. I told myself it was just my imagination and all the talk about car-jacking that made me nervous. I waited a few minutes, and a lot more vigilant, headed on toward the highway entrance and home.

I reached home in record time and turned on the television to the news. I always recorded it on my DVR. I set about my usual night time routine to get ready for bed, including some exercises to try to whittle down my mid-section. The news was really just background noise while I waited on the weather. Halfway through brushing my teeth I heard the main newscaster say, "So, what was the uproar all about in Clearton tonight, Cassie?" I immediately left the bathroom and went into the bedroom to hear the answer.

The other newscaster, Cassie, continued, "Well, Bob, there was a town meeting and it got pretty heated. A group of local citizens are apparently very upset about the proposal to build a camp and recreation site on some of the property on the east side of town. The location is shown here on the map. The proposed site development would be a camp in the summer, but will offer activities year round. It is specifically set up for children and youth with disabilities. Funding for this would come from a private foundation, and some of the ranchers are very supportive, particularly with regard to equine therapy." The camera had left Cassie's face and a video of ranchland was showing on the screen while she talked. I couldn't tell if it was Doug's ranch or not.

She continued, "Others are not as supportive. They argue that the zoning for this land is residential and agriculture. They seem to think that a camp would be considered commercial. They are afraid that once this camp is allowed to be there, other commercial ventures would be coming in. If you watch this video clip, you can tell the argument got pretty heated." The video on the screen changed to a scene inside and showed a crowded room with an animated man speaking at a microphone in the aisle. I watched the video clip, and sure enough there was Doug and some other ranchers in the audience. They looked pretty calm. Then the video zoomed in on a few of the attendees who looked angry. At least one was shaking his fist in the air. The camera panned the gathering and the screen returned to showing the news desk with Cassie and Bob.

"In fact, Bob, I'm not sure I have seen this many people at a Clearton town meeting in a long time!" she ended. I just about dropped my toothbrush at what I thought I saw in that last sweep of the audience. I had to rewind the video a few times to be certain, but sure enough, there was Paul Harbinville sitting at the back of the gathering! Car-jacking, my foot! I picked up my toothbrush, finished my routine, and went to bed. My last thought was that I definitely needed to get the real story from Doug at the dance tomorrow.

I remember my parents commented on some line in a movie, "If it's Tuesday, I must be in Belgium." Well, it was Tuesday, so I was calling in Clearton again. Strategically I arrived early enough to stop at the café in hopes that my now favorite waitress, Sadie, was working again. Lo and behold, I lucked out, or maybe she worked every day.

"Well, howdy, Miss Square Dancer. Come on in and set yourself down. Coffee?" Sadie didn't so much as blink as she grabbed the coffee pot and showed me to a corner table.

"Coffee would be good. And I would like a BLT on wheat if I could," I responded.

"No problem. Be right out with that," she added as she poured the coffee.

As I waited on my sandwich, I wondered how to broach the subject of last week's incident at Doug's or the problems at the town meeting. I wanted to know what she had heard. My sense was that if there was talk in town, Sadie would have her finger on the pulse.

"Here ya go." Sadie placed my sandwich in front of me. "How does that look to you?" she asked.

"Mmm. Looks good, thanks. These fresh tomatoes?"

"You bet. The owner of the café grows his own. Good, huh?" she added.

"Great. Any excitement I should know about, Sadie?" I asked.

"Nope, pretty quiet. You asked about car-jacking last week, so I guess you were ahead of me on that news. I heard it through the grapevine a couple of days ago, nothing official though. Other than that, nothing's happened here but the usual hometown doings, and that's the way I like it," she said.

"I saw on the news there was some trouble about some camp being established in town for kids with disabilities. What's the scuttlebutt?" I asked, hoping I wasn't pushing my luck.

"Oh that. I didn't even think about that, although I should have. Lord knows I've had folks in here all day talking about the town meeting last night. Doesn't matter to me, but some people are just plain against any kind of change. Old Jasper Crown, he let off some steam at that meeting, but that was all it was. He just has some old beliefs and fears. Some of the other folks are afraid that this is a trend though. That first, it will be a camp for kids with disabilities, and then as the cities get more crowded, they will try to put one of them prison camps out here, or some other big commercial enterprise. Silly," she said with a shrug.

She hesitated. When she continued, there was a touch of sadness in her voice that I hadn't heard from her before. "People sometimes get a little scared of what they don't understand. I can appreciate that. My daughter has a child with Down syndrome. I had some pretty strange ideas myself before little Lena came. Now I know better. She's a doll. I'm not saying that just cause I'm her grandma. You can ask anyone who works here!" Her voice had changed from sad to defensive, and I knew little Lena had one feisty protector in Sadie.

"I'm actually glad that they are talking about starting a camp here and increasing our summer trade," she continued. "I've talked to Doug Weathers to let him know I'm behind him and those other ranchers. You know him?" I nodded and she continued. "I think it would be great if he could do something to combine horses and riding to help kids. Whoever knew of a child who didn't like horses or dream of riding one? Well, listen to me, spouting off when I got folks waiting on coffee! I gotta check on the rest of the customers. Be back in a minute," and she was off to the next customer.

Her words gave me something to think about. First, she, and by generalization the locals, bought the car-jacking explanation. Second, the issue of the camp or equine therapy didn't seem to be such a hot topic to have led to violence, at least not by local folks. I continued to ponder the situation as I ate my sandwich.

"Dessert this evening?" Sadie interrupted by reverie.

"No, thanks. I think this will be it." As she wrote out my check, I added, "Sadie, does the name Nick Tricot sound familiar?"

"Nope, but I'm not all that good on names, just faces. Oh, the regulars I know for sure. He live around here? I see customers come and go, but they don't have customers wear name tags, just the wait staff," she replied with a hint of amusement. "What's he look like?"

"Point taken. I don't actually know what he looks like and he doesn't live around here. Might have some ties to the area though. Any more strangers here recently than you're used to seeing?" I ventured on a whim.

"An occasional passerby, but center of town is kind of off the path. Maybe six months ago there were some business types. I think they were developers but I'm not sure what they were developing. Then, like I said last week, there were some official types in early summer. And then one guy last week after that car-jacking. He was nice-looking, blue eyes, coffee black, okay tipper. But no, not other than that," she responded.

"Ok, well thanks. Maybe I'll see ya next week!" I paid the check with a good-sized tip. Both because she had given me some information and been pleasant, but also if she described me to anyone, I wanted to be sure I was an "okay tipper." I was off to the Clearton Squares.

Clearly, Sadie had a good memory for her customers, even if she couldn't remember their names. She knew their business and whether they tipped well. I bet that the man she described had been Harbinville.

Even with my conversation with Sadie, I arrived at the Clearton dancehall in plenty of time to set up without feeling rushed. We were still learning Right and Left Thru, but at least tonight lessons would only be the first half of the night. Most of the students had been here for the previous lesson, and this time they picked up the move like a charm. I was relieved and moved on to teaching other dance steps.

After a bit, I put on the next song and called the same patterns again so they could practice. "Good job! Let's take a break!" I said.

Doug and Carlotta had both arrived during the tip, and I was looking forward to chatting with them. As I walked toward the coffee pot, Doug smiled warmly in greeting, and gave me a lingering hug.

"Long time no see, Darla! I think it's been three whole days, huh? Barely time to recover from the Hoedown for me. I must be getting old. How about you?" Doug bantered easily.

"Oh, yeah, it does seem to take longer to catch up on that lost sleep than it used to. I saw you on the news last night. Was it as bad as they made it sound?" I asked.

Doug smiled. "Nah, you know how things can get blown out of proportion. I mean, we don't usually get a lot of excitement out here in the boonies. A few people got excited and expressed their opinions. No big deal."

"Doug, I was just chatting with Sadie at the café and she said something about developers. Anyone trying to buy that land y'all are planning on using for the camp?" I asked on the off chance that real estate was at the root of this.

"No offers that I am aware of. There were some developers who wanted to see about putting in high rises and shopping malls, even asked about some of my property. The town fathers basically told them that we liked being unsophisticated, and they left," he answered with a chuckle.

"Anything new on Nick Tricot or the car-jackers?" was my next question. I felt like I was interrogating him, and added, "Sorry so many questions, I am still trying to get my head around this."

Doug smiled and said, "The car-jacking gossip is still big news around here. But, no, I haven't heard anything new or more legit. Sheriff Lorys hasn't come looking for me. No one else has shown up unconscious on the ranch, and that's a good thing!" He continued, "I think Carlotta has tried to find out more about Nick. Here she comes now. You and Carlotta are really into this investigation thing, aren't you? I'm ready to let it go. I don't see a big car-jacking crime spree ahead for Clearton, ya know." I nodded in reply.

"Darla, I was thinking of heading up toward your way later in the week, say Thursday. Any chance we could grab a bite, you know, just the two of us?" he asked as he leaned in just a bit and kissed my neck, out of Carlotta's view.

"That would be great!" was my quick response and I was sure I was blushing as Carlotta walked up.

"Hi Carlotta, how are you doing?" I said as I gave her a hug and tried to recover my composure. "I hear that you are becoming the super sleuth, so what did you find out?" As soon as I asked the question, I made a mental note to ask less questions and make more small talk. I reminded myself that I was no longer in the investigating business. Small talk had never been my strong point, and I realized I could come across a little brash sometimes.

"Hi Darla. I tried calling a couple of the dancers I know in the Dallas/Fort Worth area, even though they aren't in the Stepping Squares. I had hoped to see them at the Hoedown, and that was my excuse for calling them. Anyway, there apparently was another dance going on in Amarillo, and they were up there. I managed to ask if they knew this Nick Tricot guy. Jenny said she knew of one guy named Nick, but she wasn't sure what his last name was. She said she really only remembered him because he seemed somewhat quiet, and, obviously, because he was a solo dancer. The guys didn't remember him at all. That's not surprising, if he is quiet. So all my sleuthing didn't add much. One of these days, we may have to just get a chance to talk to this Nick fella ourselves," she added by conclusion with a shrug of her shoulders.

"That would certainly be helpful," I said. I saw Doug roll his eyes, so I added, "Probably time to move on and let the police do their thing. I know it's time for me to do my thing again." With a smile, I headed for the microphone and the front of the hall. Back to work.

On the next tip, the last of the lesson tips, I reviewed Right and Left Thru. We made it through the singing call with almost all the students able to do Right and Left Grand, Right and Left Thru, and Weave the Ring. Success! "Take a break. Next week is a lesson night, so we will work hard next week and review these calls again then! Next tip is a club tip, everybody!"

The rest of the night went by pretty much on schedule. Lots of coffee for me, easy going conversation with Sam, Doug and Carlotta, and the night came to a close. Doug and I chatted a little after he helped me put my stuff in the car. He confirmed that Paul Harbinville had been at the town meeting.

He reassured me that he really didn't think he had been the target, and nicely suggested I let it go. We settled on what time he would come by on Thursday evening. A lingering hug, an even more lingering kiss, and I was on my way.

Back to the normal routine instead of the excitement of just a week ago. I was glad about that. On the trip home, I thought about Heather, wondered about her new friend Micah, compiled a to-do list in my head, and didn't dwell any more about the Clearton Caper, as I had begun to call it. I contemplated whether instead of coming up with a place to eat out on Thursday, I should just make dinner. Would that be too intimate? And what would I cook?

Chapter 6

Time passes quickly, but especially in the Fall when there is so much to do what with getting the gardens cleaned out after the weeds have their way with it in the summer heat. I try to get the house cleaned and aired out on the occasional nice day when I can open the windows. It's always refreshing to let in some outside air instead of relying on air conditioning or heating all the time, I think.

Today I was focused on cleaning up the house, not one of my favorite chores when the phone rang. Caller ID indicated it was Heather.

"Hi Mom! What are you doing?" Heather's voice greeted me as I picked up the phone.

"Hi Heth! I'm trying to get this house clean. Have you learned where dust comes from at that university? It certainly is defying my every effort to keep it under control. And what are you up to?" was my reply.

She laughed. "No, mom, I don't know where dust comes from, but it doesn't only thrive in Isquith. Dust is thriving right here in Austin as well." She continued a little more seriously, "Don't you know someone named Doug Weathers? Isn't he one of your square dancer friends?"

A little taken aback, I responded, "Yes, Heather, I know Doug. He's a square dancer and a friend of mine from Clearton. Why do you ask?"

"Well, there's an article in the Austin paper about Clearton and Doug Weathers and some kind of camp. Apparently some splinter group calling themselves 'concerned citizens' had a meeting to try to get other people to sign a petition to stop the State Rehab people from using the land for a camp for kids with disabilities. Mr. Weathers is reported to not only be 'an active supporter of the camp, but a staunch advocate for individuals with disabilities.' The article goes on to talk about his plans to start a program with horses to provide therapy for kids with spina bifida and other problems. Anyway, it's a pretty interesting article and you call down in Clearton, so I figured you might know some of these folks. Apparently, the protest meeting got a little out of hand. The paper says one of these 'concerned citizens' became agitated and had to be restrained. I know you don't get the Austin paper, but if you're interested, you could read it on the web. Is this Doug the same one you had dinner with here in Austin one time?" she asked curiously.

"Yes, it is the same Doug. He's been talking about equine therapy for some time. It's really too bad there's so much ignorance out there. Some people are afraid of what they don't know or understand. A camp sounds like a pretty harmless endeavor to me. I understand part of the concern was that fear that all the big city problems would follow right after the camp."

Heather laughed again. "Well, mom, you're a trip. After I met him at dinner that time, he seemed nice and interested in you! So I was kind of hoping that you and he were, you know, an 'item.' Now I find out he's an activist. You know I get concerned about you being lonely now that I'm in Austin. You really need to do stuff for fun and find someone special – but not some crazy activist, that's for sure! And I'm the one in Austin, where it's supposed to be filled with activists. Go figure. Anyway, now that I've read this article I'm kinda glad you don't know him that well. I'd be worried about you all over again. Just for different reasons."

Was it ironic or alarming that my daughter was worrying about her mom instead of the other way around? I was pleased she cared. We were working our way back to each other.

"Well, I wouldn't exactly call Doug an 'activist,' honey. He has a ranch and lots of land, and lots of horses. I think he was just trying to put some of what's his into something that could be beneficial to others. You know, give back to the community? Not exactly radical. But anyway, you worry about you, Heth, not me," I replied. I changed the subject, "So how is Micah these days?"

"Oh, he is just wonderful," she hummed as she spoke. "He is kind and supportive, and we have lots of fun together. And, mom, I want to assure you, he isn't keeping me from my studies. He's a good student. It's been a long time since I've been able to feel good about life and everything. Seeing Micah helps. I'll never forget Dad, but we need to let other people into our lives, don't you think? Don't you think Dad would have wanted that?" she asked with obvious emotion.

Her reference to her Dad and her need for reassurance caught me off guard. Almost too choked up to talk, I responded, "Oh, Heather, yes, your Dad would want you to be happy. I want you to be happy. With Micah or some other guy. But honey, I need to take my time and you do too, you know."

"Okay, mom. But I'm gonna keep bugging you!" she teased.

"Yeah, yeah. And I'll keep reminding you that you have plenty of time before you get too serious. We'll keep each other in line, okay?"

"Yeah, right. I gotta go. Love you." The dial tone came through before I could respond.

I sat there and thought about life, my life, Heather's life, and Clint's life and death. That brought me right back to my life, living alone, and putting obstacles in the way of what could be a relationship with Doug. Could we be an "item," as Heather had said? So, what should I do next? Instead of continuing down that line of thought and trying to imagine what being an "item" might mean, I got on the internet and pulled up the Austin paper so I could read the article myself.

Heather had pretty much summarized the whole thing. I wondered if there was any room in square dancing for kids with disabilities. It's an audience I should look into. I didn't remember any callers ever mentioning anything about working with kids or adults with disabilities. I do remember seeing a video of wheelchair square dancers, but they had special chairs to pivot and turn, and non-wheelchair bound partners.

I read through the article again. The picture that went with the article was of two policemen restraining someone who appeared to be yelling at Doug and some others. A nearby was overturned. It occurred to me that the local TV news had actually downplayed the meeting – as had Doug when he told me about it. This version looked more volatile.

It had been two weeks since my discussion with Sadie about the town's reaction to the proposed camp, and I hadn't given much thought to the incident in Clearton. The article and its hint of hot tempers related to the camp brought my fears about Doug as the intended victim to mind. The leader of the 'citizens committee,' one George Butard, and the director of the County Rehabilitation Office, Jerolyn Ambia, were the only other ones named, except for the man named Jasper Crowne that Sadie had mentioned.

Having found a way to yet again avoid confronting my own feelings, I decided to search the net and see what I could find out about this Butard guy and his group. A cursory search didn't yield much on him. There was a picture and a family website that may or may not have been the same Butards. I certainly didn't find anything that would suggest a history of violence. I resisted the urge to try to access some of the more restricted sites I was aware of from my previous life.

Instead, I moved on to my 'curiosity' search. I went to the various websites that cater to callers and checked bulletin boards to see if I could find anything on teaching or calling for children or adults with disabilities. I checked out the individual sites of some of the caller/teachers I knew the names of and sent some of them an email. I asked if they had any suggestions or experience calling or teaching individuals with disabilities to square dance because nothing immediately jumped out at me. Pretty simple searches, but the next thing I knew, as often happened with the internet, I realized I had spent over two hours surfing with very little information gained.

About the same time, I realized that my stomach was growling and that Doug would be at the house in less than an hour. I hadn't come up with any great ideas for what to cook for dinner or how to impress him with my domestic side, which if truth be known is pretty limited. That was probably a good thing. An hour was plenty of time to shower and dress, but not enough to come up with a gourmet dinner. I picked out my clothes with care. I didn't want to be too dressy or too casual. In all, I think I changed about five times easy. In the process, I had to remind myself I was not a teenager going on her first date.

Once I was ready, I tried to figure out how to broach the subject of the article in the paper and get more information. I could just wait until I went to Clearton on Tuesday. Then I could stop at the café and hope Sadie was there. I'd see what she knew about dear old Butard and the 'concerned citizens.' And I could ask about it between or after tips at the dance. Who was I kidding? I didn't want to wait that long. My next option was to, casually of course, ask Doug about the article. He would probably just brush off the whole thing as silly and tell me to leave it to the police. Okay, easy to talk myself out of that one. So that left Carlotta. Thank goodness for cell phones and another 20 minutes before Doug and dinner.

"Hi Carlotta, Darla here. Is this a good time to talk?" I asked when I heard her hello.

"Hi yourself. Time is fine, what's up?" was her upbeat reply.

"Well, it's just that I read this article about Clearton in the Austin paper and was wondering about it. It doesn't say very much about the people in the article, but Doug is mentioned. Bottom line, I'm looking for the inside info on this. What do you know?" I haltingly explained about the news report from two weeks before, along with this article and my interpretation of it. I felt a bit sheepish at dragging the whole thing up again.

Carlotta just laughed and interrupted, "Darla, you don't need to hedge with me. I haven't seen the Austin paper, but I'm guessing that the article had to do with another town meeting about the camp they're trying to get zoning for. There was another meeting this week. The people protesting the rezoning actually aren't against the camp, but against the other possibilities the rezoning would open the area to. George Butard is the most vocal in his objections. He used to live in another town. When they rezoned to allow for a recreation hall, somehow that allowed some "adult" establishments to be in that same area. He also did his research and has a couple other examples where residential zoning was changed to accommodate one purpose, but inadvertently the change in zoning also resulted in the establishment of some enterprise not otherwise foreseen. You might say he sees himself as something of a savior. He's saving the community from some unknown evil that the zoning change, not the camp really, would open us up to. And he gets very passionate and worked up about it. I think only those of us who actually have read all his information realize that he doesn't have a problem with people with disabilities." She paused to take a breath after her usual breath-taking run then asked, "So what were you thinking, Darla?" she asked.

"Oh, I was just toying with the idea that if this Nick person wasn't the intended victim…maybe Doug was the intended victim. This Butard guy or one of the other 'concerned citizens' might figure in the assault somehow," I explained lamely.

"I don't think so, Darla. I've known George for a couple years, and I don't know of any time when he's had trouble with the law. He's a family man, has a wife, a couple kids. He's actually pretty boring. Not exactly the town bully. And Jasper is just a blowhard, so don't worry about him. Crotchety, but lovable," she elaborated. "In fact, I can't think of any of the folks in Clearton that would go after Doug. Not to mention, that if it was someone local after Doug, they would have known his car and certainly would have realized it wasn't Doug before they almost beat him to death! Doug is pretty well respected by the locals even if they do get a little hot under the collar once in a while!"

"Okay, back to the drawing board. So in the meantime, anything else exciting going on in Clearton? Any more car-jackings that involved square dancers?" I joked.

"Nothing exciting going on here, I'm afraid. I am heading into Austin this weekend for a singles dance. Want to go?" she asked.

"Afraid not, Carlotta. I just don't know where you get the energy or the time. I'm going to relax and work around the house this weekend. Leaves are starting to pile up, and I have some fall planting going on. Who's calling the dance down there?" I asked.

"Ben Brideir. He's not my fave, but at least it is an opportunity to meet other singles, and dance even if Prince Charming doesn't happen to show up. I plan on being at the club dance on Tuesday, and then I'm going to a dance weekend, Oktoberfest, the next weekend in Rosenberg. Have you ever made it to that one?" Carlotta asked.

"Nope. I'm thinking that with the number of weekend dances coming up I have to go to, I may take that weekend to go visit my daughter. I think Tom Greenville is one of the callers in Rosenberg though, so I know you'll enjoy it. Anyway, I guess I will let you go. Get some rest for your heavy social calendar," I jested.

"Okay, Darla, I'll see ya on Tuesday, and don't you worry so much about Doug. I don't know about a car-jacking, but I don't think he was the target," she reassured me.

We hung up, and I again found myself wondering again if she or Sam knew that Doug and I had gone out a few times. No time to worry about that right now as the doorbell chimed and it was date time. Why was I trying to hide it, there was no reason they shouldn't know. With a sigh, I went to the door.

"Hi, Doug! Come on in. How was the drive?" I greeted him. "Why don't we sit down for a few minutes, unless you're in a hurry. Would you like some coffee? Water?"

"Thanks, Darla. Water will be fine," Doug replied as he took a seat on the sofa. I noticed he seemed a little tired. He was dressed in casual pants instead of jeans. I realized I didn't really know why he had been coming in the direction of Isquith. As I handed him the water, I asked, "So Doug, were you up this way on business? You look a little tired."

"Well, thanks a lot! I thought I was looking pretty good! But, yes, it has been a long day. I wish I could say the only thing that brought me here was you Darla, but the fact is I had some business to take care of with a developer near here. I know I told you no one was trying to buy the land designated for the camp."

He hesitated before continuing, "Well, they didn't want to buy that land, but a couple of other parcels and I really don't need all that land. But the developers were trying to insist on some legal jargon in the sale contract that would restrict what I could do with the adjoining parcels and access."

He sighed and shrugged his shoulders. He continued, "So, I went to a meeting with the developers and their lawyers and my lawyer. After two plus hours, the legalese was mind-numbing and we were still at an impasse. No sale. I was hoping to use the proceeds from the parcels to help with the construction of the camp."

"Oh, Doug, I am so sorry. Will this stop the camp then?" I asked as I sat down and put my hand on his arm.

"It won't stop it completely, but it means it will take it longer to be fully functioning. I have been working so much on this project. It really has become a passion for me. I have already had a couple of the kids come out to the ranch and given them rides in the corral, but the camp would be a lot bigger and have more activities than just the equine therapy. And we'd have to get a couple more horses that were well disciplined. Some of the horses in my stables wouldn't be appropriate for these kids. Even I have trouble with a few of them!" he ended with a smile.

He pulled a drawing out of his pocket while he talked and showed me rough sketches. The drawings were complete with a mess hall, activity room, and handicap accessible stables. I could hear his passion for the project through his words.

"The idea would be to get them to the point of being able to ride a trail of sorts, nothing too challenging, instead of just going around the ring. Give them some control. Of course, that would depend on each child and their abilities. We'd have to have a professional evaluate their capabilities on a one-to-one basis," he continued. He shook his head and laughed at himself.

"But I'm getting carried away. This evening is for us, not just me." Leaning in, he slid his arm around my shoulders and added, "If we don't go get some dinner pretty soon…" and he leaned in a little more and kissed me thoroughly. His hands were stroking my back. I felt him offering an alternative to dinner if I wanted to take him up on it. I leaned into him and touched his back, enjoying the kiss while at the same time feeling a little nervous. Not nervous about Doug specifically, just about getting too close to a relationship.

We came up for air, and he looked at me with those heavy eyes barely masking his fatigue, and asked, "Dinner or…?"

I laughed, a result of my nervousness, and responded in what I hoped was my most endearing voice, "I'd hate to take advantage of your current exhausted state, Doug. I think dinner. Then maybe we can think about dessert."

"You got a point, Darla! But no more discussion of the camp, the car-jacking, or anything related, okay? Where to for dinner?" he asked. After a brief discussion, we settled on the local barbeque place. I don't think there is a town in Texas that doesn't have at least one! We headed out to Magnums for dinner and I did my best to keep the conversation light. We talked a little about the Hoedown, the dances coming up, and of course, Heather. I told him I was a little worried she was getting serious about Micah. I didn't tell him about the article she called me about.

By the time we finished eating and returned to my house it was getting late. I realized I was a little nervous about the 'dessert' option now. I didn't need to worry though. When we got to the house, Doug walked me to the door. As I opened the door and invited him in, he took me in his arms. After demonstrating his great kissing ability once again, he said, "Darla, I think I'm gonna have to pass on that dessert offer this trip. It's getting late, so I am going to head home. Can I have a rain check?" I was relieved and disappointed all at the same time.

"You gonna be okay to drive? I have a guest room you could stay in," I offered as my acquired southern hospitality kicked in.

"Now, Darla, I'd love to spend the night, but when the time comes for me to spend the night, I don't have the guest room in mind," he said with his eyebrows wiggling comically. I got the feeling he was only half teasing. "I'll be fine driving, but maybe next time? We really need to get our schedules in sync."

I laughed out of embarrassment, blushed several shades of red, and tried to keep things light. I went to give him what I intended to be a quick peck. He countered and met the 'peck' and I felt the tingle go down my spine. I watched him get in his car and head out, and then went inside.

I wasn't exactly sleepy, so I decided to try again on the computer and the internet. Despite my resolution to leave it alone, being with Doug had rekindled my interest in the attack on his property. I still didn't quite buy the car-jacking explanation. So, what else might catch the attention of the FBI? As I read the website, I figured that a lone square dancer, however he ended up on Doug's property, wouldn't likely warrant FBI investigation as a terrorist. Of the likely domains that might immediately draw the FBI's attention, that left organized crime and white collar crime.

Then it hit me. Maybe the difficulty in figuring out who the man was, was all an attempt to maintain a cover. Maybe this Nick Tricot was actually an agent working undercover. Then his assault would definitely generate an immediate response from the FBI. I mean, I never even met the man, just looked at his clothes. I guessed he could have been involved in organized or white collar crime, but with the immediate presence and follow-up by Harbinville, first at a square dance and then at a local town meeting, my money was on his being an agent. Maybe he was investigating the camp to be sure it really was a camp, and not some scam. I'd have to find out from Doug more about this foundation that was funding at least part of the camp. Maybe there was some organized crime connection there.

Feeling very proud of myself for putting two and two together, but not quite ready for sleep, I decided to put aside the Clearton Caper and check my calendar. I needed to figure out what else was coming up before the holidays. They always seemed to sneak up on me, and this had been even more of a problem since Clint died. I looked ahead. I had my weekly Tuesday commitment in Clearton, and alternate Mondays with the Forsby Footstompers. I had a couple of other calling jobs in October. One next week, in fact, was in LaGrange, and then one the following week was in Sugar Land. Then the Houston Regional job, Thanksgiving dance, and the Winter Solstice weekend. These, of course, would be followed by Christmas and New Years holidays, not my favorite days lately.

As a wave of loneliness came over me, for about the hundredth time, I seriously considered venturing to that singles dance in Austin that Carlotta had mentioned. Then I remembered who the caller was, and he was not one of my 'faves' either. He was just a little too pushy and 'hands on' with the ladies for me. I did my share of dodging roaming hands when I was in high school and college! That was good enough reason to stay far away from that dance, as if I needed a reason not to get involved with anyone. And things were moving forward with Doug, albeit very slowly. Despite what Heather said, I wasn't sure I was ready to move on from Clint just yet. With her on my mind, I headed to bed.

I had a not-so-restful night's sleep, got up, and started on yard work. Well, most people would call it yard work. I called it "therapy" and "exercise." My three-bedroom house with lots of extra rooms is about 2400 square feet and sits on about one-quarter acre. The yard has multiple gardens, an outside pond complete with pump and fish, wooden deck, and lots of trees that are slowly but surely dropping their leaves.

Of course, the neighbor's trees are also dropping their leaves, and they end up in my yard. It's like the dust. Any reasonable explanation escapes me, but everything seems to end up in my lap, on my property, in my house. So I have lots of therapy, exercise, or work ahead. It really becomes therapy when I get to sit on the deck in my porch swing and look out at how great my corner of the world looks, and see what I have accomplished. Now that's satisfaction.

I cleaned out the pond first and checked on the acidity levels and the fish. I worked my way from the back edge to the deck and fence line, just bagging leaves. After about ten large bags I was at my limit and I called it quits. The difference was pretty amazing, and with the same effort tomorrow the back yard should be leaf free – for a while anyway. After some cold lemonade, I went to the front of the house and cut some flowers. I pulled the worst of what had died out and tried to visualize how I wanted to do my fall planting.

The small community of Isquith was populated mostly by families. On my street, there are about three of us who really work at our gardens and often we share our finds at the various garden markets. As I looked down the street, it felt good to see that my yard looked at least as good, if not better, than some of the others. For me, it was a matter of pride. Some of my neighbors had already put up their harvest decorations and pumpkins. I was a little behind.

The rest of Isquith, all 20,000 residents, kind of sprawls through hills and vale, with the homesteads getting smaller toward the center of town and more expansive toward the fringes. You can tell you are approaching the center of town as the houses get closer together and closer to the street. Lately, the major business in Isquith is technology. A big company, Technocorp, established a manufacturing plant and research center on the southern outskirts of town.

Even though a few of the old guard of Isquith are still here, the majority of my neighbors are engineers, programmers, and software developers. Many of the rest are company employees and townies who comprise the infrastructure to support commerce, education, and finance. Blue collar or white collar, people know their neighbors and the crime rate is low. These had been some of the reasons I chose Isquith when I moved here with Heather after Clint's death. Unfortunately, my lack of active involvement in the community kept me from knowing anyone well and I knew most folks as acquaintances only.

There wasn't a square dance club in Isquith, and I hadn't known when I moved here that I'd be wanting one. So far I hadn't found anyone in Isquith who square danced and the closest clubs were the two I called for regularly in Forsby and Clearton. At one point I had checked into teaching a class at the local community center, but the folks who planned the programs didn't think there would be enough people, They suggested I do a line dancing class instead. One of these days, I might just do that, but I would have to learn how to do some before I teach them!

Having tired myself out in the garden and cooled off with lemonade, I opted to shower and play around with some choreography and new songs. I'd need to practice a few times without dancers, and then I could try them out on the Clearton Squares on Tuesday. That would give me a chance to make adjustments before the next big dance. Sooner or later I would have to increase the number of clubs I called for on a regular basis, both to keep myself busy and to keep the bank account paying Heather's college expenses. With Clint's life insurance and pension still hanging in there, money isn't a major problem right now. I am able to work part-time and put a daughter through college. But money isn't growing in my backyard and incoming funds would help keep the current stash active and able to support us over time.

The hardest part of calling was not becoming too content to do the same old songs and patters each time. That and trying to include contemporary songs from various categories – easy listening, rock, show tunes – that might appeal to different age groups. Part of the training for callers is how to break down a song and put the different square dance moves together. Most of the time, callers shared what they had already figured out for songs over the years. It was one of the newer songs I set to working on. One that I could call my own and maybe even record for others to use.

#####

Before I knew it, it was Tuesday again. Back in Clearton, the lessons went with only a few hitches, and it looked like we would really manage to finish up Mainstream moves by Thanksgiving. At tonight's lesson I continued down the list of Basic and Mainstream movements, but there were still a few who couldn't quite seem to keep left and right straight. I'd asked both Doug and Sam to be in the square with the slower learners to avoid any conflicts with others in the square who were ahead of the game. There were also a few who tried to "anticipate" the call – to guess my next call before I gave it.

Tonight there was a good show of dancers from a variety of clubs. Although I had been doing the lessons for the past hour rather than a regular dance, there had been five squares of dancers. Some of the dancers I recognized; some I didn't. In between tips, I saw Sam coming in my direction.

"Darla, there's someone here I want you to meet. Nick Tricot, this is Darla King, our caller and lady extraordinaire!" Sam spouted, taking me quite by surprise. "Nick decided to try making our dance again, and this time was a little luckier than the last," he continued with twinkling eyes that told me he was tickled to be able to surprise me with his introduction.

I have no idea what my face looked like at that instant, but I can guess my mouth was hanging open. So this was the mysterious Nick Tricot! It was the second Tuesday of October, about a month since the car-jacking incident. I'd finally been able to stop myself from stewing over Nick's attack and Doug's safety. I hadn't thought about it since I concluded that Nick was an FBI agent himself and that Doug really hadn't been the target. Darn it! Now meeting Nick brought up doubts all over again. I didn't want to spoil Sam's surprise, so I didn't let on that I would have recognized Nick from the driver's license picture I'd downloaded from the web. I gathered my composure, smiled, and reached out to shake Nick's hand.

"Hi Nick! Glad you were able to make it and that you've recovered so well!" was my initial greeting.

Despite that fact that we had just met, Nick gave me the usual square dancer's hug. He was about the same height as me and had a friendly smile. He looked a bit pale, and I wondered if that was the result of the accident. He was okay looking, but on the slim side, almost too thin. This might be a consequence of his assault if he wasn't fully recovered. I hoped he wouldn't overdo dancing tonight. My mind raced, and I decided he didn't exactly fit the image of an FBI agent, undercover or not. He didn't have the inscrutable aura of Harbinville for sure. If anything, he seemed a bit sheepish. The quiet demeanor jived with what we had found out about him from other dancers. Somewhere in the back of my mind I remembered my mama telling me to beware of the quiet ones.

"Now, Darla, Nick has an interesting tale to share, so I've invited him to stay after lessons and share it with us. So let's get on with it!" Sam said. I didn't have time to ask how Sam had heard Nick's tale. It was time to dance.

"You bet! Let's go. Square 'em up, folks!"

It was a "club night" so lessons were limited to the first hour and the rest of the night was dancing and not lessons. The first tip was members and students, with only moves the students knew. Then the rest of the night was a combination of Mainstream and Plus tips. Back to the predictable pattern of two-dance tips with one patter call and one singing call. Usually within the same tip, the call combinations are the same. It was a challenge for me to call the right dance for the dancers, but I love a challenge.

Tonight I wasn't sure enough of my new song and choreography to use it though, so I was sticking to the tried and true even when it was time to switch from lessons to regular club dancing. I concentrated on keeping everything straight, but my mind kept being pulled away from the job toward the story I would hear from Nick later. My curiosity would finally get satisfied, not just sidelined.

After the dance, I lent a hand as we finished putting away all the club gear, banners, and roster. My curiosity gave me an extra jolt of energy. I was eager to hear the story straight from the source. When the musketeers were the only ones left, we grabbed our beverage of choice – coffee for Sam, Nick, and Carlotta and water for Doug and me. We pulled up chairs around the one table we hadn't put away.

"Okay, Nick, we're all ears. Tell us your story. Just what were you doing down here in Clearton when those car-jackers got to you?" Doug asked.

"Yeah, Nick, spill it. What really happened out there?" Sam put in his characteristic two cents worth.

"Well, parts of it I remember fine, but others?" he shrugged. "Well, I was out cold for most of the show. I was on the road to Doug's farm, going slow by every gate to see if I could figure out which one was his. I'm embarrassed to say I didn't plan any of it very well. It was just a spur-of-the-moment thing when I saw the exit sign for Clearton on the bypass. I didn't remember Doug's name or I would have called first. I just decided to see if I could find his place, introduce myself, and see if he had any suggestions on a wild idea of mine. So, anyway, I was inching down the road…"

"Hold it, Nick. If you didn't know my name, how'd you know where to look for me? And why were you on the bypass in the first place?" Doug asked the questions before I could even get them figured out in my own mind.

"I'm a long-time insurance man. I'm used to hunting down potential rural clients without much more than a route number or a few landmarks to go by. A friend and I had been talking and he knew Doug. Gary Andrews, Doug. After Jack told me to see Doug in the first place." I remembered Doug had told us that one of the state officers referred a person to him Doug when he asked about club outfits.

"I had Doug's name, but of course it was at home," Nick continued. "I hadn't had any reason to think I'd be planning to stop by that day so I didn't bring it with me. I was going to Houston to a dance. But I did remember Clearton and the fact that Gary said Doug's place was about 20 miles out past the high school and had a helluva lot of cactus at the entranceway." Nick shot a look at Doug and a smile bent his lips. "And man, what a helluva lot of cactus it is. I'd just recognized that grand stand of cactus at your lane when it all started. Have to say I'm glad I didn't actually end up in it when I went down."

Doug's prickly pear stand was notorious. It started as a volunteer plant and he just never got around to cutting it down. Then Clearton had a couple of dry summers and everything but the cactus died out while it thrived. By that time, it had become a county landmark. Over the last ten years or so, it had grown so huge I'd believe Doug was feeding it just for the heck of it.

"So now, that's the part I want to hear. How'd you 'go down' as you put it?" Sam prompted Nick.

"I get a little fuzzy there. As I said, I was poking along trying to find Doug's place. I'd noticed a vehicle behind me. I figured they were pretty annoyed with me for speeding up and slowing down so much. When they started around me at Doug's gate I assumed they were finally passing me. But instead they steered over toward me. I had to head for the ditch. My Rodeo tilted at a crazy angle and I barely got it stopped before it flipped. I was mad, I tell you. But before I could even get out and give them what for, one of the guys ripped open my door and grabbed me by the shirt."

"How many guys were there?" I garnered a bunch of dirty looks from the others and realized I'd interrupted Nick at the action-filled part of his story.

"Who cares, Darla? Let him talk," Carlotta griped.

"I know there was more than one, that's all I remember. One of them grabbed me and pulled me out of the SUV and another, or several, hell I don't know, started in whaling on me. I remember being surprised as hell and thinking that was some road rage. I don't remember much more than that before I went out cold. I put up some fight, but I didn't do myself very proud. I just didn't realize how serious they were. Apparently one of them crowned me with a pipe or a bat or something and that's all she wrote." Nick rubbed the back of his head and I wondered if it was an unconscious gesture or if his head was still tender from the hit.

"So did you see their car or recognize them?" That was Sam getting into the story.

"No, I didn't really see much. I've given the cops all I can. I gave them a hazy description of the car and the man I saw. But it's way too sketchy to do them any good," Nick explained.

"You figure it was a car-jacking like they're saying?" Again Doug asked the question forming in my mind.

"Well, I guess it must be. Don't know why anyone would be after me. Although I must say that's how it seemed to me. It was like they wanted me more than my Rodeo. They left it down the road where the sheriff's men found it. If that's the case, I don't know why they left me alive though. If it's supposed to be a warning I sure didn't get the message. I guess if they meant to shut me up permanent they could've been scared off before they finished by a passing car or stray coyote."

"Or they thought they had finished you off. You were pretty far gone when I found you," Doug put in. "If I hadn't gone out the drive that evening, and lots of evenings I don't, you sure wouldn't have lasted till morning."

"You're right about that, Doug. I owe you my life. 'Thanks' isn't enough for me to say," Nick offered genuinely.

"Just glad it all worked out, Nick," said Doug.

"Well, that explains part of the story, alright, but I still don't understand why you were looking for Doug's in the first place," Sam pressed Nick. Nick cut a look at his watch.

"That's an even longer story. I better be leaving for to Fort Worth or it'll be morning before I get home. I'll go into it all later if you're still interested," he said as he stood.

After Nick left, I was curious about the rest of the story. I felt like I was left hanging. Sam was obviously unsatisfied as well. He prowled around the room, filled his cup and picked at some leftover chips on the counter.

"So, what'cha think?" he asked.

"I think Nick thinks there's more to the story than a car-jacking, but I wonder why," noted Carlotta.

"Nick seems like a straightforward guy, but we don't know much about him," added Doug, a little suspiciously. "I'll give Gary a call and check out that part of the story."

"And I think I better be heading home or I'll never get up in time for work," added Carlotta. "Darla, you staying with me tonight or hitting the road?"

"I better head home, too, I guess. I've got a gig tomorrow night and I need to get ready for it. See you guys later," was my parting comment as Carlotta headed out.

Sam grumbled that he wouldn't be able to get to sleep with all the coffee. I offered to stay and help Doug finish the cleanup, but Doug told me to go on. Everybody hugged each other and left Doug alone with the remaining mess. I found I was a little disappointed that he didn't help me out to my car. I had started getting used to those lingering kisses. I sure hoped I hadn't completely blown it by offering him the guest room last time. But he hadn't called, so I thought maybe I had.

Chapter 7

I got home close to 1 a.m. and just about fell into bed. Unfortunately, the phone rang first thing in the morning. Just someone trying to sell me something or other. I couldn't get back to sleep so I made myself some coffee and a light breakfast, thinking over Nick's story from the night before. If he was an undercover FBI agent, his cover story wasn't very well conceived. Of course, it may just be that I didn't know what the focus or goal was. On the other hand, if he wasn't an FBI agent, then why was Mr. Suit involved? 'Mr. Suit' was the substitute alias I'd given Harbinville to keep myself from thinking of him as the Harbinville Hunk.

Not coming up with any ready answers, I decided to tackle my plan for the dance tonight. I had never called for the LaGrange club before, but their regular caller, Jerry Jamison, had a family engagement tonight and so I was the "pinch hitter" so to speak. Like the Clearton Squares, the contract was for three hours with a combination of Mainstream and announced Plus tips. I felt like I had the first time I ever called in Clearton. My adrenaline was pumping and I was fueled by anxiety.

I reverted to my safe haven, the internet, and checked out the club I'd be calling for, the "Grand Grangers." Apparently the club had been around for some time and had about 50 members. Good thing I checked. Listed among the club VIPs was "Laura Jones, line dancing." That made it look like the club also did line dancing in addition to square dancing. That might mean I'd call fewer tips and need to coordinate my timing to include line dances in between tips. It also meant that I probably needed to have a back up for any of the songs I might use that are frequently used in line dancing. It's always important to be prepared and to extend the courtesy to other callers and club officers to contribute to the evening.

By setting up a tentative set of tips, with substitutions, I felt a little more confident. I rechecked to make sure I had phone numbers and the complete address for the dance hall. GPS systems like the one in my vehicle were wonderful, but did require a destination. LaGrange is an old town established in the 1800s by immigrants, mostly German, on the Colorado River. Later, other immigrant groups moved in to the area. LaGrange has its fair share of fairs and festivals to honor the respective cultures and peoples who populate the area. With the web information about the place and the square dance club, I felt a little better.

After donning a long skirt and top in an attempt to make a favorable impression, I gave myself a once-over in the mirror. I decided to add a pair of pettipants under my skirt just in case I got to do some line dancing and kicked up my heels a little too high. I smiled at myself for being a prude. Lord knows, today anything goes in the way of clothing, or lack thereof, and yet I worry about showing a little too much leg. It wasn't the amount of leg I show, I thought wryly, it was the amount of leg I had to show. The older I got the more pounds seemed to apply themselves to my hips and thighs. Twirling once more in front of the mirror, I shrugged and set out for LaGrange. On the way, I tried calling Heather, but ended up getting her voicemail and leaving a message.

The Grand Grangers danced in the hall attached to the largest church in the middle of the town. I knew I was in the right place because of the banners and signs inviting dancers to come in. That was an advantage of combining dance types like line dancing and square dancing in one club. Some people came to do one and watched the other, and vice versa. At a time when clubs were having trouble making ends meet, this was one means of increasing membership. As I entered the building, carrying my equipment, I was greeted by a blonde woman about 25 years old and a man about the same age, who I assumed was her husband. Jenny and Stan quickly introduced themselves, and added that they were responsible for the dance tonight. That meant they were in charge of the refreshments, set up, clean up, etc.

"So if there's anything you need Ms. King, you just let us know. Can we get you some coffee or iced tea? Water?" offered Jenny.

"Please call me Darla. Thank you, water would be good. But what I really need to do is get set up and check the sound system and stage area. Where does Jerry usually put his gear?"

"Over here. Let me help you," Stan said as he took one bag, and led me to the opposite end of the hall while Jenny went for my drink. "Do you need anything else?" he asked as he put the gear down.

"Actually, Stan, I think I'm all set here, just need to hook up a few things. While I'm working could you tell me a little background about how your dances usually go, what the dancers will be expecting, and so on? That would be helpful. You know, like do you have a set time you do announcements, that kind of thing," I replied, wanting to boost my confidence as the hall started to fill with lots of unfamiliar faces.

"Oh, yeah, we just thought Jerry woulda filled you in. We will introduce you, and then you will do a tip. Then Laura will do a line dance when you take a break. Then you call again, then Jerry usually just puts on a waltz or a two-step after that and then he does his first Plus. Then Laura, then you, then a break, then you, then Laura and like that until the end of the night. Two Mainstream and one Plus for tips. About 8 or 8:30, we'll make some quick announcements, you know, the usual things. That help?" Stan paused for a breath.

I laughed and added, "Yeah, that helps a lot. Now, Stan, I gotta tell you, I am a little surprised at the age of folks I see coming in. The clubs I usually call for are the parents and grandparents of these folks. I hope they like oldies!" As I looked around at the people filtering in, many of them looked to be about Heather's age or not much older.

"Not a problem. As long as we get to dance, the music doesn't really matter," Jenny interjected as she walked up and handed me a big jug of iced water. She added, "Need anything else?"

"Not right now, thanks. But later I'd sure like to know how you manage to get so many young people involved in your club," I said as I smiled and turned to check out the equipment and the time. I got my first CD cued up, and announced, "Ok, let's square dance!" That was Jenny and Stan's cue to introduce me and then we were off. The first tip went well with about four squares, and Laura had a good number for line dancing. By the second tip, we were up to five squares. I found a waltz and put it on, turning away from the dance floor to look through the CDs for my first Plus tip.

"Hi Darla! Surprise!" greeted Carlotta with a hug and big smile. "I noticed that you were scheduled tonight and decided to surprise you! Looks like I probably should have checked to see how many singles there were though. I may not get to dance. How's it going with this young crowd?"

"Good so far. I am surprised. I have seen a few men standing out, but I've never called here before, so I don't really know if they are singles or not. Jenny and Stan seem to be the ones in charge here. They could probably tell you for sure, make some introductions, even," I offered as I pointed out Jenny and Stan to her. Jenny was coming toward us, and I introduced her to Carlotta and excused myself to go talk to a few of the dancers. I tried to get a feel for how my calling was fitting the crowd.

As dancers squared up for the next tip, I noticed that Carlotta had found herself a partner and I smiled to her. She never went long without a dance partner. Her man this tip was a teenager just about her height. I had a sense of the crowd and I had adjusted my music to be a little more upbeat, a little quicker. Not exactly contemporary 'popular' music, but some of the songs I shifted to were the 'tried and true' songs that everyone could recognize. I was checking out the squares and the dancers, when a movement caught my attention. I saw Nick Tricot walk into the hall. What was going on here? Now we just needed Paul Harbinville to show up to make a full house! I went through the tip with no hassles.

"Darla, you are doing just great!" Jenny exclaimed as she came toward me when the tip ended.

"Thanks, Jenny. The feedback is helpful. Line dancing now?" I asked.

"That's right! Stan and I wondered if you would be interested in coming back this way in the future. It's not very often that we need a guest caller, but if we do, we would like to be able to call on you again," she continued.

"I'm enjoying calling for your club. Yes, I'd love to if the scheduling works out. It's encouraging to see some younger dancers involved in square dancing. Your club and other young clubs are the future for square dancing, so if there's anything I can do to help." Jenny squeezed my arm and headed to the refreshments. I checked my equipment quickly as the line dancing started and then turned to get some water myself.

"Darla, look who's here?" Carlotta quipped as she and Nick met me near the water station. Nick smiled and extended a side hug.

"Hi, Nick! What brings you to LaGrange?" I asked, not wasting any time before trying to satisfy my curiosity. Not being a fan of coincidence, it seemed a little odd that they had both shown up here.

"Darla, after the other night, I was curious about how Nick was doing and the rest of his story, and so I called him up," Carlotta offered.

"Well, Carlotta mentioned that you were calling here tonight and that she might be coming," he responded with a shy smile. Continuing, he added softly, "I was on a business trip not far away. I'm still trying to make up for a month off work and a month of no dancing! I only wish I had managed to get here a little earlier. This is a pretty up-and-coming club for being so far out in the country." He spoke so quietly I had to strain to hear him.

Somewhat surprised by his timid nature, which made me even more sure I had been on the wrong track when I thought he was an FBI agent, I responded, "We probably have only one or two tips left, but I'm glad you could stop by." I gulped a drink of my water and went back to work, fleetingly wondering how it came up in conversation for Carlotta to let him know I was calling here. I was beginning to wonder if perhaps Carlotta was taking the amateur sleuth idea a little too seriously, or maybe the shortage of men was really getting to her. Carlotta and Nick partnered up and took positions in the front square. They seemed to enjoy the tip and as I put a two-step record on after the tip, I noticed they stayed on the dance floor. I had to admit, Carlotta's petite build and Nick's slim physique were a good combination. They made a cute couple.

Before long I was calling, "Square 'em up for the last tip folks!" and none too soon. I had pretty much run through all the songs I was sure this crowd would like. After the usual individual thank you's, the dancers all faced me, led by Jenny and Stan, and thanked me as well. That was one of the up-sides of being a caller. Lots of warm fuzzies came your way interacting with positive folks. As I packed up my gear, Jenny and Stan and several other dancers came by to tell me how much they had enjoyed the dance. Carlotta came by as well.

"Darla, Nick and I are going to stop for coffee up at the Country Diner on the interstate. Care to join us?" Carlotta asked.

"Thanks, Carlotta, I think I am going to pass. If I drink coffee now, I will never get to sleep. I am just going to head home, but you two enjoy the coffee." I responded, wondering at the pace of this fast friendship between my friend and someone new to our scene. It occurred to me that perhaps he was more than just a victim. "Carlotta – call me if you need me."

"Okay, I will. Drive safe, and I'll see ya next week in Clearton!" Carlotta said as she gave me a hug.

"Yeah, Darla, drive safe. Good to see you again. I'll catch you at another dance, I'm sure," was Nick's farewell comment as he also gave me a quick hug, and took Carlotta's arm.

I watched with some concern as they walked away, and reminded myself they were grownups, and just going for coffee after all. I packed my car and drove home. My mind once again was in overdrive while, as usual, I replayed the night and identified which songs or calls had or hadn't worked. Tonight, though, I quickly found myself instead thinking of the whole Nick Tricot thing. It was now potentially getting more complicated with Carlotta's apparent interest in him. Her interest in Nick seemed to trigger all my maternal instincts. Even though it was late, I called Heather again and was a little concerned when she didn't answer.

The rest of the week went by with very little excitement, and disappointingly, no contact from Heather. Heather and I had been talking at least once a week so far this semester. I was getting worried that I hadn't been able to reach her in over a week. I didn't want to become one of those overbearing mothers always calling her and checking up on her. I worked on the gardens and the yard, and reworked some of my choreography and music that hadn't gone so well at LaGrange. There were a few I considered trying out in Clearton before taking to the special dance in Sugar Land. October was one of the bigger months for "special dances." The harvest theme, Oktoberfest, and the dropping temperatures made dancing much more comfortable. Now, don't get me wrong; all the halls we dance in are air conditioned, but some are better than others. And getting to and from dances in Texas heat can be wilting.

Seeing Nick at LaGrange brought the car-jacking and assault back into my mind. I didn't hear from Doug or Carlotta, and didn't have any more brainstorming ideas that might explain it. I thought about calling Doug to suggest getting together. It was, after all, okay in this day and age for a woman to call a man, but I just couldn't bring myself to do it. Over the weekend I rescinded my vow not to nag Heather, and called her several more times with no success. By the third time I stopped leaving messages. If I didn't hear from her soon, I'd drive over to Austin to make sure everything was okay.

By the time Monday came, I was looking forward to going to the Footstompers' dance and being on autopilot. As I entered the senior center and said hello to Flo, Hal, and

Lenore, I was struck by the extremes of age as compared to the LaGrange group. Here I was calling to the Grange Grands grandparents' age again.

Flo asked about Sam and Nick, though she couldn't remember Nick's name. She asked me what I thought about one night stands and I fumbled for an answer, trying very hard not to giggle. Then she commented on one of the men's butts and headed in his direction. All in all, the night went smoothly with nothing out of the ordinary and no excitement. As I drove home this time, I recalled my sense of being followed the last time. I was very careful to check as I drove home, but didn't notice anything. Life seemed to be settling down once again, at least as far as my professional life was concerned.

Before I knew it, it was once again Tuesday, and I was heading fo Clearton. I arrived and exchanged greetings with Sam and others as I made my way in with my gear. Tonight I would introduce the star formation and star promenade. These are relatively simple moves compared to all the 'Thru' moves. Looking around, I noted that neither Doug nor Carlotta had arrived yet. Given the circumstances of the last time Doug didn't come to a dance, and the last time I'd seen Carlotta as she walked off arm-in-arm with a stranger, my anxiety immediately jumped up. I reminded myself that this was a lesson night and still fairly early.

"Let's square them up!" I called out, and dancers arranged themselves accordingly. Sam, giving me his characteristic wink, smiled as he joined a square. For the first tip, I reviewed and got everyone warmed up. We went over "Right and Left Grand" and "Right and Left Thru" and "Slide Thru," and after the singing call, took a break. As I put on a waltz for those who wanted to dance and turned, I did a double-take as Carlotta and Nick walked in together, followed by Doug. I headed toward the coffee and tried to keep my curiosity under control.

"…the crowd was pretty good overall, and the callers were good. Rosenberg is such a quaint town with great family-owned local restaurants. We had a good time," Carlotta stated as I walked toward them.

"Hi Darla. Carlotta and Nick were just telling me about the Rosenberg Oktoberfest dance this past weekend. Sounds like we both missed a good time," Doug commented. He looked surprised – whether surprised that they had gone to a dance together or that they were here together, I wasn't sure. Myself, I was surprised at both.

"Hi yourself. Glad to see you," I said. I meant it more than they knew. I tried not to show my surprise and to keep my mind open.

"Nick and I had a great time, but I did miss you guys. I've kinda gotten used to the "gang" all hanging out together. And, no excitement, just dancing," Carlotta added. "Nick and I met for dinner tonight and that's why we were late. We ran into Doug in the parking lot, only figuratively speaking, of course! What held you up, Doug?"

"Yeah, I was getting a little worried when you weren't here," I added.

"I just got hung up at a meeting with the mayor and town council folks around that camp we're trying to get approved. It looks like it will go through this time, with lots of restrictions in the rezoning wording to keep people happy," answered Doug with a sigh. "It looks like the financing is pretty well set too."

"Doug, that's great! I want to hear more about the meeting and plans, but right now, it's back to work for me."

"OK, let's square them up." I varied the calls a little and made a fairly smooth transition for the singing call.

At the breaks, I chatted with Doug about the camp and the rezoning. He was so excited and pleased with the progress the council had made that he really couldn't talk about much of anything else. Sam, Carlotta, Nick, and I barely got a word in. Then, of course, I was back and forth between the conversation and my calling.

I noticed that Nick and Carlotta danced together fairly consistently. Doug and Sam danced with the students. As much as Carlotta seemed to like Nick, I was still a little unsure of his motives. One thing seemed for sure, if the camp proposal had been related to the supposed "car-jacking" of Nick, then there was no longer any reason to think that Doug was in danger. That was comforting. I hadn't come up with any other reason someone would be out for Doug. Sam certainly hadn't offered any possibilities. And there was always the possibility that it really was just a car-jacking of a square dancer on the way to a dance out of town.

On the other hand, maybe we didn't know all that there was to know about Nick. The night ended with the gang, and Nick, helping me pack everything up. Doug lingered some, but not with the same level of interest as the last few times. I hoped it was that his attention and focus was still on the camp and the realization that it would come to be. Still no alone time with Doug, and still lots of questions. I headed home.

#####

A few days off, and I was back on the road. The next job was a special dance in Sugar Land, another club I hadn't called for before. The drive to Sugar Land wasn't that much longer than to Houston proper, since its actually a suburb of Houston. I tried to go through the tips I had planned out in my head as I drove, but I had trouble concentrating.

My mind kept returning to Heather and the fact that I still hadn't talked to her. She hadn't even emailed me. I'd left her a message telling her in no uncertain terms that she should call me to let me know she was okay, and I'd sent her an equally strong email message.

Now I found myself debating whether to drive over to Austin after the dance and go see her in person. Or I could call her roommates' parents, the only contact I had for her, or check with the university administration to see if she was attending classes. Any of the choices would infuriate Heather and qualify me for interfering mother of the year, I knew. Not that I minded the title terribly, but I did wish Clint was still around to help me decide how to be a parent. Of course, if

Clint was still around, chances are Heather would be a lot easier to be a parent to. I reined my anxiety in and refocused on my driving and upcoming gig.

As with my trip to LaGrange, I felt a bit nervous. This was the club's Oktoberfest Harvest Special and everyone anticipated a big crowd on a Saturday night. That wasn't what made me nervous though. The Sugar Land Singles was one of the few square dance clubs that catered to solo dancers, although not all the members were singles. That put an added "zing" into my work as most of the dances I called were couples oriented. I usually used a 'pilot square' to monitor how dancers were handling my calls. With couples, I could easily match up partners by coordinated clothing. At singles' dances, however, no one matched.

But that challenge wasn't the scariest part of this gig. When I had first started calling, I had attended one caller lab with the club caller for the Sugar Land Singles, and he was going to be a hard act to follow! He had a great voice and did mostly singing calls. He used a variety of music types that were phenomenal. He even moved dancers from square to square in what is called progressive movements. I had only heard him that once, but he left an impression on me and on the other caller students. You might say that TJ Guirion had become a legend in my mind. The potential for these dancers to be comparing me to TJ put me in panic mode.

I stopped going over the tips in my head and tried to think peaceful and positive thoughts. My mind wandered to Doug and I wondered if there was any chance of our getting together before the Houston Regional or if we would have some time alone at the Regional. He hadn't mentioned coming to Sugar Land, so I was pretty sure he wouldn't be around tonight. The last few weeks hadn't helped to grow our relationship. Houston Regionals would definitely provide us with an opportunity to spend some time in between dancing. Okay, not such a peaceful and calming thought. I redirected my unruly brain once again.

I just had to find the hall in Sugar Land and think positive! After all, I reminded myself, I couldn't remember ever being at a square dance where they booed or threw things at the caller. Just the image of dancers throwing cookies or pies at the caller made me smile. This was a good thing, and I let my mind play with the vision. I located the hall, unpacked my gear, squared my shoulders, and went in the door.

"Hello and welcome to Sugar Land Singles! I'm Neta and I bet from all that stuff you're carting that you must be our caller tonight. Let me give you a hand," offered a 40-something blonde. She was wearing the Sugar Land Singles club dress with bluebonnets in bands alternating with white and blue bands on the skirt. She had on a white flouncy peasant top with bluebonnets embroidered on the collar. She had the traditional version – short skirt and crinolines – and sported a garter peeking out from under it all on the left leg. In her case, it wasn't hidden and it didn't look tacky at all. It also was just above her knee, not exactly risqué. Add a pair of white dance boots, and you have Neta.

As she extended her hand and took one of my cases, I responded, "Hi Neta, I'm Darla, and yes, I am your caller tonight. Just tell me where to set up and give me a hint of what to expect, and I'll be on my way!"

"You'll be setting up right over here," she explained as she led the way to the left of the room. A table and stage were set up between stacks of hay and adorned with a lady and man scarecrow. I actually don't remember ever seeing a lady scarecrow before, but there was one over there. "As you can tell, not many folks have arrived yet, so you can take your time getting set up. We usually get started around 7:15 instead of 7. Somehow, that's just the way it works out," she continued with a shrug and smile.

"So do you expect a big crowd tonight?" I asked, hoping not to sound too anxious.

"We certainly hope so. We only dance every other week. There are so few singles dances in the area that when there is a special one the crowd tends to be greater than usual. Now of course, not everyone who comes will be solo dancers. We throw a fine dance here and everyone comes. We need to have good crowds and lots of involvement if singles clubs are going to survive. For me, square dancing is my social life. With the regional dances coming up, it's helpful to meet some other singles so there are options at those larger dances."

Neta stopped to breath and then continued, "Darla, are you single?" Seeing my nod of acknowledgment, she continued, "Well, then you know what I'm talking about. Particularly at our age, there is a shortage of men out there. Maybe some time you can come back and as a dancer. You might meet someone. Hmm, I guess as a caller, you get to view the field from a different vantage point tonight!" she added with a smile. "I'll leave you to get your stuff ready and I'll go greet folks as they come in. We'll have time to talk a little more later."

Neta walked away, in the direction of the door. I tried to get my bearings and check out the crowd as I set up my stuff. I always felt self-conscious when people suggested activities, even dancing, as a means of meeting someone. The hall had been decorated tastefully, consistent with the fall theme, and it was good sized with some tables off to the side with refreshments, all those cookies and pies I imagined being thrown at me if they weren't pleased with my performance. There were chairs along the walls for those who chose to sit out.

Looking around, I saw there were probably about 30 people already here, so about three squares. I almost laughed out loud as I glanced around and was reminded of junior high – with a few exceptions, the ladies were all on one side of the refreshments and the gents were on the other. So far, most of the men had on the shirts that identified them as being with the Sugar Land Singles, while at least half the ladies did not sport the Sugar Land club dress. I busied myself trying to get both my equipment and my energy going. I put on a popular country western CD as I checked the sound system and how well I'd be heard at various spots in the hall. I rarely got this obsessive, but when I was nervous, I reverted to checking everything. By the time I was finished, it was approaching 7:15.

"Darla, right? Glad you could make it! I'm JJ and this is Ken. We're the co-presidents of the Sugar Land Singles. If you are all ready to go, I'll introduce you and we can get started." JJ was a stocky woman with a no-nonsense demeanor that belied her frilly crinolines and the ruffled bands of her skirt. Ken was tall and lanky. He gave me a quick hug and tentative smile, as JJ took the microphone.

"Welcome everyone! Tonight we have the pleasure of dancing to Darla King! She is the regular caller for Clearton Squares and Forsby Footstompers. We are very excited that she is here with us tonight!" As the dancers clapped, JJ handed me the microphone and I fell into routine with "Ok, folks, let's square up and get dancing!"

For the first tip, there were four squares, some folks sat out, and more arrived mid-dance. With my nerves in high gear, I focused my attention on being sure that I was getting partners back together, and trying to gage if I was going too slow or too fast. I tried for a middle ground for the first tip. I planned on changing if the dancers were getting lost or seemed to need more of a challenge.

So far, so good. All four squares stayed with me and everyone seemed to be smiling, and I reminded myself that I needed to be smiling too! As I brought the singing call to an end with "Promenade home, swing your partner, and let's take a break!" I took a long breath, chose a waltz for my break song, and grabbed a cup of coffee.

"Hi Darla! We heard you were calling here tonight! Isn't this a great crowd," Carlotta chimed as I turned with my coffee in hand.

"Hello yourself! Why didn't you tell me you were coming here? Are you just taking in every singles dance these days or are you becoming my groupie?" I teased.

"A little of both," she answered. "Trying to get to know as many of these guys as I can before Regionals, though I'm not sure I'll be partner-less anyway," she added with a mysterious smile.

"Carlotta, did Doug come with you tonight? Or Sam?" These were my first guesses for what was behind the mysterious smile. Carlotta didn't have a chance to respond before Nick came into sight and gave me a hug. Although they had been together the last two times I had seen Carlotta, it hadn't occurred to me the partner she referred to would be Nick.

"Hi Darla! Good to see you again. Can't wait to dance the next tip! We were a little late getting here," he added.

"Good to see you too, Nick. You're a long way from home," I responded and then realized my waltz had ended. Whew! "Gotta get to work. Catch you after the next tip!" I covered my surprise with a smile and headed back to the microphone. This time we had six squares and I tried to change things up a little to keep it interesting. Nick and Carlotta danced together each tip after that. It was pretty clear now what she meant about probably not needing a partner for the Houston Regionals. In the meantime, other dancers changed up their partners and I concentrated on my pilot square. Neta came by and introduced some of the others, including some who would be in Houston.

I felt pretty good about how the night was going. So good, I braved trying out the new sequence I'd worked out on the computer and tried out in Clearton. It was a big hit, if for no other reason than that it wasn't the same old tried and true. It did present a challenge for some of the dancers without being too difficult. I chatted a bit with Carlotta and Nick, and some with JJ, wondered at how Ken managed to be co-president and so quiet, and made it through the night.

"I'd like your attention everyone before the last tip tonight," JJ said as she commandeered the microphone. "We are so glad that you all could make it tonight! The next time we'll see most of you is at Houston Regionals. Hopefully, we can continue to have a good singles presence. In the meantime, I want to take this opportunity to thank Darla for some great calling tonight. I know we will all look forward to dancing to her calls again in Houston! And when she's not calling, remember, she's a solo dancer too!"

As she finished, everyone again clapped and smiled. I took the microphone back and gave the usual "Let's square them up for the last tip!"

I decided to end with two singing calls and the dancers seemed to appreciate the change from the pattern-singing duo I'd done all night. I ended with, "Promenade home and swing your partner! Thank you for having me call for you tonight! I really enjoyed it. See you all in Houston! Now how about making one big circle, and a Grand Right and Left Grand as you say good night to each other." Everyone joined in the circle, including me, and we did the "g'nite" most of the way around the room before people started breaking off. I was packing up my gear when Carlotta and Nick walked over.

"Great dance, Darla," Nick offered with a hug.

"Yeah, ditto," added Carlotta. "Can you do more of that new stuff for us in Clearton? I love it when you try out new stuff on us! And with lessons almost over, you could do that more and more," she continued. I started to answer, but Ken and JJ walked up.

"Darla, I just wanted to thank you again on behalf of Sugar Land Singles," JJ said as they joined us. "I may have to come to Clearton one of these days for the change in pace," she added with a smile. "We sometimes get a little too used to dancing to the same caller, so change is always good."

"Well, thank you. I'm glad you were pleased. T.J. is a fabulous caller, so I was a little nervous about filling in for him. I take that as a real compliment. I hope to see you at the Regionals! And let me know if you need a caller any time in the future," I replied as she handed me my check for the night, which I noticed included a bonus.

"Nick, it was good to see you again. You haven't stopped in for one of our dances in a few months. No business bringing you this way these days?" JJ asked.

"Thanks, JJ. Unfortunately I was laid up for a bit, and so cut back on my travel. Now, my schedule is pretty busy again. I always like to stop in here for a dance, so don't you worry, I'll be back!" was Nick's response. He gave JJ a hug and turned to leave. Nick and Carlotta walked out with me. We exchanged good nights with each other at my car as I loaded my gear.

"See you in Clearton on Tuesday, Carlotta, and at Regionals, Nick," was my parting comment. Well, Nick apparently got around and did make a habit of stopping in at different clubs when business brought him to an area. That was somewhat reassuring. Of course, that would also fit with my theory of a cover, but it's not like square dance clubs were involved in nefarious activities that would warrant investigation. Most clubs don't exactly make money. In fact, most of them barely break even with the minimal dues or guest fees by the time they pay for halls, liability insurance in case anyone gets injured at a dance, and the fees paid to the regional and state associations.

When I got in my car, I burrowed into my totebag and pulled out my cell phone. I usually left it in the car when I called dances so I wouldn't run the risk of forgetting to turn it off and getting a call in the middle of a call, so to speak. My heart fluttered when the phone flickered to life and signaled a missed call. Tapping the magic series of buttons, I saw it was Heather's number and she'd left a message for me. Another series of buttons and I was hearing her voice, "Hi, Mom. I know I haven't gotten back to you in a while. Sorry if you were worried." If I was worried! Isn't that what I'd told her in the several messages I'd left her? I couldn't exactly read her voice, but there was something in it as she continued her message, "My computer had a virus so I couldn't send you an email, and I've been so busy I didn't want to call you by the time I remembered late at night."

I was breathing a sigh of relief that everything was okay, but now I was worrying on another front. Last year she'd hit academic probation because of her lack of studying and I thought she was doing so much better this semester. Now it sounded like she was going down the same road again. Well, I just couldn't be happy, could I? Wasn't it just possible she was busy studying? Maybe. I tried harder to read between the lines as she finished up her message, "So anyway, everything's okay, Mom, don't worry. I'll send you an email soon, promise. Love you. Bye." I told the electronic menu voice to save her message. I planned to listen to it again later to see if I could divine any more hidden meanings in it. Then I buckled up and headed home.

I called Heather again on Sunday, again with no luck. Monday night's dance at the Forsby Footstompers went smoothly, but there was a small group. A cold front was on its way through and the weather was cold and drizzly, keeping some folks snugly at home. We had twelve dancers, so four took turns sitting out each tip. That was no fun. Square dancers come to a dance to dance and even the usual dominoes crowd was somewhat thin tonight. Somehow, without Flo being there, it was a very tame and quiet night. I asked about her, and Hal and Lenore assured me that she was healthy enough, just not up for venturing out in the cold. With older dancers, concern is not light when they miss a dance.

By Tuesday evening, though, the front had passed through, and the weather was cool and crisp for my drive to Clearton. In fact, weather was just as it should be for the middle of October. When I arrived, Doug had opened up the hall and was the only one there so far. He gave me a quick hug and then helped me get my equipment set up as we visited. He grabbed one end of a long table and I took the other end. We lifted and scooted across the floor with it.

"So, Darla, how's it been going lately?" he asked across the table's length.

"Fine. I've been getting a lot of invitations to call lately. Guess my name's getting out to the clubs. Not sure how, though. I haven't done any advertising." We set the table down at a 45-degree angle so I could stand behind it to start my music and then walk around in front as I called.

"You don't have to advertise, Darla. You're a good caller. And fun to dance to. People hear you once, they're gonna get their clubs to invite you. I can't recall, do you want these speakers at the end of the table?" he asked.

"Well, thanks for the compliment, Doug. I hope you're right. No, if you would please, put the speakers behind the table. That way I'm less likely to bump them when I move around." I plugged the speaker wires into my CD player. Out of the corner of my eye, I saw one of the tall speakers wobbling as Doug placed it on top of the other one. I lunged for it to stop its fall just as Doug stepped over to catch it. The speaker fell squarely between us and landed unhurt on both our outstretched arms. We fumbled a little over the speaker and finally got it stabilized on the table. Instead of turning to the job of placing it on top of the other one, Doug reached for my hand and kept me within reach. He put his arm around me with just enough weight behind it to make sure I knew it was intentional.

"Darla, I haven't told you how much I appreciated your listening to me rant and rave when I came up for dinner. Somehow things seemed more manageable and positive with you around. Thanks," he said, looking into my eyes.

"You're welcome, Doug. I'm glad you feel that way. Glad I could help," I said laughing a little. I almost said something about the guest room again, but caught myself in time.

He tightened his grip and pulled me closer to him. "What's up with us, Darla? We seem to get something going between us, then it just disappears. You sending me a message I'm just too dense to get?" We were facing each other with our faces just a few inches apart. His eyes held mine and my heart skipped a beat. I thought a minute before I answered.

"No, you're anything but dense. Me, on the other hand, I'm pretty stupid at this dating thing. I enjoy being with you, you know that. I'm just not sure I'm ready for anything serious in my life, and I don't know how to respond sometimes. So I end up backing away instead. Make sense?" I asked, a little uncomfortable. I almost wished he had just pulled me into an embrace and kissed me, long and hard. This thinking thing was too stressful.

"Darla, I enjoy being with you, too. Don't stress out on me. It doesn't have to be serious, okay? Just wanted to be sure I wasn't overlooking your signal to bug off." His eyes smiled even though his mouth didn't. "So, if you say that's not the case…." His hands slid to my sides and rested at my waist. He pulled me to him for a soft, tender kiss. Then he pressed a little further and I tensed up. He pulled away and put a little space between us.

"No?" he asked, looking a bit disappointed and confused at the same time.

"Yes," I answered. Then I rolled my eyes, disgusted with myself. "You'd think I was raised by wolves, wouldn't you, by how skittish I am? I remind myself of when I was in high school and my first date. Sorry, Doug. If you can put up with me, let's keep trying to get together. My mind and my emotions just aren't communicating very well. What do you think? Is it worth it to you to keep trying to get on the same wavelength?" I asked.

He shook his head, but his smile stayed in place, "Good thing I like you," he said, "or I'd have gotten fed up long ago. Yeah, let's keep working at it. I've always welcomed a challenge."

The hug came naturally and we both stepped into it. I heard the door open and pulled out of his embrace, feeling heat come to my cheeks. Of all the stupid things, I thought, a 45-year-old woman blushing to be seen hugging a friend. Dadburn my old-fashioned sense of propriety. I heard Doug chuckle as I turned around to welcome the first dancers of the evening.

"Good evening! Good to see you. I'm just about set up over here, so it looks like we'll be starting on time tonight," I said heartily. Behind me I heard Doug lock the top speaker into its place with a sigh. The dance went well, and Carlotta, Sam and Doug were a great help with the lessons. Between tips, I played waltz, two-steps, or polka music. I was relieved and pleased when Doug asked me to dance one of the waltzes. He was a good dancer and easy to follow. It also meant there was still hope that we could eventually hook up, if I could just loosen up. I thoroughly enjoyed being in his arms.

#####

I'd been looking forward to the first weekend of November and the Houston Regional workshop and dance. I called at the Regional last year and enjoyed the crowd that came. This year I would be calling with one of my favorite callers, Slim Boyer. I assumed Slim got his name when he was much younger, because it certainly didn't fit him now. He was generous around the waist and always wore suspenders. Not just for appearance, I always thought, but in their original functional role. Slim had been calling for about 30 years now, and pushing 60, he frequently talked about retirement. He was a lot of fun to work with, and one of the best and most entertaining callers in the country. I always learned something from him when we worked together. I certainly hoped he didn't retire too soon.

Slim and I arrived about the same time for the Friday night dance. On Saturday we would share duties at the all-day workshops and evening dance, then close out on Sunday morning. It made a full weekend, but it paid good money. And I counted on mixing in some fun with my work. Again, the Clearton Squares group indicated they planned to come for the weekend and I supposed Nick would be here as well. He was getting to be a pretty solid member of the dance group, and he seemed particularly eager to be at whatever dances Carlotta went to.

It was already November, and I still hadn't had the chance to hear the remaining part of Nick's story. I wouldn't be satisfied until I did, so I planned on making time at the Regional to hear it so I could finally let it go. My mind kept returning to the events of the night Nick was injured at Clearton. I was ready to put my curiosity to rest and get focused on other things.

It was all squares tonight, no rounds. Cuers for tomorrow's round dancing would arrive in the morning, but tonight Slim and I alternated or called together and kept the tips going, so I had only short breaks. I concentrated on the job at hand and it was well into the evening before I felt like I had a chance to catch my breath. On one of Slim's dances, Carlotta found me at the water cooler.

"Man, what a crowd! This is a great dance. I can't believe how many people are here tonight! How's the calling going?" Carlotta's enthusiasm, as usual, overflowed.

"Fine so far, but busy. Who's here from the Clearton Squares?" I asked.

"We've got about three squares, I think. Oh, and Nick made it down from Fort Worth. I think there are a few more Stepping Squares here too," answered Carlotta. "Some of the other singles from Sugar Land are here. I haven't seen anyone from the Promenaders though."

That was all the conversation my short break allowed us. I nodded, chugged my water, and made my way to the stage. During the next tip I noticed Carlotta partnered with Nick and I picked out most of the other Clearton Squares. I didn't locate any more Stepping Square outfits, but did see some of the Sugarland group. The dance was over before I had a chance to visit with any of the dancers. Carlotta, Doug, and Sam found me next to the stage while I packed up my sound system.

"Darla Darlin' – didn't get to dance a tip with you all night. I'm heartbroken," said Sam.

"Sam, the ladies line up to dance with you. You probably wouldn't have had a tip for me even if I had time for one," was my quick and honest response.

"Darlin', I'd always make room for a tip with you," Sam answered with a grin.

"We going out to eat? We barely had time to make it up here in time for the dance. I'm starving!" suggested Doug.

Carlotta looked over at Nick before answering, "Yeah, I'd like that." I don't think Nick noticed Carlotta's inquiring glance, but he agreed he'd like a bite. Before the group split up we decided to meet at the front door of the hotel in fifteen minutes.

I didn't need the extra time. I'd be using my sound equipment on Saturday, so I could leave it where it was. I'd taken advantage of my last calling break to make a bathroom stop. Impressed by the elegance of the hotel, and with a few extra minutes on my hands, I took a quick tour around the lobby and atrium. A group of three men caught my eye at a table in the lobby bar. They were obviously dancers, and I waved at them as I passed by. None of them saw me because they were looking past me toward the elevator. I realized they must be waiting for some more dancers to join them following the dance. Probably their partners. Something felt wrong about the group but I couldn't put my finger on what. They had on the 'right' clothes, but seemed out of place.

As I walked on toward the atrium, I couldn't get the trio off my mind. I chewed on it like a stringy piece of brisket. Then it clicked into place. What was wrong was that the men weren't sweaty. No one could dance three hours of non-stop tips and end up looking that fresh. There hadn't been time to change clothes since the end of the dance, and besides, that's how I'd known they were dancers. They were will wearing their matching shirts, so they hadn't changed yet. It would be surprising for men to sit out enough dances that they wouldn't look at least a little disheveled or wilted after an entire evening.

I shrugged it off. Too much imagination. Maybe the group had arrived too late to do much dancing and planned to go to Saturdays' dance instead. As I rounded the corner and left the atrium, I walked toward the front of the hotel. I spotted Carlotta standing with Nick and Doug at the front door.

I headed toward them and my mind telegraphed a visual connection to me. It brought up the image of the group of four men smoking outside the Cracker Barrel near Dallas. I realized these three could have been cut from the same bolt. But I still couldn't place the shirt patterns and hadn't seen them with any women dancers, or any women at all, for that matter. Of course, there were gay square dance clubs but these guys didn't seem to fit that bill either. They just didn't fit with square dancing at all. But then they were here and had their club outfits on so it just left me confused. Hah, what did I know? I arrived at the door at the same time Sam arrived from the other direction, pushed the distractions out of my mind, and all five of us headed out for food.

At the restaurant, we all ordered meals, except Nick, who ordered a piece of pie and coffee.

"Pie! All you're getting is pie and coffee?? The rest of us are starving!" teased Sam. It was clear Sam didn't care what Nick ate. He was just giving him a rough time to make sure Nick didn't feel left out.

"Well actually, I had time to eat before the dance. I was already in town for a couple of appointments." Nick hesitated, then lowered his gaze to the table. "I really just came for the company." In case there was any question what he meant, I thought, Carlotta's beaming smile in response answered it. I wasn't sure Nick saw the smile. He found something fascinating with his pie about then, but I think everyone else at the table felt it. I was a little uncomfortable with how fast Nick was ingratiating himself into our little group, but Carlotta had always been a pretty good judge of character. And, after all, she was a bright and capable lady. If she liked Nick I figured that was a good recommendation.

"Well, pieman, the rest of us are eating man-sized portions, even the ladies. You'll need to carry the conversation while we chew," Sam said. "You can start where you left off last time we were all together. Why did you want to see Doug the night you were attacked?"

"Like I said, I was on my way to Houston for a dance. Jack had suggested I try to catch up with Doug to answer a question I had. When I saw the exit marked Clearton, I remembered that was where Doug lived. I had a little extra time, so I detoured to swing by his place to see if he was home," Nick explained. "I don't have any idea where my attackers started following me, but I guess Doug's land was the easiest place for them to dump me," he added with shrugging shoulders.

"What was the question you had for me?" Doug asked, his brows knitted in consternation.

"This is probably no big deal. I'm in the insurance business and an actuary by training. Anyone who does a lot of work with numbers, well, it almost becomes second nature to look for patterns, kind of like square dancing. There's something mathematical about actuarial tables as well as square dancing, wouldn't you agree, Darla?" he asked.

"Well, yeah, everything in square dancing is based on eights and combinations of steps that all come down to eights," I offered.

Nick nodded and continued, "Anyway, these patterns, sometimes they mean something, sometimes they don't. Well, I'm on the road a lot, and go to a lot of square dances when I go to different towns. With my social life pretty much limited to square dancing, I also make an effort to get to the bigger dances, regional events, state events, and national events. People at square dances are generally friendly, and as a single man, I usually don't have any trouble finding a partner." He shot an embarrassed glance at Carlotta. She smiled back.

"Over the last year, it seemed like every time I was in a larger city for a square dance event, I ended up being paged by the main office to go see one or more of our corporate clients whose security had been breached. Sometimes it was a museum and part of their inventory would be stolen. Or one of the more prestigious jewelry designers would be burglarized. Or multiple thefts at a single major hotel. Different places – Houston, San Antonio, Austin, Dallas, Fort Worth, Galveston – and different businesses. Nothing that ever seemed to be consistent, and no headway on the cases from the police departments in any of these." He finished with a sigh and a shrug.

"So what does this have to do with me?" Doug interjected as Nick paused to take a bite of his pie.

"Okay, yeah. Well, the fact that these were all major losses, that is what they are classified as by the industry, means that they are all listed together in the quarterly and yearly loss reports and recoveries. When the second quarter reports came out and I was scanning the list, I noticed that for each and every one of the losses, I was at a square dance in that location. That seemed a little too coincidental for me even though I obviously went to other dances in towns that didn't have any losses. So at the last few special dances and regional dances, I tried to keep my eyes open."

"Open for what? Get on with it, Man!" urged Sam.

"I wanted to see if I could come up with anything that might link specific dances with the location of the losses. The easiest way to identify where square dancers are from is by their clothes. When I asked Jack about a directory of club outfits, he said if anyone knew of such a record, it would be you, Doug. I don't know why. So I figured I'd come down and talk to you about the history of square dancing and the club outfits. I'm not sure what I hoped to accomplish, but figuring out the pattern is like a burr in my boot, and I can't help but think I'm missing something!" Nick concluded.

"Did you ever mention this to the police or investigators?" Carlotta asked.

"Well no. Who would I tell? All the cases were in different towns, and there is the confidentiality issue for me as an employee of an insurance company. Besides, I'm sure they'd just think I was dreaming it all up. Or worse, somehow involved in the burglaries," he answered with a sigh.

"Whew! That is an interesting story. But, heck, there are probably lots of large events in major cities in Texas and all across the nation that have nothing to do with square dances there. I bet you could find a similar pattern for say, health care conferences. Sounds a little stretched to me! You can't really think that square dancers are involved in these crimes?" Sam responded.

"Well, coincidence or not, I don't think I can help you much," Doug offered without giving Nick a chance to respond to Sam's question. "The history I researched didn't really detail the actual pattern or design on the dress or shirt, just the idea of the short, full skirt, the crinolines, and such. Much of the history had to do with dancing etiquette of the time. It centered on the concern of men and women having physical contact, hence the long sleeves of the men's outfits and the traditional three-quarter sleeve of the ladies' dresses. I discovered quaint customs like the rules against the ladies wearing black hose because they might be too tempting to the men, and other such rules. But a club can go and pick out any material, add whatever emblems or designs, and call it their own. The club dress or costume is to identify club members. The only time club members wear the club dress is usually at special events as a show of power or membership present as it were. I don't remember seeing or reading about a record of different clubs and their dresses." Doug responded to Nick's query. "That would be an interesting historical project, though," he added. I could tell Doug's active mind was off and running. While mysteries grabbed my attention, Doug's interest lay in histories.

"Anyway, that's the answer to why I was at your place. Now you know," Nick said. "I came down to talk to you about your history research. But you don't have what I need, so I may just have to start one of those directories myself! If you have any entries, send them my way!"

It didn't seem like a fun project to me, but to each his own I suppose.

"I just can't imagine all the combinations you'd find," I said. "I'm always seeing new patterns, emblems or designs. There are fabrics with different colored flowers, birds, eggs for Easter. Literally everything the fabric designers have been able to come up with and then variations on those are used! Such a project could certainly keep you busy for a while!" I paused and continued, "Well, I have a long day ahead of me tomorrow. You guys ready to go back to the hotel now that our mystery's solved?" When everyone agreed they were, I gathered up my things and paid my part of the tab. Once again,

I thought that I'd heard the end of the mysterious Clearton Square Dance Caper.

Chapter 8

The phone rang as I was walking out of my hotel room early the next morning. When I answered it, Carlotta's voice sounded a little higher than usual. "Morning, Darla. I…um…need some advice," she said with some hesitation. Not like her normal exuberance at all.

"I don't know what kind of advice it'll be this time of the morning, but shoot," was my leery response.

"Oh, I'm sorry Darla. I know it's early. Did I wake you up?" Carlotta asked apologetically.

"Nope. I was just on my way down to breakfast. What's up?"

Carlotta continued, "I don't know what to do about Nick. We…um…stayed out pretty late last night after we left Denny's. When we called it a night we agreed to phone each other this morning to make sure we got up in time to make breakfast before the first workshop. I've been calling his room for about an hour and he doesn't answer. I don't know if I should go pound on his door or just not worry about it. What do you think?"

"Well, Carlotta, I think Nick's a big boy and should be able to get out of bed on his own. It wouldn't be the end of the world if he missed the workshop," I advised, somewhat relieved that she was not calling about something more serious.

"Oh. Okay. Thanks, then." Carlotta was obviously ready to hang up. I still didn't know why she'd really called. Surely it wasn't just about Nick's wakeup call?

"Sure thing. That'll be two cents." Before she could put the phone down, I went on, "Carlotta? Did you call just to ask that? You seem upset and I guess I don't see why you'd be worried about something like a wakeup call."

"Well, I am, dammit. Darla, I feel silly. Last night Nick and I got pretty serious…"

"Oh? Really?" I interrupted. "Wanna tell me the details?"

"Not that serious, smartmouth. We've kinda been heading toward some kind of relationship since he's been coming down to Clearton. Last night was the first chance we'd had to get, well, romantic. That's all. But now I don't know whether going over to his room and waking him up seems too pushy, or too familiar, or assumes too much, or … I know, I know, it's not as big a deal as I'm making it. Forget it. Thanks for the advice, and you're right. I called him, so I did what I said I would. The rest is up to him. He probably forgot all about our agreement and he's already down having breakfast while I'm sitting here stewing. Sorry to bother you. You going downstairs?"

"No bother, Carlotta. But I will expect to hear all the juicy details of your evening at some point. Yeah, I'll meet you in the coffee shop in a few minutes," I said.

A few minutes later, I met Carlotta at the hotel coffee shop. We grabbed breakfast and headed toward the workshops. As we suspected, Nick slept through the first workshop. It was a busy morning, but my workshops went smoothly. I even got in a little dancing during my off times. You'd think that square dance callers would get enough of square dancing just from calling, but most of us never do. Instead, we end up on the dance floor in a square as often as not.

Lots of things attract people to the profession of square dance calling. It may be the thrill of performance, the chance to meet new people, or to travel all over the world. But to be a caller, one thing you've got to enjoy is the challenge of moving dancers smoothly around the floor to the right place. It's one thing to watch from up on stage as the dancers follow my instructions, but it's totally different to experience it at floor level. When I get a break from calling, you often find me, and many of the other callers, in a square. It helps us to become better callers to actually do the dancing, as well as the calling.

During one of Slim's sessions, I tracked down Doug and asked him if he'd like to be my partner for a couple of tips. He agreed. As Slim warmed up the crowd, he sounded almost like an auctioneer as he invited couples to square up. Doug and I took to the floor in search of a spot. I saw Tom and Stacey Greenville move onto the floor and motioned them over. Jerry Jamison and his wife saw us and came our way. While Slim continued to fill the floor, Tom held his hand in the air in a signal letting folks know we needed another couple to finish out our square.

A smiling couple appeared and slipped into the open spot. The woman wore a bright blue dress with ruffled collar and gold edging around the hem of her circle skirt. The man wore white pants and a blue shirt that exactly matched the color of his partner's dress. He wore a white ascot tied around the collar of his shirt with a gold ring holding it in place. I wondered if the shirt and skirt had been handmade from the same bolt of material or if the dancers were lucky enough to find a matching shirt. Unless a couple's dance clothes are made or bought together, it's usually easier to match the man's shirt to the most prominent color in the woman's dress than vice versa.

Both of them had full white hair and they made a striking couple. I didn't have time to find out their names before Slim launched into his first call of the tip, so I just shot them a friendly smile. I've learned never to anticipate Slim's calls, and sure enough he didn't start with a common one. Instead, he began a singing call and sent us straight into a Plus-level move called Teacup Chain. You could hear surprised laughter around the room as dancers revamped their expectations to respond to the sometimes tricky movement.

"I didn't know this was a Plus dance," Jerry said as he turned me around and sent me to the center position. "Did Slim announce it?"

"I didn't hear it if he did. We'll see if the floor is up to it," I said. I sailed into the center of the square and hooked elbows with Stacey. Slim sang out "Help Me, Rhonda" as we teacupped our way through the move.

You might expect callers to be great dancers. After all, we have to know all the calls. Most of us are acceptable but rusty. Unfortunately, we're most often standing still instead of dancing. Square dancing relies heavily on muscle memory, and callers' muscles haven't been drilled in the calls as much as frequent dancers. I was proud of the dancing ability of the callers in our square. We came through the Teacup Chain smoothly, ending up just where we should when we should. I couldn't say the same for the other squares.

"Left Allemande and Right and Left Grand." called Slim, mixing the words of the song with the dance calls. Slim sang, laughter in his voice as he watched the dancers on the floor.

He went easy on us for the rest of the tip and we were feeling pretty pleased with ourselves by the time he ended his second singing call. As was customary, we joined hands in our square and took a bow together. As I hugged and thanked the others dancers quickly, I glanced at the nametags of the couple I didn't know.

"Sam and Julia, nice to dance with you. Good job on those tricky calls!" I said.

"I've been dancing a long time," he said. "I knew what was coming," he responded.

Jerry leaned over and held out his hand, palm up. "Sam and Julie, you may not know it but you've just earned yourselves a purple heart. This was a square with three callers in it. When you dance in a square where everyone but you is a caller, you take your life in your hands. Make it through, and you earn a purple heart dangle! Want them?" Two miniature plastic purple hearts rested in the palm of his hand. Julie laughed and scooped them up.

"You bet!" she said. "We keep every dangle we get in a display case at home. With as many different ones as we've collected over the years, we learned it can be dangerous to slap around a long string of them while we're dancing. But we love 'em. Each one represents a memory for us."

As we cleared the floor and round dancers took our place, Julie turned to Doug and asked, "So where do you call?"

"Not me. Darla's the caller in our pair," he answered.

Julie turned to me. "I'm sorry. What a silly assumption for me to make. I've danced to many a fine woman caller. Do you have a home club?" she asked.

"No need to apologize," I assured her. "I've only been calling a few years. I call for several clubs north of Houston. Where are you folks from?"

Turns out they had come all the way from Minnesota. We chatted through the round dance, then Sam and Julie joined Doug and I in the next square as Slim drew the dancers together again. Jerry and Tom had drifted off so we had two new couples in our square this time. Two short tips and I'd already had the opportunity to meet six new people. For me, meeting people was truly one of the joys of square dancing. I wasn't good at small talk, so dancing gave me something to talk about when I met new folks.

Doug, Sam, Carlotta, and I met up at noon and grabbed a quick bite in the hotel coffeeshop again. When Nick hadn't shown by then Carlotta didn't know whether to be irritated, hurt, or worried. I left them digesting their lunch over coffee while I took off to find Slim and determine which room I was calling in for the afternoon sessions. I had just finished setting up my equipment when I looked up to see a familiar face. It took me a minute to place it. Even when I did, my mind took another few beats before it sunk in.

"Paul? Paul Harbinville? For Pete's sake, what are you doing here? Decide to take up square dancing after all?" As soon as the words left my mouth, I realized they were way too flippant to match the expression on his face. "What's happened?" I asked, more seriously.

"You haven't heard?" He looked genuinely surprised. It eased my mind a little when I saw a smile tug at his mouth. "I thought your grapevine worked better than that. It's Tricot. The local police called me down here when he went downtown last night."

If my bewilderment made him smile before, he must've gotten a real kick out of the blank look on my face this time. I didn't even have to ask anything for him to know whatever he told me would be news. But I stammered out, "Downtown?"

"Down to the precinct. He'll probably need a ride to the hotel soon, if you or your friends want to help him out. He rode down in a patrol car after they answered the call," he explained, clearing leaving out some pertinent details.

I understood his words, but not his meaning. I couldn't connect the dots. I guess he wasn't used to actually giving out information, because he wasn't doing a very good job of it. I'd given up working on my sound system and had moved around to the front of the table to lean on it.

"Okay, Paul, you're gonna have to take it slow for me. What the heck are you talking about? When and why were the police here?" I asked, beginning to get a little perturbed and worried.

"I really did think you knew about this. That's why I came out to ask you a few questions. Thought you might be able to shed some light on the situation. But you don't. You know I can't tell you much more. Especially because right now it's still in the jurisdiction of local enforcement. But your friend's okay. Not hurt. He just had a scare, that's all. Had a close call late last night and he thought he ought to report it, given recent events," was his response.

A few dancers had wandered into the room during our conversation and now I saw Sam and Carlotta talking with a group by the entrance to the hall. Apparently they hadn't realized who I was talking to, or I know they would have made a beeline over to find out what was going on. Doug came in as I was looking toward the door and either he recognized Harbinville or he figured something was up by the expression in my face. He headed over our way without missing a step.

"Doug, Paul has just been telling me Nick had some trouble last night. I've got to get things going here, but it sounds like he may need some help. Catch me up later." I wanted to find out the rest of the story, but I had a contract to fulfill. I knew Doug could handle whatever needed to be done. I stepped up on stage and spoke into the microphone as Doug tried to pry information from Paul. He looked a little frustrated, threw up his hands and then walked over to Carlotta.

"Welcome back after lunch! Let's get this afternoon going. Square 'em up!" I exclaimed from the stage. As folks began to form into squares, there was one square that was short a couple. "OK, we need one more couple in the back and we can get started. Here we go. My name is Darla, and I plan on taking you through your paces this afternoon."

I continued to mix up some of the Basic moves, calling moves when they were least expected, and working with them on mastery of the moves from any position for the patter part of the tip. With breaks, by the time I was relieved by Slim, I was pretty well spent. I'm not sure I could tell a Right and Left Grand from a Right and Left Thru myself! It didn't help that my head was spinning with questions about what had happened to Nick.

Six hours later Doug and I sat across the table from each other picking at the last of supper and waiting for the waiter to refill our coffee mugs. Nick was in his room, undoubtedly fast asleep after more than 36 hours with little more than a few minutes nap. Sam had gone to visit friends who lived out in Deer Park, and Carlotta swore she planned to soak in a hot bath until the knots in her shoulders eased and her skin shriveled. I was determined Doug wouldn't get away without a debriefing, so I'd offered to treat him to supper. While we ate, Doug had filled me in on the events of the last day and a half.

Over our coffee refill, he looked across at me. "Ya know, Darla, I'm just having trouble believing all this. Nick seems honest enough, and Lord knows I have no idea what he has to gain by getting us to buy a story like this, but it's so farfetched. We all took him pretty much at face value and befriended him without checking into his background at all. I'm just thinking he may be more involved than he's letting on."

I had no reason to doubt Nick. On the other hand, I'd known Doug a lot longer than Nick and trusted his instincts. And the events were strange. According to Doug, Nick had been on his way out to his car after he dropped Carlotta at her room late Friday night. Well, actually, early Saturday, about 2 a.m. Nick said he'd forgotten one of his bags in the car and went out to get it before he went to his room for the night.

While he was rooting around in the trunk of his car, he saw headlights coming toward him for all the world like the driver intended to run him over. He stepped quickly between his Rodeo and the pickup next to it and, fortunately as it turned out, stumbled over the bag he'd just placed on the pavement. As he banged a knee on the ground, a bullet hit the rearview mirror above his head. A second bullet pierced the door of the pickup. When he realized what was going on, he rolled under his car, then scooted forward until he was between the rows of parked cars. He crouched there and listened to determine where the car went.

The car circled around and came down the next aisle, so Nick dropped and rolled again, this time stopping motionless until he heard the vehicle pass. When it did, he poked his head out far enough to catch a glimpse of the car from behind. He said it looked like it could be the same SUV he saw in Clearton, but he couldn't tell. He was able to read a few numbers off the license plate under the light from the parking lot, but he wasn't sure about those either. Apparently, Nick had some military training and so he hadn't hesitated much in his response. Hard to believe from the timid insurance agent he'd led us to believe he was, though.

He'd waited until he thought the SUV was gone. He knew the driver could just have cut the engine and be waiting for him, but he made his way into the hotel. He called the police, and a couple of squad cars came out to take the report. Nick felt sure enough of a connection to suggest they contact the Clearton sheriff's office, and Lorys called in Harbinville. It had become pretty evident now we weren't looking at a simple car-jacking.

And now Doug's instincts were telling him there could be more to the story than Nick let on. If he was right, we couldn't really trust anything Nick had told us so far. If Nick was on the up and up, though, he needed our friendship, and maybe our help, more than ever. My brain rehashed the idea that he was an undercover agent of some sort. My imagination tends to run full speed ahead when faced with ambiguous situations, and the next thought that popped into my head was that maybe he was in the witness protection program. In either of those cases, why would Harbinville need information from me?

"What makes you think Nick may not be telling the truth?" I asked Doug.

"Nothing I can put my finger on. For one thing, I haven't been able to reach Gary Andrews yet to verify how Nick was able to make it out to my place. And then it's just that nothing that's happened seems to have a reason, if you take Nick's word for it. Why would someone attack him in the first place? And then again in the parking lot of a hotel in Houston? If he didn't know he'd be there, how did they? And why are they after him? And who are 'they'?"

"It's confusing, all right. In fact, I was just thinking last night that we've all gotten pretty friendly with Nick pretty quick, especially Carlotta. But he seems like such a good guy I'd hate to think he was playing us," I said.

"I've been thinking, Darla. With your skills from working with the State Attorney's Office and my experience in military intelligence, we ought to be able to establish Nick's bonafides. And I think we should. If he's legit, we can throw our skills behind him to help figure out who's got it in for him. If he's not, we could be putting ourselves in harm's way, if not from Nick himself, then from his 'friends.' Now, mind you, I am not suggesting any active involvement, just a little internet and database checking, well out of harm's way!"

I couldn't keep the twinkle of mischief out of my eyes. "I've already done some of that," I confessed. "When we first found out who he might be, I went online and did a little background check on him. Of course, I was only trying to establish his identification. I wasn't looking into his activities or the company he keeps or how long he has been around, you know like if he suddenly came into existence like a protected witness or something."

"Well, hell, Darla! Why didn't you tell me? As usual, you're way ahead of me. While I've been wondering which road to take, you're already on the journey. Okay, let's decide where we go from here," he suggested.

"The first thing that comes to mind is that we ought to see if Nick's connected in any way to the group you mentioned. The ones that don't want you setting up a camp for disabled kids," I said. "Or those developers who wanted to buy some of your land," I continued. I saw Doug open his mouth to protest, but I plowed on, "Okay, okay, I know you don't think it's related. Or if either of them is even an organized group to start with. But say they are. Say the developers are trying to force Clearton into becoming more urbanized. Say Nick is an agitator for one of the groups. It's something we have to consider."

Doug shrugged. "Well, okay, if you think so," he said. "I really don't see the connection. But it wouldn't hurt to check out Nick's affiliations, at least. To see if there are any red flags."

"I can do that, Doug. And I can check and make sure there's a record of his paying taxes, etc. back at least 10 years. And we need to see if he's got any connections to Clearton that he hasn't mentioned." I stopped for a minute, then continued, "Remind me, Doug, why we're spending so much time invading Nick's privacy? I'm starting to feel a little sheepish about doing this in the name of 'friendship'."

"Not me, Darla. We live in a world where things are not always what they seem. Things, and people have gotten downright scary lately. I try not to be paranoid, but I do want to follow up on this one. After all, he showed up on my property and now he's kind of latched on to our circle of friends, especially Carlotta. He knows pretty much where we're going to be when, and who won't be at home, so I'm not at all hesitant to do what we can to make sure he's who he says he is. You read the papers, listen to the news. You know there are lots of crazy people are out there – and they can look perfectly sane. I just don't want to get caught unawares by someone who might be one of the crazies," Doug concluded, looking a little less cheery and a lot more serious. Probably because of both our histories, even though we usually wanted to look for the positives in people, in the back of our minds lurked the possibilities

We talked at length about how we would divide up the duties and go about checking out Nick's background and the story he'd told us so far. It still felt awkward and yet, I didn't like the idea that Carlotta could have been with him when that SUV tried to take him out.

"I don't have any real reason to doubt him," Doug said. "I'm just trying to make sense of it. And, darn it all, this isn't how I'd pictured this weekend at all." He reached across the table and rested his hand on my arm. "I'd hoped we'd have some time to spend together. You and I haven't had time to visit, just the two of us, in way too long. And I hadn't planned on the topic being another man," he added with a chuckle.

I ran the idea around in my head like you do when you run your tongue around your mouth feeling for a rough tooth. I tried to find a niche that would let me respond to Doug's overture but my mind didn't have any extra slots this evening. Even I was disappointed, and I was the one turning down the invitation.

"I'd like that, too, Doug. I just don't think tonight's the best time. I'm physically worn out from working all day, but really more than that I'm emotionally exhausted. I don't think I could focus on a rational conversation, or anything else, much as I'd like to. My mind's too tangled up in everything that's going on. Something always seems to get in the way of 'us.' Can I take a raincheck?"

"Sure, Darla, you know that. You're probably right, anyway. Let's call it a night," he answered, with some disappointment evident.

After the obligatory wrangle, I won the bill. I paid the tab and as we walked toward the elevator Doug slipped his arm around my waist. I leaned into him, enjoying his solidness. In the elevator, we leaned together against the railing without talking while the car made its way to the third floor. At my door, Doug at first gave me a friendly hug, then changed his mind and stepped in closer. I moved into him again, encouraging the kiss he gave me. He took off and I went into my room alone and locked the door behind me.

Okay, I wasn't really that tired. I could have let Doug come in. Would have liked to, at least on an emotional and intellectual level. The problem was on that other level, the intimate one. At this point, while I enjoyed the closeness with Doug, enjoyed the affection, I just didn't seem to feel the chemistry I should. I assumed it was my fault. Ever since Clint had died, I'd built an ever-growing barricade around any romantic feelings that might poke their heads out of my emotional shell, and I'd squashed any semblance of my sex drive as well. Losing my husband hurt too much. I wasn't ready to put myself in a position to feel that much pain again.

So I pushed away any desire I might have to be with Doug, or any man, and bolstered my confidence in being alone. Doug had managed to punch through my defenses a couple of times, and he seemed to be determined to try again. I was surprised he continued to put up with me. I'm not sure I would have.

Before getting into bed, I called Heather. No answer again, so I left a message. What good was paying for her cell phone if she never answered it? I spent a fitful night, alone again, despite my exhaustion.

Chapter 9

The front square was made up entirely of men, there were no women in it. They wore matching shirts and did the moves carefully. They had to be careful. Each held a cigarette between the fingers of his right hand as he turned and twirled and wove among the others. They were keeping time to the music, but they weren't following my calls. I'd call a Scootback, they'd do a Spin Chain Thru. I'd call a Right and Left Thru, they'd do a Track Two. I'd call a Weave the Ring, and they'd Promenade. I kept trying to get in sync with them, to see if maybe they were doing a pattern I ought to know, but I couldn't see it. I just couldn't see it…

I awoke with a start, sweating and disoriented. The lighted numbers of the bedside clock bought me back to reality and I saw it was 3:15 a.m. At the same time, the dream registered. I knew who the dancers were and why they were out of step. I worked my way back through the theory looking for holes, but couldn't find any. Then I worked my way forward through it, trying to see what it meant. No luck.

My mind was whirring and there was no way I was getting back to sleep, so I rolled out of bed and headed for the bathroom. Fortunately, this was one of the hotels that offer in-room coffee makers. I brewed up a pot and took it over to the small table by the window. They didn't have creamer, of course, only that awful powdered stuff that turns your coffee white in an attempt to fool you. Oh, well, it would have to do.

Each night the hotel slid a newspaper under my door, and each morning I had little interest in reading it. I was awake when it appeared under the door this morning, so I picked it up and idly scanned the headlines. I tossed it on the dresser like I always did. Then I stopped. I went over to the dresser and picked up the paper. The headline was on the front page, just below the fold: Security Guard Killed, Hofheinz Museum Loses Treasures.

I thought of the question that Nick said brought him to Doug's ranch in the first place. In his explanation to us, he'd mentioned that he always noticed major losses in the towns where he'd gone to dances. This one was certainly in the pattern. And had escalated from robbery to felony murder. I remembered reading about another murder associated with a museum heist about the time when Nick had been found on Doug's land. I wondered if the Hofheinz was a client of Nick's company. Nick had run the stats on claims from his company correlated to his dance trips. But probably he hadn't had access to claims from other companies. If there was a pattern, it would lead one way if all the claims came out of the pool of one insurance company's clients.

But a much bigger picture would emerge if multiple companies were experiencing similar strings of burglaries. The latter would pretty much vindicate Nick having any involvement, while the former… I didn't want to go there. If Nick was setting up the crimes against his company, he wouldn't have told us about them, would he?

I doodled on the hotel stationery until I thought it was an acceptable hour to call Doug. It was finally 5:30. Yeah, that ought to be late enough.

"Doug, it's Darla. Want to get an early breakfast?" After listening to a few choice words about the early hour from the other end of the line, followed by a proposition that made me blush, he finally conceded that breakfast was the only thing on the menu. I tucked the newspaper under my arm and went down to the hotel coffee shop to meet Doug.

We were keeping that place in business. There never seemed to be enough time to go somewhere else to eat. It was your basic hotel coffeeshop, overpriced but reasonably good coffee, efficient but not particularly friendly wait staff. This morning we beat the staff to the punch and the coffeeshop wasn't even open for another 15 minutes. Doug and I located a private spot on a couch in one of the lounge areas and I laid out my ideas for him. It wasn't formal enough to call a theory, really. I hadn't tied any of the loose ends together, but I knew

Doug could keep up with me and see if it was a direction worth pursuing.

I told him about my dream, looked around to make sure we were alone, then went on, "What clicked into place when I woke up was that I've seen the same group of men at the last two major dances I've called. That's not unusual of course. I'm more surprised when I don't see the same faces at each dance. But there's just been the feeling of something wrong, something out of place, with these guys. For one thing, they haven't had any women with them and that's unusual. Most dancers come in couples or even more women than men in the group. And then they're smokers. Again, not that unusual, but most square dancers aren't. I've never seen them actually at a dance in progress. I've only seen then just around the periphery. Sure, their schedules could just be different than mine. These big dances have multiple dances going on at the same time. Maybe they just don't like my calling. I don't recognize their shirts as any club I know, but maybe I just don't know it. See, Doug, it can all be explained away. It boils down to a gut feeling that they are 'masquerading' as square dancers, but aren't really square dancers after all."

I took a breath. I'd been sifting through my thoughts for over two hours, and now they poured out of my brain like spilled flour. I kept spilling.

"The main thing to me, I guess, is that they just don't seem open and friendly. That's one of the things I like most about square dancers. They're usually smiling, willing to visit and meet new people. I've never seen these guys talking to anyone other than themselves. I just can't figure out why some group of men would decide to try to pass themselves off as square dancers. It's not like police or fire or even ambulance personnel, where the 'masquerade' might get them in somewhere without being questioned too much." I finally stopped talking so I could catch a breath.

Doug had listened closely during my spiel, but I could tell he wasn't really on the bandwagon with me.

"So, Darla, what are you saying?" he asked. "Who do you think these guys are?"

"I have no idea. I feel like I have a bunch of miscellaneous jigsaw puzzle pieces with no picture to go by. I'm not sure they're even part of the same picture. First, we've got Nick coming to see you when we don't know him from Adam. Then we've got the attacks on him for no apparent reason. We've got Harbinville, who won't give me the time of day, and initially says 'case closed – car-jacking,' but keeps showing up in the thick of things. We've got a bunch of guys who don't seem like square dancers coming and going at the major dances. And now we've got this."

I plopped the newspaper up on the coffee table in front of our couch. I could tell Doug caught the significance of the headline as soon as he read it. He picked up the paper and read the first few paragraphs.

"You're thinking of Nick's idea about burglaries that tie into his dancing schedule, right?" he asked.

"Yes, that's what came to mind when I saw it though this time there is a murder as well. And I remember reading about another one earlier this fall, also a museum curator killed. But how does it fit into the puzzle any more than any of the other pieces?" I asked. "Like I said, being dressed like square dancer isn't exactly gonna get you into an art museum or past security."

"I don't know. But I do know I won't come up with any good ideas until I get a little caffeine in my system to jumpstart my brain. Come on, the restaurant's opened up. Let's grab a table and hash this out over some hashbrowns," he said, shaking his head.

Doug and I tried to hash it out over breakfast, but we still come up empty. We had a lot of apparently unconnected pieces that may or may not be part of a bigger picture. Kind of like the way teachers always gave you extra, and irrelevant, information in math word problems to see if you could figure which information to pay attention to and which to ignore. After breakfast, I chatted briefly with Carlotta who was still pretty upset. She was understandably concerned about Nick rather than upset that their relationship was going south before it really got off the ground. She had called around 10 to see about breakfast and seemed to need to talk, so I obliged. Well, another cup of coffee wouldn't hurt.

We met after I finished calling the trail-out dance. She was as confused as I was. She was upset that she had doubted him and felt guilty about that as well. I didn't bother to tell her she wasn't the only one wondering what was going on, but I assured her that I was gonna keep pondering the problem.

In the meantime, I needed to call Heather. I was eager to try to reach her again, but wanted to make sure Carlotta was through talking things out.

"What do you think, Carlotta? What's your schedule for today? The trail-out dance was the last of the scheduled events. Are you planning to hang around awhile?" I asked.

"Geez, Darla, I don't know what to do. I rode over here to the dance in Sam's truck, and knowing Sam I'm sure he's itching to get on the road. I'd really like to stay and talk to Nick when he gets up. What about Doug, you think he's staying any longer? Maybe I can catch a ride to Clearton with him." Carlotta rolled and unrolled her napkin for about the hundredth time. She didn't say anything for a minute, then took a deep breath and let it out. "I can't sit here all day, that's for sure!" she said. "I guess I'll track down Doug and Sam and see what's what. You leaving, Darla?"

"Not just yet. Pretty soon. I'm going to make a call first, but I may not see you before I head out to Isquith. You need me to wait?" I asked.

"Thanks, Darla, but no. I'll get it all worked out." Her smile was weak, but in place. I half stood and gave her a hug goodbye, then sat down and dialed Heather's number, for what felt like the millionth time. I almost expected her voicemail to kick in, so I was surprised when she answered.

"Hi, Mom. What's up?" she asked.

"Heather! I've been trying to get hold of you. Is everything okay?" I tried to keep the mounting frustration with her out of my voice.

"Sure, Mom. Everything's fine. Didn't you get my voicemail? Really. Everything's just fine." Her extra assurance had exactly the opposite effect on me. There was something she wasn't telling me, and I didn't know how to get it out of her.

"Heth, please tell me what's going on with you. Is it classes? Micah? Don't shut me out, please," I asked in my most motherly tone.

"Mom, it's okay. Really," she said. I still didn't believe her so I stayed silent, using the time-tested Mom technique of getting teens to fill the silence. Sometimes it works, sometimes not. This time it did.

"It's just…well, we've got midterms going on so I'm at class at weird times and I'm at the library a lot, studying and…and at Micah's place and…" her voice trailed off. I stepped in with the place she hadn't mentioned.

"Why aren't you studying at home, Heather?" I asked. Her long pause told me I'd hit the target. She finally answered.

"See, that's why I haven't been answering my phone, Mom. I knew you'd make me tell you. It's no big deal, really. But Stacy's boyfriend's been staying at our place and, well, it's not that big and there's only one bathroom and I don't know him very well and so I'm hardly ever there and I have my cell with me but I haven't been answering because I didn't want to tell you and I knew you would be upset and please don't try to fix it for me." It all came out in one breath and I tried hard to follow her.

"Heather, honey, slow down. Do you mean you can't study at your own apartment? Can't even have any privacy there?" I asked.

"No, Mom. Not that I can't. I just haven't been. I didn't want to tell you because I knew you'd be upset. See, I was right," she said.

"Not with you, Heth, you know that. But we do need to work this out. I could talk to Stacy for you, or call her parents," I offered.

"Mom, no! See, that's just what I knew you'd want to do. Please, please let me work this one out on my own. It's okay, really," she pleaded.

"How are your grades doing?" I asked.

"Fine, Mom. Micah's really smart and he's helping me study. I'm pulling all B's except for Chem. That's a C but it's just midterm and I can bring it up by the end of semester, promise." She was pulling out all the stops to keep me from feeling like I needed to step in. I wanted to, but reined myself in as much as I could. One red flag I couldn't ignore, though.

"Sounds like you and Micah are spending a lot of time together. Aren't you moving a little fast?" I asked.

"Micah's great, Mom. You'll see next time you come over. Don't worry so much about me. I'm grown up, you know." She really thought she was.

"Sorry, hon, you'll always be my little girl no matter how old you get. You can't get out of that one. But I'll respect your judgment for now. I won't do anything about Stacy's boyfriend or yours. But, honey, you know you can talk to me. Don't shut me out, okay?" It was my turn to plead.

"Okay Mom. Are you at home?" She was good at changing the subject.

"No, I'm in Houston. But I'm about to get on the road. Did you need something from the house?" I asked.

"No, just trying to visualize you on the other end of the line," she said. "I love you, Mom, but I gotta work things out for myself, you know?"

"Yes, I do know. But you know I have to look out for you too. That's my job. I love you too, and answer your phone, will ya?" I asked or rather stated.

"I will. Bye Mom. Be careful on the road."

"Bye, Heth. You be careful too. Love you."

I closed the phone wondering if I was glad she'd answered or not. Was I happier knowing the problems she was dealing with? Knowing I couldn't protect her from them? Knowing that "spending a lot of time at Micah's place" probably meant she was sleeping with him and didn't want me to know? I certainly hoped she was using birth control. I could not handle being a grandmother right now, but I didn't think this was the time to get into it with her over the phone.

That last thought put me over the edge and I just couldn't think about it anymore. I seemed to be getting good at avoiding thinking about topics that made me uncomfortable. That thought in itself made me uncomfortable. Next I'd be talking to myself and answering! I put aside Heather's situation, knowing she was at least safe and coping, and went back to thinking about Doug and Nick and Carlotta and the Clearton Caper. I went up to the room and gathered my things, loaded the car, and checked out of the hotel.

On the drive home I tried to come up with some tactics for figuring out this puzzle. It occurred to me that while Doug was doing some additional checking on Nick's background and the link to Gary Andrews, I could see what I could come up with from the crime databases. Although I certainly couldn't access police records, I did know how to access the databases used to compute crime rates in various places. It was limited data, but data just the same. Nick, if he was telling the truth, was only basing his suspicions on crimes that affected businesses insured by his company. The databases would be more extensive. Even then, there would be no way to control for however many other activities or events were also occurring at the same time as a square dance. Sam really was right about this idea of Nick's being pretty far-fetched. Or a red herring to distract us from the real issue, whatever that was.

When I got home, I put my stuff away and decided to relax for a while before going on the internet. The population of Isquith is about the same as Clearton, but Isquith's city limits are a little more confined so it seems more crowded. The streets are wide and the town beautification committees have been hard at work with various foliage and trees along the main thoroughfares. As with Clearton, Isquith has the sense of small town, but is relatively close to the city, in its case Houston instead of Austin. The weeks had flown by, and fall was well upon us, even in Texas. Physical exertion had always seemed to help me release tension, and not being prone to jogging, I got out the rake, bagged leaves, cleaned up the gardens, and did general yard work. Yard work and the improved appearance of the place always helped me to clear cobwebs from my brain and gave me a sense of accomplishment. Now my yard didn't look neglected next to the finished lawnscaping of the town streets. I showered, and with a clearer head, sat down at the computer.

Accessing the databases for crimes in Texas for the past 6 months, and then focusing on larceny, I pulled up the stats. I found locations, dates and type of loss, solved or unsolved, and even clicked to the local "crime stoppers" on those that had links. Not surprisingly, I found the earlier museum burglary that ended up with the curator being killed. The problem that immediately came to mind was that for the unsolved larcenies, including that one, there was no common element immediately apparent. The items stolen were very different.

Working any investigation, police and most government agencies tend to look for a pattern – jewelry, antiques, negotiable stocks and bonds, art collections, etc. Most professional thieves stick to one kind of merchandise and associate with already identified fences to get rid of the merchandise. This actually is what makes it possible for some of the merchandise to be recovered. Come to think of it though, Nick had mentioned variable merchandise when he brought up his theory. I transferred the larceny data to a new file, arranged it by date and place with a click of the mouse, and went to the next step.

I pulled up the calendar for the state and regional square dance associations, and then checked some of the other calendars for any big dances that would have attracted multiple clubs and callers. I did some fancy rearranging and had these dances in chronological order back to April with the locations. Now for the real magic. I transferred the dance calendar to the crime file and put them side by side. It took some manipulation, but sure enough there it was right before my eyes!

For each and every date I had noted a dance, there was a coinciding major larceny in the location of that dance. In some cases there were two dances at different parts of the state, and only one unsolved larceny for a date, but that only happened twice in the six months. I hadn't accounted for all the unsolved larcenies, but that wasn't particularly surprising. Although I wanted to jump up and down, I reminded myself that these were fairly large cities and square dancing was not necessarily the only activity going on in these locations on those dates. If I had the ability to cross-reference the crimes with other conventions or conferences, I might see the same pattern.

On a whim, and to check on chance occurrence of the 'coincidence' of square dancing and larcenies, I went back to the crime databases and the square dancing history sites, and pulled up the six months. I put these side by side and the frequency of 'coincidence' seemed to be less for the previous fall and winter as compared to the more recent six months. In fact, the co-occurrence of unsolved larceny and a major square dance seemed very random until early spring or March. Somehow, this didn't quite seem like chance, but I had no other data to show that it wasn't just that. No way to prove that Nick's theory was right and the authorities were missing something.

Having printed out multiple pages of data I wasn't sure were even going to be helpful, I turned to my other question. I put 'car-jacking' into the search engine and waited to see what came up for Texas in the last six months. Sure enough, there was a record of the car-jacking in Thornton in July, and it was unsolved. Although it was now nearing the middle of November, I was surprised to see that Nick's car-jacking in Clearton wasn't showing up. That was kind of strange. Not to mention that a single car-jacking didn't quite add up to a series. So while the statistics really did jive with Nick's theory, they didn't match with what Sheriff Lorys and good old Harbinville would have had us believe about the car-jackings and Nick's 'accident.' Hmmmm.

I'd have to share this information with Doug when I was in Clearton this week and see what luck he had reaching Gary. In the meantime, there wasn't exactly a directory of people in witness protection. I again checked the databases of public information on Nick himself, just to see if I could find out anything about his past, like that he had one and didn't sprout as an adult. Sure enough, I could find where he had a driver's license and even had won awards and been a speaker in various places for at least five years back. It seemed a little too much to request one of those background checks available for a small fee. That would make me feel like I had gone too far. I would just have to wait and hope that Doug was able to get more information from Gary.

Exhausted, I turned off the computer and went to bed. My eyes were burning from reading the screen and my muscles were beginning to complain about the unaccustomed paces I'd put them through this afternoon. I took a couple of ibuprofen and curled up in bed. As I was falling asleep I tried to think back to the guys I had seen smoking on those two occasions. More specifically, I tried to remember what the pattern on their shirt was, but the pattern was elusive, and nothing was ringing any bells. I told myself it was all my over-active imagination and went to sleep.

Chapter 10

Monday morning came way too soon. It was Mondays like this that made me wonder how Slim and others worked full-time jobs and still called at weekend dances. Here I was calling at one club weekly and one club every other week, and the weekend of work just about knocked me out. With the fall schedule, most of the clubs had fall themes even for their club dances, and tonight was the fall/anniversary dance for the Footstompers. I ran my errands, and then gathered up my stuff and left for Forsby.

As usual, Hal and Lenore greeted me at the door and Hal grabbed some of my gear. The hall had been decorated with haystacks and a scarecrow or two. On a table there were several scrapbooks, with years covered noted on the outside. Hal and Lenore moved to greeting the dancers as they came in, and I got my gear set up. As usual, I would start with a patriotic medley. I checked the time, smiled at some dancers as they gathered nearby and got the dance started with a "Hey there, Footstompers, let's square up!"

It was a good crowd and six squares formed with no problem. There were the usual folks playing dominoes in the back of the room. Looking around, I figured it was time. "Bow to your partner, bow to your corner," and then the CD took over. I called them through the melody, but they all were singing along, they knew it so well.

After it ended I told them, "OK, take a break. I'm putting on a waltz for any of you who want to take advantage of the opportunity," as I went for some coffee. Flo came up and gave me a hug.

"Hey Darla, are you just about ready for Thanksgiving?" Flo asked. I again remembered that aside from being outspoken, Flo pretty much knew everything about everybody, kept the history of this club, and had been an officer at the regional and state levels.

"Getting it together. Now, Flo, I got a question for you. In all your travels to various dances, have you ever seen a group of guys, two or three maybe, just hanging around at a square dance, but they don't ever seem to dance?" I asked on a whim.

"Are you looking, Darla? Usually, any men hanging around a dance would be dancing!" she answered. "What would make you ask that?"

"At the dance this weekend, I happened to notice that a few guys were just standing outside the dance and thought it odd," I responded as I drank my coffee and looked around.

"Sorry, I can't help, but if there are some single men somewhere, let me in on it huh? I'm not getting any younger here!" was her response. She turned and walked away and I got ready to call the next tip. "Let's square 'em up!"

I called the usual two more tips with a waltz and two-step to break up the venue and keep me on schedule. On the next break, Jonnie came over. "Hi Darla, don't know if you remember me. I'm Jonnie. Moved to Forsby just a while ago. Flo said you were asking about some fellas who might be just hanging around a dance? Well, that's not quite the way she put it, but I think that was the gist." He smiled and coughed, and looked a little embarrassed. I am not quite sure what Flo had communicated to him.

"Yes, Jonnie, that's right. Have you seen guys like that?" I asked.

"Well, yeah. A couple times I noticed these two fellas hanging around when there was a co-op dance of all the Dallas area clubs. They didn't seem to belong to any of the other clubs and they certainly weren't Stepping Squares. I don't think they ever came into the dance, but I used to smoke, and would see them when I was outside catching a smoke. I quit since then. Doctor said it wasn't good for me," he concluded. We chatted a few more minutes and then it was time for the last tip and my drive home. It was somewhat consoling to know that I wasn't imagining things, but that meant these guys had been around for some time. The Clearton Caper now seemed to extend to Dallas.

A good night's sleep and it was Tuesday and I drove to Clearton. Although I wasn't sure why, I didn't get out of town early enough to stop at the café and talk to my friendly waitress, Sadie. I got to Clearton and set everything up for lessons night. Overall, lessons were progressing fairly well. For a lesson night, there was a pretty good turnout, including Nick, who had driven down from Fort Worth once again and was keeping Carlotta pretty busy! He seemed to have recovered from last week's excitement and their relationship was certainly moving along faster than mine with Doug. The new dancers had finally mastered Right and Left Thru and the various other Thru and Star moves. Tonight we were working on the Chain moves. Gradually, we would work through all the moves for Basic and Mainstream.

We continued to work through the new moves, and then to review the previous moves. I put on a singing call that included the various chains so they could practice during the break if they wanted to, and told everyone to take five. I noticed Sam talking to one of the men, apparently explaining to him that his hand was supposed to be in the small of the lady's back, not lower. Square dancers observe a tighter level of decorum than the mainstream of today's society. I chuckled but knew that Sam could explain it diplomatically.

As I left the small stage area, I noticed that Gary Andrews had come in during the last tip and was chatting amicably with Doug. Gary and his wife Pauline were mainstays of the square dancing community. They'd both held almost every office of associations at regional and state levels. He was a big bear of a man, well over 6 feet tall and so stout that my arms didn't reach around him when I gave him a hug. But his size didn't keep him from moving quickly on the dance floor. He could dance any calls you threw at him, and he and Pauline often requested a "hot hash" tip. Hot hash means fast-paced calling that keeps the squares moving at racing speed. I wasn't advanced enough in my calling abilities to do a "hot hash" number, but I had a few quick songs that usually pleased the hot hash fans without being too fast for the other dancers.

When I located Pauline visiting with Nick over by the refreshment table, I caught her eye and waved. She beamed and waved back at me, her round face all smiles under her short gray hair. She was average height and obviously worked out when she wasn't square dancing. She wasn't skinny, but she certainly wasn't fat either. Gary and Pauline were both retired, probably in their late 60s, and they followed the square dance circuit across the country in their RV. I hoped I had as much energy and happiness as them in another 20 years or so. I walked over toward Gary and Doug, curious what brought the Andrews this far south of Dallas.

"Hi Gary! What brings you down here to Clearton? First Nick starts coming and now you. It's not like Dallas is right next door!"

"Hello yourself, Darla!" he answered with a hug and a smile. "Nick's been telling me what a great caller you are, and I haven't had a chance to visit much with Doug here, so I decided to come on down. Pauline and I are on our way down to Rockport for some winter dancing, so we thought we'd swing by Clearton on our way. That's okay with you, now, right? I wouldn't want to cause you any trouble," he joked.

"No problem with me, Gary, glad to have you here. It's good to see you again. Missed you in Houston! And you certainly missed some excitement!" was my response.

Nick and Carlotta came over and joined us to catch up with Gary and Pauline. I figured it was time to get my cup of coffee if I was going to before it was time to square up again. It certainly seemed like Nick and Gary knew each other, and whatever doubts Doug had raised in my mind were fading pretty fast as I watched them all interacting and joking around.

Doug and Gary had served together as officers on several state boards over the years, and they'd struck up a friendship. Doug had a deep respect for Gary's judgment. Plus, Gary had at least a passing acquaintance with just about everyone who'd been square dancing in Texas for any amount of time. If Nick had been dancing in the Dallas area for a while, Gary and Pauline would know him. I was sure Doug felt he could rely on Gary's gut feeling about Nick.

I made my way to the front for the next call. As I faced the room and said "Let's square 'em up!" I noticed Doug and Gary headed out to the hallway. Pauline noticed too, and snagged Nick for the next tip so she wouldn't miss a dance. The rest of the night went well, in part because I opted not to try to teach too much more. Around Thanksgiving there would be a break in lessons for a week, so to try to teach too much before that with little chance for review wouldn't be productive. The time went by quickly, and it was soon time to pack everything up.

"Hey Darla Darlin', how about joining us for some java?" Sam asked as he walked toward the door and grabbed one of my bags. He smiled and his eyes sparkled like always.

"I'd love to Sam! But I can't be hanging around all night now!" I answered. Doug had joined us by then.

"Come on you slow pokes, Darla has a long ride home yet!" Doug called to the group of Nick, Carlotta, Pauline, and Gary as we cleared the door and headed for our cars. "We'll meet you at the diner," he yelled to the trailers.

Doug and Sam helped me carry my equipment to the car. Doug put his arm around me and suggested we all ride together. The three of us got into my car and drove downtown.

"Well, Darla, as you can tell, I contacted Gary. And sure enough, just like Nick said, he had floated his idea about the thefts and square dances by Gary. Gary didn't think there was any connection. When Nick asked about the club patterns on dresses and shirts, Gary suggested he contact me 'cause he remembered my article in the newsletter a few years back. Gary said he never gave it another thought. Gary said Nick is genuinely a nice guy, but like all accounting types can be a bit boring. I assured him that hanging around with Nick these days is anything but boring!" Doug laughed as we pulled into the parking lot. "I did check around with my connections, and I have to say that Nick seems clean. Nothing suspicious."

"Whoa! What are you talking about? You guys been checking on Nick? That's not very neighborly!" Sam chortled. "But I must say I'm glad you did, to be honest. I was getting a tad worried about our little Carlotta. It seems things are moving a mite fast there, don'tcha think? On the other hand, I guess I better watch out in case you decide to check on me!" he added.

"No point in it, Sam. We all know you're a ne'er-do-well from way back, even without checking on you! But yes, Darla and I have done a little checking on Nick. Everything seems to check out. Darla was following up on Nick's robbery theory, too," Doug explained.

"I checked the crime databases, and first of all, there is no series of car-jackings that I could find. In fact, they didn't actually file Nick's accident as a car-jacking no matter what story Lorys and Harbinville would have us believe. The other thing I found out is that there is a pattern, not necessarily of Nick's insured businesses, but of larcenies and square dances. I can't say that the evidence is conclusive though, it may just be random." I added to bring Doug and Sam up to date as I parked my car.

Carlotta pulled up in her car followed by Nick, Pauline, and Gary in Nick's Rodeo, and we all went into the diner. While we were deciding on our orders, I looked inquiringly over at Doug. He raised his eyebrows and shrugged, leaving the decision up to me whether to fess up to Nick on our private-eye work. I opted for half a confession and left out the part about checking on Nick's background.

After the waitress left with all our orders, I said, "Well, Nick, I don't know if anyone told you that in my previous life I was an investigator of sorts. After the incident at the Hoedown, my curiosity was aroused and I followed up a bit on your theory. Seemed to me the attack on you in Houston made the first one a little more than coincidental, so I checked out the correlation of dances to burglaries. I think you may have hit on something. Now, I didn't check to see if there were any other conferences also happening at the same time. It may just be that the big dances are in big cities, and big cities have high crime rates. And I obviously couldn't access information on which of those places were insured by you. The question now seems to be: Is that what's making you a target and, if so, why?"

Nick responded, "I am so glad that someone at least is taking me seriously!" He actually seemed more animated than I had ever seen him before. He continued, "I had no idea you had an investigation background or I would've thought to ask you sooner. I don't know why I would be a target. It's not like I actually know anything, or the same companies are involved and the fact that I am nearby when they get hit makes them suspicious. Everything seemed unrelated until I noticed a possible pattern. I was only looking at my attendance at dances and my getting called about a loss."

"Nick, have you noticed anyone or a group of people at the convention centers or hotels that stood out to you? Like a group of men in square dance clothes who don't seem to dance at all?" I asked.

Nick avoided looking at Carlotta and very sheepishly responded, "I'm sorry to say Darla, when I attend dances, I don't usually notice the guys, dancing or not!" We all laughed, including Carlotta. Nick added, "Not sure I'll even be noticing the ladies anymore," and looked over at Carlotta, who, surprisingly, actually blushed.

Discussion shifted to the business at hand with Carlotta's pointed question, "Ok, Darla, what's the plan?"

I didn't realize I even had a plan, but as I related more of the details about the unsolved larcenies and various square dances one took shape in my brain. When I mentioned my uneasy feelings about these solo male dancers I had seen at two dances this fall, Nick jerked up his head.

"I never thought about it, Darla, but now that you mention it, I ran into three men at the hotel restaurant when I was at a dance in August. They weren't particularly friendly and didn't seem exactly 'right.' I looked for badges or other indication of their home club, but I didn't see any. They could be your group," Nick said. "I wouldn't remember, except the guys got pretty angry with me. I guess I tried a little too hard to be friendly."

He smiled a shy smile. "I've been told my social skills aren't always the best. When I saw these guys, I went up and started talking to them like I would any group of dancers hanging around after a dance. I asked where they were from, but they always sidestepped the question. Mentioned west Texas and I said something like, that was a long way to come to the dance. One guy bristled at that and asked me if I was calling him a liar. Took me by surprise. I was just making conversation. The more I tried to smooth things over – making small talk, asking where they were going after the dance, what have you – the more they took offense. I finally said something like, 'well, I know y'all have business to take care of' and made my exit as gracefully as I could." Nick looked distinctly uncomfortable as he related his experience.

"One guy stood up out of his chair to come after me. One of those angry drunks, I guess. I pretty much convinced myself that they weren't square dancers, just happened to be wearing similar western style shirts and jeans. The one guy woulda come after me, but his buddy put a hand on his shoulder and told me to have a good evening. I never did figure out what I'd said to rile them up, and it worried me for several days. I'd forgotten about it all till you mentioned those guys you saw."

The light had dawned about halfway through Nick's story. "If they're connected in any way to this string of burglaries, pretty major ones at that, I think you may have just hit on the reason for your troubles, Nick. They think you're onto them! And even if you don't remember seeing them at other dances, they may have seen you. And obviously enough times to remember you. Not sure how they managed to follow you to Clearton and Doug's though." I said. "Nick, I need a list of all the dances you attended in the last year. I think I may have a plan after all, Carlotta."

The first weekend of December was the Winter Solstice dance for the mid-central portion of the state. Hosted by two regional clubs and the state association, as well as local clubs and callers, the purpose of the dance was to collect small gifts for children and adults to be distributed to the various shelters in four counties. Instead of a monetary cost for entrance to the Friday and Saturday dances, each person had to bring a wrapped package of estimated $5 value labeled for the most appropriate type of recipient. To attend the afternoon workshop, three cans of food or equivalent were required for entry. Club presidents and delegates then were responsible for distribution of the canned food and the gifts in the surrounding areas. The callers, including me, would all volunteer our time, and the convention hall was charging a minimal rate to help the cause. Each year, the attendance and the donations grew, and all else aside, a good time was had by all!

With multiple clubs, associations, and callers, this was the next big dance. If the pattern held true, there would be an unsolved larceny in Austin. So the Winter Solstice became the location of our plan. Each of us would write down the patterns we identified as a club outfit and the club associated with it. At the same time, we would make it a point to notice any single males, keep track of the patterns on their shirts, and try to make conversation with them.

The plan meant that the Clearton crew couldn't all stay together or with Gary and Nick. Everyone needed to be mingling and circulating. Easy for the others, not so easy if you're the one calling the tip! At any rate, our plan was to gather information, especially about any smoking males we noticed. If nothing else, it would serve as the basis for an article or paper on club dress and emblems for Nick and Doug! The media would tell us the other bit of information we needed - if a major burglary occurred there over the weekend.

Well, that was my plan. I finished laying it out for them and then shut up to wait for their responses. All I got was dead silence for a good while. Then Sam spoke up.

"Well, I can't see a thing wrong with that, Darla. You know me. I don't have a speck of trouble being friendly and making conversation with strangers. I might leave the recordkeeping to the rest of you, though. I'm not much on that part," Sam added.

"Not a problem, Sam. That's the part I like," said Nick. "And Darla, I have that list in my car. I keep track so I can get my Friendship Bars." Friendship Bars were 'dangles' that dancers could earn by visiting other clubs. As a caller, I didn't get these bars and if I did they would sit in a box. I don't usually sport one of the name tags that the bars hang from.

By the time we finished dessert, we'd fine-tuned my ideas a little and everyone had bought into the overall plan. We didn't have long to wait to put it into action. The Winter Solstice was coming up fast, right after Thanksgiving. It would probably amount to nothing, I told myself. It was now pushing on midnight, and I still had to drive home to Isquith. Under normal conditions, I might have stayed over at Carlotta's place, but, I didn't want to ask and then have an awkward situation if Nick had been planning on staying over.

Doug gave me questioning look, and I hesitated, but there was just too much on my mind. "Now it's my turn, Darla. I do have a guest room, you know, and you are welcome to it. It's really pretty late, and I don't want you to fall asleep driving home," Doug offered quietly. "I promise I'll behave," he added with a smile, as if I had any doubts. It also dawned on me that his making the promise was somewhat disappointing. Anyway, I decided he was right, and accepted his offer. I drove Sam and Doug back to the dance hall, and then followed Doug home.

All the way to his ranch, I had misgivings, came up with a million reasons why I shouldn't spend the night, even in the guest room. I still hadn't gotten around to packing an emergency overnight bag, although I did keep a few extra clothes in the trunk. As I passed his cactus stand and proceeded down his drive, I remembered the night Nick had been left for dead off the side of the road and shuddered. I parked my car next to Doug's and grabbed my extra set of clothes. Well, at least after sleeping in my clothes, I could put on clean ones for the drive home.

"Need any help with anything Darla?" Doug asked as I hesitated at the entrance way.

"Nope. I do appreciate your letting me stay here," I responded shyly.

"I don't think you've ever been to the back of the house, so let me give you a brief tour. This door leads to what was called the private quarters back in the day," he explained as he indicated a door from the living area opposite the open archway to the kitchen. He opened the door and we walked into what was probably called a sitting room in days gone by. Like the living room or great room we had just left, it had a sofa and some chairs. There were three doors off of this room. Doug indicated the farthest door straight ahead and said somewhat wistfully, "This door leads to the master suite, quite impressive actually. I haven't changed it much since my parents passed on. I guess one of these days I will. I don't use it. The one on this side is my room. The one over here is the guest room. I have updated both of these rooms. Some time back, my parents renovated and both have private baths."

He opened the door to the guest room and I noted it was tastefully decorated in blues and golds. "The bathroom should have everything you need," he added. As he looked at me, he started to laugh. "Really, Darla, you look scared to death! I don't bite!" he added as he chuckled, and I blushed, probably to my toes.

"I know Doug. This is just a little weird. I'm sorry," I stammered and then I started laughing. Doug put his arms around me and rubbed my back. It felt good. Then he tilted up my chin and kissed me long and hard. I was starting to warm up when Doug pulled back and raised his arms. "Sorry, I promised to behave," he said with a laugh. "Now, Darla, do you need anything?" he asked with a smirk.

"Well, I, uh, no, uh, I think I'll be okay, Doug," was all I managed to stammer out. He kissed me again, just a brush this time, and then walked over to the door to his room.

"G'nite Darla, see ya in the morning," was the last he said before opening and closing the door. I walked into the guest room and closed the door. I checked out the bathroom and lo and behold, there was even a robe hanging on the door. I almost felt a twinge of jealousy, but then realized it was a unisex robe. It was probably bought for whomever happened to be the guest and no one in particular. I undressed and climbed into the bed still reeling from the kiss and the realization that I was sleeping at Doug's but not with Doug. I was still pondering this as I fell asleep. When had I become such a shrinking violet?

When I got up in the morning, I showered, changed, and found my way to the kitchen. Doug was sitting at the table reading his paper and drinking coffee.

"Good morning, Doug. Got enough coffee for two?" I asked.

"Help yourself, Darla. Did you sleep well?" he countered.

"Yes, I did. And you?" We chatted a little more and then I finally made an awkward exit. I really had to get home. All the way home, I kept replaying the night, always with different endings. Before I knew it I was home and contemplating Thanksgiving.

Chapter 11

Heather and I decided to have Thanksgiving Day dinner at her apartment in Austin. She wanted to cook her first holiday dinner and invite Micah over to show it off. I was pleased she wanted me there. At least I thought she did. It was hard to tell by the phone conversation we'd had about it.

"Mom? Can we do T-day at my house this year?" Heather's tone had been tentative, afraid, I guess, that I'd say she ought to come to Isquith instead. It would be so much easier if she did. I could prepare a lot of the meal on Wednesday night. Then she and I could finish up on Thursday morning and have a relaxing visit. I felt far away from her lately.

But I hadn't wanted to squelch her efforts at being grown up. We'd come pretty far with each other in the past year and I was conscious of giving her some measure of control over her life.

"Sure, honey," I replied. "What do you want me to fix for the meal?"

"Gosh, I don't know." It was evident she hadn't thought I'd agree so quickly. I was sure she had oodles of plans for my "No" response, but apparently she hadn't prepared for my "Yes" reply.

"Well, when do you want me to come over?" I asked her.

"Thursday morning, early, Mom. How early can you be here?"

We negotiated a little and we agreed I would come over on Wednesday night. Then we could get up early and start the turkey together. She made me promise to come late on Wednesday, however. She clearly wanted to spend the evening with Micah, not Mom. I tried not to let it hurt my feelings.

"Isn't Micah going home for the holiday?" I had asked.

"No. His parents are coming for the game on Friday. So he's staying here instead of driving back and forth to Dallas," she answered.

'The game' was the annual football rivalry between The University of Texas and Texas A&M University. It had been held on Thanksgiving weekend as long as anyone could remember. As Turkey Day approached, 'the game' could only refer to that particular event. Some years it was on Thanksgiving itself, some years on the Saturday after the holiday. Most years it occurred on Friday, as it did this year. The location alternated between Austin, home of the UT Longhorns, and College Station, home of the A&M Aggies. This year it was Austin's turn.

So here I was on my way to Austin late Wednesday night, the back seat and trunk filled with things for delivery to Heather or things I thought we might need for cooking the requisite feast. My roaster pan and a multitude of disposable food storage bags and bowls were stashed in the trunk with my overnight bag. The back seat held two bags of groceries, a stack of books Heather had asked me to bring (a good sign regarding her academic discipline, I thought), two boxes of Heather's winter clothes, some homemade cookies (okay, not made at my home, but homemade by a local Isquith bakery at least), and my CD equipment for calling a dance. I didn't know of any reason I'd need the CD equipment, but a caller seldom goes anywhere unprepared to take the stage.

I'd stashed an emergency bag of items in the trunk that I didn't plan to take in right away. Things like spices, recipes, pie pans. I was walking that fine line again, making sure I didn't overstep my boundaries with my own daughter. If she'd gone out and bought sage and poultry seasoning, I didn't want her to think I didn't trust her to get them. On the other hand, I wanted to have it on hand in case she'd forgotten to get it so we wouldn't get caught with a dish full of raw dressing while we ran to the store. Momhood – ever the juggling act.

I avoided I-35 like the plague and drove the city roads toward her apartment, pulling into the parking lot at almost 10 o'clock. Her freshman year she'd lived in a dorm near campus, my preference, not hers. Over the summer she'd convinced me to let her move into an apartment with a girl she met somewhere.

I met the roommate, Stacy, when I helped Heather move in to the apartment in July. She seemed nice, and we'd visited about her parents and where she was from. To Heather's absolute mortification, I'd verified names and addresses online when I got home, then called and introduced myself to her parents. I didn't volunteer what I'd done to Heather, but Stacy's parents told their daughter they'd talked to me. Stacy relayed it to Heather. Heather was convinced it looked like I was checking up on them and was embarrassed, but I was unapologetic. A mom's gotta do what a mom's gotta do. And now Stacy or more accurately, Stacy's boyfriend was creating conflict in the domicile.

I left everything but my purse in the car and made my way down the winding sidewalk to Heather's first-floor apartment. Feeling like an intruder in my own daughter's life I was unsure whether to knock, call her on her cell phone, or try the door. I chose the latter, mostly to make sure she was keeping it locked. She was. I knocked three times and held back the "Hi, honey, it's Mom!" that was on the tip of my tongue. Just when I was thinking maybe I ought to opt for phoning, Heather pulled the door open and threw her arms around me. I caught a glimpse of her wide eyes and splotches of flour on her red t-shirt before she gave me a bearhug.

"Mom! Thank goodness you're here! After Micah left, I decided to bake a pie and it's a disaster! You've gotta help me!"

"That's why I'm here, honey," I said, squeezing her in response to her hug and feeling warmed by her pleasure at seeing me. My mother's heart was just a little happy to hear Micah had already left for the night and I hadn't interrupted a moment I might not be ready for. Not that they couldn't have already had lots of moments, I just wasn't ready to see them.

"Do I need to come save you right away, or do we have time to get stuff out of the car first?" I laughed.

"Sure, no problem, I'll come with you. I just took the crust out of the oven, so it won't burn, at least not any more than it already has. I think I made cement instead of pie crust," she said, pulling away and closing the door behind her. When I heard the click, I prayed silently that it hadn't automatically locked behind her.

We ended up making three trips to the car and back, finally emptying all the contents into Heather's bedroom and kitchen. The apartment was small, and Heather's bedroom was crowded with the new clothes and books when we finished.

"Stacy went home for the holiday. She's not into football, so she won't be here for the game. She might have stayed, but she and her boyfriend broke up last week," Heather told me as we deposited the last stash. "She said you can sleep in her room if you want."

"I'd rather stay with you if it's okay," I said. "We get so little time together, I hate to miss any opportunity for girl talk."

"Sure, no problem," she said. "I hadn't changed Stacy's sheets yet. I figured you'd probably say that."

I was surprised she'd even thought of changing the sheets. Maybe I wasn't giving her enough credit for growing up. Then I remembered our conversation about Stacy's boyfriend and realized he'd probably been sharing the sheets, making Heather very conscious of needing to change them.

We spent a few hours on pie-making and planning, then hit the sack. By the time we went to bed, we had three passable pies – two pumpkin and one apple. We were both tired enough that we didn't get much girl talk in. The tired part was a good thing, since I'm prone to claustrophobia and the crowded room would normally make me want to stay awake and clear out the clutter to open up some space. Instead, I reminded myself it was Heather's house and talked myself into a sound sleep – which didn't take much talking.

The next morning we rose early to start cooking. I like to eat dinner close to noon, so we put the bird in the oven about 8 a.m. It wasn't too big, just for three of us, but big enough that we'd have plenty of leftovers. Leftovers are the best part of Thanksgiving as far as I'm concerned. Well of the food part of Thanksgiving, that is.

"What time is Micah coming?" I asked. Heather was still in her nightgown and didn't seem in a hurry to change clothes.

"I don't know. He said he'd call this morning and see how things were going. I couldn't tell if he's nervous about meeting you or if he's not sure I can cook. Maybe both," she laughed.

"Well, tell him to come over between 12 and 1," I suggested. "That'll give us time to get everything almost ready and you can look in complete control of the kitchen. Plus, it won't give us much time to fill talking before we sit down to eat. He won't be nervous once he starts chowing down."

"Cool, mom. Thanks. I'll go call him," she said.

She returned to the kitchen dressed in capri pants and a layered tank top that didn't quite reach the waistband of her pants. Of course, she was cute as a poppy, but I immediately opened my mouth to tell her she needed to put on something a little less revealing if Micah was coming over. I shut my mouth before the words leaked out, realizing she was dressed more conservatively than the majority of teens I'd seen lately. Besides, she was beaming.

"Micah says he'll be over about 1:00," she said. "So now you can show me how to get control of the kitchen, or at least make it look like I have control. While we do, catch me up on your life. Anything exciting going on lately? What's happening with you and that Doug guy?"

I suspect I blushed at the last question, but proceeded to catch her up nonetheless, censoring it for any potential mom romance that I was sure neither she or I was ready to talk about. "Well, I don't know how exciting it is, but remember me telling you about the dancer who was attacked in Clearton last September? I've gotten to know him. Do you remember my talking about Carlotta? Well, she and he are now going out. There's something weird going on, and a group of us are planning to collect information that might help figure out what's going on," I told her.

Heather rolled her eyes. "Mom, can't you ever leave well enough alone without investigating everything you come across?" she asked. "…like with Stacy's parents?"

"I hadn't thought of it that way," I laughed. "But I guess, now that you asked, the answer is no, I can't! I guess I have a curious mind. Now let me show you how to carve a turkey."

We spent the morning laughing, talking, and cooking. I learned a lot about her classes and a little about Micah. I'm not sure how much she learned about making Thanksgiving dinner, but she ended up feeling like the cook, which was what I'd hoped.

At a break in the conversation, I brought up her roommate situation, very much on my mind. "Heth, how's it going with Stacy and her boyfriend? I know you said they broke up, but before that and in the future. What have you worked out?"

"Mom, can you get the milk out of the fridge for me? I need some for the potatoes," she said. I knew a stall technique when I heard one, but I let it go. She'd answer when she was ready. I took the jog of milk from the fridge and placed it beside her.

"You need a measuring cup?" I asked

"I don't think so. Just tell me when you think the potatoes look right." She poured a little milk on the boiled spuds and then dropped in almost an entire stick of margarine. They were going to be really buttery potatoes, but I didn't say anything about it. I waited her out, and finally she answered my question.

"I talked to Stacy. She said Jeff had three roommates. That's his name, Jeff. So she couldn't stay at his place. They really want to be together, so he stays over here a lot. She says it's her place too, so she should be able to have company over whenever she wants. But now they broke up so …" Heather's voice held both defeat and defiance.

"Well, Heth, it's true that she can have company over, but maybe the two of you can sit down and define what company means. When does company become another roommate? Or maybe you could set ground rules for everyone, like a duty roster or privacy requirements," I suggested.

We talked some more about it. I tried to walk the line between giving her helpful advice and staying out of it as I'd agreed. When we finally changed the subject, nothing had been resolved. We had everything ready for about 1 o'clock as planned, but no Micah. While we waited, I suggested to Heather that she call her grandparents, Clint's parents, and wish them a Happy Thanksgiving. They had never been real close to us while Clint was alive. After Clint died, I moved to Texas to be near them. Heather and I were just starting to develop a relationship with them when they retired to Florida. I no longer felt like the rift between them and Clint had been all his fault. I had given him a hard time about it the whole time we were married, another reason for me to feel guilty about unresolved issues.

Heather called them as I suggested, and I heard snatches of the conversation even though I really wasn't trying to. They clearly pressured her to go out to Florida for Christmas break, and she did her best to weasel out of it. She ended the conversation on a weak note, but flipped her phone shut harder than she needed to.

"Oh, mom, I just hate calling them! I love them and all, but it's almost like they expect me to be dad, or make up for dad, and that's not gonna happen," was Heather's initial comment as she hung up the phone. "And now, I suppose, you want me to call Aunt Nita, right?"

I nodded affirmatively, and chuckled. Nita was Clint's sister and actually Heather was a lot like her. Nita lived in Seattle for the past 10 years, and weddings and funerals were about our only contact. In between were the requisite holiday phone calls.

"Hey, mom, Aunt Nita wants to know if you have found a substitute Mr. Right. What shall I tell her?" asked Heather, laughing and then handing me the phone. I wished Nita a happy thanksgiving, listened to her telling me to get on with my life or join a convent, and then hung up.

"So, mom, tell me about this Doug guy? Is this serious?" Heather asked. About then I really wished Micah would hurry up and arrive.

"No Heather, it's not serious, at least not yet. We've gone to a few concerts and such. We dance sometimes at the dances. Not quite what I would call serious," I responded. I really hoped to avoid any further discussion of my nonexistent romantic life. We continued to chat and check the food while we waited on Micah.

Micah finally made it over about 2 o'clock. Heather hadn't told me much about him, other than how wonderful he was, which I wasn't sure I'd agree with. I didn't know what to expect when he came in. We were in the kitchen trying to clean up whatever we could before the meal, so we wouldn't have so much to do afterward when he walked in. He hadn't knocked, so I knew he must feel at home in Heather's apartment.

I'd steeled myself for everything from a jerseyed jock to a pierced punk, but I was still surprised by Micah's appearance. He wasn't really short and was probably taller than he looked. His thin, wiry frame made him look small. He had black hair cut short around the sides and back, but it tumbled in curls over his forehead. He had a patchy beard that matched his hair and gave him an overall unkempt appearance. He did have a nice smile and judging from his teeth, his parents had spent some money on orthodonture. And he had very blue eyes.

"Hi Heather, hi, Mrs. King. Nice to meet ya. Sorry I was late, I was working on something and lost track," he offered with a shrug.

"Hi Micah, nice to meet you too. How about we sit down and eat?" was the best I could do for a response.

With Micah's late arrival, the turkey was a little overdone, but neither he nor Heather seemed to mind. I quelled my inner clock and made an effort to stop trying to control the day. It was a holiday, after all. I also tried not to interrogate Micah like the lawyer that I am, or the mom that I am, either, for that matter. Micah made all the appropriate positive noises as he ate and Heather looked very pleased with herself. She absolutely beamed when he complimented her on the apple pie!

As we finished eating, I asked, "So Micah, what were you working on earlier?" I hoped this was sufficiently oblique and general that Heather wouldn't call it 'investigating.'

"Mrs. King, I was working on a project for my engineering class. Need to write a computer program to solve a problem. I kept working and getting error messages, and was trying to figure out what the problem was. The project is due next week, and it just isn't coming off as I wanted," he answered shaking his head. Okay, so he was determined and motivated and didn't give up easily. These were good traits.

"Yeah, mom, Micah is a very good student and the stuff he does is way beyond me," Heather chimed in. "And, you'll be happy to know that he is very serious about studies and keeps bugging me to stay on track."

Micah cleared his throat. "Don't go making me out to be a saint, Heather! But yes, school is important. And so is having some fun – like the football game tomorrow! Will you be here for that Mrs. King?"

"I will probably take off before the game. I assume it's on TV. What time is the game?" I asked.

"It's at 2 o'clock and yes it is on TV. I plan on watching it as well. The tickets were just too expensive! Micah's parents got tickets so they are coming in tomorrow," explained Heather. "Besides, I'm not much of a football fan. Micah tries to explain it, but ..." she added with a sigh and a shrug of her shoulders.

Micah smiled and shook his head. Obviously, this was not news to him. We continued to have some stilted conversation. Then I suggested they go in the other room and watch TV and I would clean up. I didn't get much of an argument, and as I cleaned up after our meal it occurred to me that Heather and I had just moved to a new phase in our relationship. I still remembered the first time I met Clint's parents. Even 25 years later, I wasn't really comfortable conversing with them. In fact, I still felt like every comment his mother made was a direct criticism.

As I cleaned up, my phone rang. My sister Julia was calling to wish us a happy Thanksgiving and catch up on the past six months. She was a sales representative for one of the major communication conglomerates and was constantly traveling. Whenever we talked she had found a new Mr. Right, and this time was no exception. I listened to her glowing description of her new-found love, and squeezed in a word or two about my life. After we talked for a while I wished her a happy Thanksgiving and then yelled to Heather to come take the phone. I was afraid to walk in unannounced on her and Micah. Heather laughed and joked with Julia for a few minutes. She gestured to me to silently ask if I wanted the phone back. When I shook my head, she said goodbye for both of us.

We both went into the living room, and joined Micah. Not much later, he took his leave to go work on his programs some more. Heather and I spent a quiet afternoon and evening and then I headed back to Isquith. I was grateful for the mother-daughter time together, and relieved that maybe we were getting past our emotional distance. On the other hand, I hadn't asked any questions I didn't want to know the answer to. I would find out soon enough if Micah was a serious contender.

Chapter 12

Back home Friday afternoon, I was pursuing my own projects while Texas A&M beat UT. They had a long history and UT had won the more recent years, so I guessed it was A&M's turn. Other college games continued and provided some background noise as I worked. Computers are amazing things, and I'm not sure I could be a caller without one. I rely on mine for internet access about everything from the clubs where I call to ideas for new calling arrangements. Using my CD player for music at dances lets me avoid carrying all the cumbersome equipment used by callers in the past. My GPS gets me where I need to go with only a few bumps here and there. But when it comes down to it, you can't get by without plenty of time-honored rehearsal time.

Before a big gig like the Winter Solstice, I always set aside a significant amount of time to practice calling, usually in my living room. Anyone watching would get a kick of seeing me direct invisible dancers through the movements and respond to the laughter of a non-existent crowd. So here I was, the week before the Solstice and another trek to Austin, with my sound equipment set up in my living room and a smile etched on my face. I didn't feel the need to dress the part, so my sweats added an offbeat, if comfortable, aspect to the scene. I mentally created a crowd of colorful dancers and smiled to each one across the dance floor. My active imagination helped.

"Good evening, ladies and gentlemen. Welcome to Austin and to the Winter Solstice. I know we're gonna have a great weekend, so let's get started. First, though, I'd like to thank…." Uh oh. Who was I thanking this time? Good thing I rehearsed. It made me realize that I didn't know exactly who had organized the Solstice. I reached over and grabbed my notepad and jotted down a reminder to myself to check what committee or club I needed to thank in my opening comments. I started over.

"Good evening, ladies and gentlemen. Welcome to Austin and to the Winter Solstice. I know we're gonna have a great weekend, so let's get started. First, though, I'd like to thank the XYZ club for doing such a great job pulling this event together." I waited for the imaginary applause to die down, then started up my CD. "And here we go! Bow to your partner, bow to your corner. Left Allemande and Grand Right and Left…."

I carried the patter call all the way through to the end of the music. Even though I'd been calling for several years, I still had to think about making my transitions smoothly. I held the microphone near my mouth while I talked, at the same time making sure I didn't turn my back to the dancers as I started the singing call for the second half of the tip. I'd found a call for a little known Reba McIntyre song that I really liked. I planned to try it out for the first time at the Solstice.

The music led me into the song, and I mixed the calls with the lyrics. It was a good thing I had this chance to practice. I had to start over a few times to make the words fit with the calls, but finally made it through the entire piece. I liked it, that was certain, but it would be a while before I could do it with anything less than full concentration. And then the usual, "Great dancing, folks. Thank your partner, thank your square."

The rest of the practice took me all morning, but when I finished I felt that I'd prepared as much as I could for the weekend. Unless something unexpected came up, I was ready. I had some tried and true, and some brand new. And this was after all supposed to be recreation, well, for the dancers anyway. Now to my other project.

I took the list Nick had given me and created a database with that information just like the burglary database and the major dance database. This time I merged the Nick dance database with the burglary database, lining them up side by side. If I thought that merging the major dances with the burglaries produced surprising results, well, this was beyond coincidence for sure. Every single dance on Nick's list was associated with an unsolved burglary in the same location, even when the dance he attended wasn't a big dance! Now, he tended to go to dances in cities, and there were often burglaries in cities, but…

I found myself wondering if Nick wasn't somehow connected to these burglaries. Maybe his assaults were because of some parting of the ways among the thieves. Or maybe Nick had tried to get out of the business and they weren't thrilled with that. As much as I was beginning to like Nick, who would be better positioned to cue some guys how to dress, maybe even what club dress to don, and at the same time to be able to identify potential targets with all the information an insurance company might have with regard to security measures?

All these thoughts came flowing full tilt, and I was pacing and not sure what to do or who to share my fears with. There really would be no way to figure it out unless the thieves were caught and ratted him out. I also reminded myself that he could be innocent.

I continued to remind myself of that all week before the Solstice. It was actually an easy week, with calling only in Clearton. Neither Carlotta nor Nick was there so I was spared trying to be civil while thinking that Nick could be criminally involved in all this, potentially the leader, rather than an innocent bystander or victim. Doug and I chatted briefly, back to our comfortable level of discourse, and Sam just kept talking about the Solstice. The week flew by fairly quickly and then I was heading to Austin Friday afternoon with hopes that Heather, with or without Micah, might stop by the dance.

With a pad of paper to write down shirt patterns mixed in with all my usual gear, I walked into the convention center right behind Carlotta and Nick on Friday evening. Watching them walk together, arms entwined, I found myself hoping that Doug and I could find some time to be alone and get reacquainted this weekend. Maybe if there was no excitement, and just good fun! I also hoped that Carlotta didn't get terribly hurt in this whole mess. Nick seemed genuine enough. There had to be some reasonable explanation. I waved them off as I reached the area set aside for callers so I could find out where I needed to be and when. Horizon Ballroom after the Grand March, invocation, and presentation of colors in the Main Ballroom. It looked like I would be calling with Tom Greenville tonight, mostly Mainstream, with announced Plus. Tom was always a lot of fun, and we could even duet some calls instead of just taking turns. I went to Horizon to get the sound system set up, and then to mingle with folks until time to go to work.

"Hey Darla," called Tom as I walked into the Horizon. "I already got stuff set up, and once I realized it was the two of us down here, I pulled a couple CDs that we've done together so we can mix it up a little. What d'you think?"

"Sounds good to me, Tom! I was thinking that when I saw your name. Great minds must think alike! Need any help getting set up? You want to start out with a tip with us both and then break it up or the other way around?"

"Let's start together, and then we can take turns. Stacey is here and hopes to do more than just sit and watch me work. If we take turns, Stacey and I might even get to dance once and a while. This lone wolf coming this way your partner tonight, Darla?" Tom asked as he tilted his head to indicate I needed to look at someone coming up behind me. Tom walked over toward the wall to finish hooking up the sound system.

"Well, well, hello…Paul. You know, for the number of square dances you seem to be attending lately you might want to take a few lessons," I said facetiously, and felt my stomach do little flip-flops as I remembered, too late, what he'd said in response to my last gambit about dancing.

"Hello, yourself, Ms. King. Has it occurred to you that maybe I keep coming to the square dances because of you?" he answered, surprising me by being flippant in return. He took a step closer and I thought for a moment he might actually be flirting with me. He added quietly, "I did some checking and I know your background. Don't be getting involved in this investigation, you hear?" With that, I quickly dismissed any thoughts that he might be trying to flirt with me.

"Investigation? I thought this was a solved case? A car-jacking gone south. Is there something to investigate?" I asked innocently. His facial expression didn't change but I thought I could see a spark in his eyes. I couldn't tell if it was my imagination, if he was angry at my retort, if he was trying to flirt, or if he was making fun of me. I had no doubt that he had checked all of our backgrounds early on.

With a curt, "Stay clear, Darla, I mean it," he turned and walked away. Well, he was a single male, so I added him to my "suspect" list! And he certainly was right up there on the strange scale. But what a hunk! And those blue eyes…

"Darla, who was that dude?" Tom asked out of curiosity.

"He's some government type. He was part of the accident investigation I told you about a while back at Doug's place. For some reason, he just keeps popping up even though they say the case is closed." I responded, keeping my voice level. I didn't say anything else. As much as I liked Tom and trusted him, I figured the fewer people who knew our plan for the weekend the better.

"Well, I gotta tell ya, Darla, that is one fine looking man,. Does Doug know he's hanging around making eyes at you?" Stacey chimed in with a laugh.

"No worry on that score, But I am going to go see if I can find Doug before the Grand March, and see who else is here already. You and Stacey behave down here in Horizon now!" I teased back.

As I walked out of the room, I remembered to check my cell phone to make sure it was off. I seldom kept it with me while I was calling, but tonight I had slipped it in my skirt pocket when I got out of the car. I didn't want to take the time to run it out to the car.

We'd all driven in from different directions to arrive in Austin today. Like most times, we'd called back and forth while we were on the road to find out where everyone was, and just to pass the time. When I'd arrived in Austin I found myself stuck in the university area and unable to locate the hotel, so I'd called Doug's cell number and he'd talked me right into the parking lot. I didn't like leaving the phone in my hotel room. It was too easy a target to steal. So I just turned off the power and left it in my pocket. I'd treated myself to one of these miniature flip-phones and hardly noticed its light weight in the folds of my gathered skirt.

Without too much difficulty I found Doug and Sam, and then some of the folks from the Footstompers, including Flo and Jonnie. Hal and Lenore were probably part of the opening ceremonies or helping get things set up. I also saw Gary and some other dancers in Stepping Squares colors. So far, I didn't see any guys off by themselves in nondescript colors. I made sure Doug knew which room I would be calling in and that I was available if he needed a partner whenever Tom was calling. That was more of a hint than anything else. Solo males never have to look far for a partner! I was hoping that it might lead to something more, at the very least a little time together. Doug was stable, caring, protective, and intelligent. Not to mention that Heather was right, it was time to move on with my life.

The first tip went very well with both of us calling. The next tip, Tom called and I walked around the hall checking out everything. It was a good crowd and a large hall, which meant I walked around the hall and made sure the sound system was working in all corners. At the same time, I tried to identify as many of the clubs present by their dress, and jotted down some of the ones I didn't recognize as well.

The next tip was mine, a Mainstream, and it also went well. We were starting out with a patter call and then a singing call. Tom had already indicated that if the dancers seemed not to need the patter call for a quick review, we might shift to all singing calls. He even had hinted that he might try calling a progressive tip. Normally, all the moves called are done within a square and each dancer ends up in their home position at various points in the dance process. Ultimately, a progressive works the same way. The intent is still that dancers end up in their original position in their original square, but with specific calls couples move from or progress from one square to the next, going through multiple squares as the tip progresses.

Through the caller's skills and tracking of the dancers, everyone ends up in their original square. It is all based on mathematical patterning and combinations, and not something I am ready to attempt, but very impressive when done well.

The third tip was a Plus one, and Tom was calling so I looked around to see if I could spot Doug, but didn't see him. Since it appeared I wasn't going to be dancing, I took time to try and read the pins of the folks whose club dress I didn't recognize, and updated my notes. So far I had identified clubs from Arkansas, Oklahoma, New Mexico, Louisiana, and Michigan, in addition to clubs from all over Texas. As I made my way toward the sound stage and Tom, Flo called my name in a very loud whisper.

"Darla, shhhh! Darla!!! I have to tell you something!" she said in a low tone but that wouldn't quite pass for a whisper but communicated that whatever it was she was she was saying, she was trying to be discreet. Now, for Flo, discretion is not always easy.

"Hi Flo! What's so important?" I asked.

"Now Darla, remember you asked Jonnie and me if we'd ever seen some guys hanging around like they were square dancers, but they weren't dancing?" she asked with all pretense of whispering lost. She grabbed my upper arm tightly. "Well," she continued, "Jonnie and me were coming over here and we passed these three guys standing in the lobby, and looking around. I figured they were just lost or something, and walked over to them, friendly like, and asked if they were going to the dance. They just said no, and started to walk away, but I wanted to be friendly, and well, one of them was kinda cute, so I just gave him a Yellow Rock. Darla, he shoved me away!"

In square dance parlance, a 'Yellow Rock' is a hug. Technically, a hug with your corner dancer but the term is frequently used generically. Callers will sometimes call "Bow to your partner, and Yellow Rock your corner." As I listened to her story, I was torn between wanting to laugh that she was so concerned about missing out on a hug and worry about her.

"Flo, are you alright?" I asked, opting to express my concern.

"I'm just fine, but can you believe that? No square dancer – hmmph – no gentleman would shove a lady like he did," she answered with a huff. Given her age, I thoroughly agreed with her, though outside of square dancing, someone you don't know coming up and hugging you like you were family or friends might be a little much.

Tom came up just then, and signaled me that it was time to call. "Flo, I gotta get to work here. You be careful, and stay away from those guys if you see them again, you hear?" I said as I turned and got ready to call the next tip. "I'll talk to you later, Flo," was my parting comment, followed by pushing appropriate buttons, turning on the microphone, and announcing, "Let's square 'em up! We're here to dance, right?" And the tip was off.

I didn't see Flo again and there wasn't anything exciting going on as far as I could tell. I wished she had come back into Horizon so I could ask more questions, but I didn't want to encourage her either. I also didn't see Doug, and I wondered where he was. Toward the end of the night, instead of a Plus tip, Tom did call progressive squares and the dancers seemed to enjoy that. Some of the dancers got confused, but most of them ended up where they were supposed to.

"Ok, folks it's the last tip of the night! Square 'em up! We want to thank you again for your donations and efforts to ensure a happy holiday season for children and families throughout Texas. Darla and I have had a great time here in the Horizon with all of you tonight and we hope to see you here at the Winter Solstice again tomorrow. Don't forget your canned food donation! Now bow to your partner, thank your corner, and let's Circle Left."

Tom and I ended as we started, sharing the calling for the last tip. Then we packed up and headed for the main entrance along with Stacey. Nick, Carlotta, and Doug were hanging out in various corners. Doug spotted me first and came forward to give me a hug and take my gear.

"Darla, it's good to see you! Sorry I didn't make it to the Horizon. I spent most of my time in the Main Ballroom with Plus only. I'll have to come listen to my favorite caller tomorrow though!" Doug said with a smile.

I returned the hug, and just laughed as Nick and Carlotta approached. Carlotta looked like she was just about to bubble over. Once again, I had to wonder at her amazing energy level. A few minutes later, Gary joined us, and then Sam. Gary was playing the bachelor this weekend. His wife was visiting some of her relatives. With the gang all accounted for, we made our way to the parking lot and then to the hotel down the street in separate cars. I followed Doug and Sam in Doug's car. Carlotta and Nick followed in Carlotta's car with Gary behind them. Nick and Carlotta had decided that in case his Rodeo was the target for some reason, there might be less excitement if they just drove her little Honda. The plan was to meet in Sam and Doug's room to share all the information we had collected. Doug was waiting by the door, alone, when I walked into the hotel.

"How about a quick stop at the hotel bar? Maybe check out the entertainment if they have any?" Doug asked casually.

"Sure, can't hurt." It didn't quite seem in keeping with the plan, but I figured I could go along and I did want to spend some time with Doug alone. It was flattering to think that that was his plan too.

We walked past the elevators and up the half stairway to the bar area. Doug had my arm and steered me toward a table in a corner rather than the bar area itself. We sat down in dim light amidst the backdrop of a piano player's rendition of a popular love song. Almost romantic, but the bar area was the only place to smoke and smoky ambiance isn't quite up there with romance in my book. I pulled my chair up close to Doug and angled my shoulder into his armpit until he put his arm around me.

"It's great to see you, Darla." Why didn't his tone sound more intimate? "But that's not really the reason I wanted to come in here." He had the grace to look a little sheepish. "This is the only place to smoke, so I figured we might see those would be square dancers in here. Unless of course, they are at a different hotel. But this is the major hotel for this dance, so it would be the most likely choice for square dancers, or someone pretending to be one."

Despite my disappointment for his ulterior motive, Doug's point was well taken. I took advantage of the opportunity to tell him about Flo's encounter and that helped ease the awkwardness I was feeling. From where we were sitting, we could see the bar area and the front lobby. There were certainly a fair number of people milling around in square dance attire now that the dance had ended. There were probably a number of "after" parties here at the hotel as well. Although there is no alcohol at a square dance and drinking before a square dance is frowned on, there are no rules for after the dance and hence, some folks have "after" parties.

"Ten o'clock. Three guys, no ladies. What do you think? Are those the same ones you saw before?" Doug directed my attention to my left and toward the bar.

"Doug, I never really paid attention to them enough to recognize them again. But I certainly will now! I suppose if you, Sam, and one of the other Clearton guys came to the bar your shirts would all match, but do you recognize the pattern on the yoke as belonging to a club?" All three had pastel colored stripes on the yoke of beige shirts, all soft colors merging with each other like a pale rainbow. They wore dress khaki pants, pressed to a sharp crease. This was not a typical pattern or a typical outfit.

All three men were of husky "cowboy" build, about 6 foot, wearing boots. One of them had blonde hair, the other two were salt-and-pepper but heavy on the pepper. All three were generally clean-cut, no long hair or beards here. I'm pretty bad at guessing ages, but judging from their hair, physical build, and lack of facial wrinkles, I guessed them to be in their early to mid-thirties.

"No, Darla, I don't recognize it. Odd for the pattern colors to be pastel and not bright. Do you still like white wine when you indulge? I think I need to go up to the bar." I nodded with a smile, and Doug walked over to the bar. He reached the bar itself just about where the three guys were smoking. Doug signaled the bartender, the bartender and he exchanged words, and the bartender went about making the drinks Doug had ordered. There wasn't much of a crowd this early in the evening, so I could barely make out their conversation above the music.

"So, what did you guys think of the dance tonight? Great crowd, huh?" Doug tapped the nearest guy as he made the comment, ensuring that the man knew Doug was talking to him.

The first man made a noncommittal response as he turned his body to put his back to Doug. All three shifted slightly so there was greater distance between them and Doug.

"Did you come far? Me, I'm from close by, so it was an easy ride," Doug added, trying to keep the conversation going, but with no luck.

"Here you go, sir," the bartender interrupted, handing Doug the two drinks. Not having any excuse to stay at the bar any longer, Doug returned to the table and recounted the conversations to me. I pointed out quietly, and with intimate whispers for effect, that the three seemed to be watching us. We got a little chummy and close, laughed and intentionally avoided looking in their direction. Shortly after that, Doug and I left the bar. The three guys still lurked near the bar, not talking with anyone, and didn't look very approachable or much like square dancers other than their matching shirts.

The hotel was a high-rise luxurious one, and Carlotta and I had decided to share a room to save money. So had Doug and Sam, and Nick and Gary. I was regretting the decision as I walked toward the elevators with Doug. We hadn't discovered anything enlightening with our clothes-sleuthing at the dance, as far as I knew. An intimate evening with Doug sounded much better than a group debriefing session right now. Especially after the wine and snuggling we'd done, supposedly for effect, in the bar.

In Sam and Doug's room with the whole crowd of us, we spent the next hour more in laughing and joking around than in any productive outcome. We'd certainly gathered a lot of information about club outfits, which clubs wore what, and even how the clubs chose their designs. As I've said, square dancers are friendly people. Get them talking and no telling what you'll learn. But we hadn't turned up anything out of the ordinary. Doug and I relayed our run-in with the group at the bar. I filled them in on Flo's experience, but it didn't seem to shed any new light on anything. It just reinforced the fact that this particular group of men wasn't looking for any new friends, or actually attending the dance. Thinking about the guys in the bar, I recalled with a laugh, "Flo did say three guys I think, though I am not sure which one of those guys she thought was cute!"

As the full day took its toll on everyone, conversation slowed down. I had another full day coming up on Saturday and knew I ought to call it a night. But I wasn't quite ready yet. I was still thinking about romance.

"Well, I guess I'm just about ready to quit," I said. "Doug, you want to grab a quick drink in the bar before we call it a night?"

I was pleased Doug didn't have to think about it. He answered immediately, "On my way."

"Darla, would it be barging in if Nick and I come too?" asked Carlotta.

Of course it would.

"Not at all. Come on. Anyone else?" I responded politely. Oh, well, it wouldn't be the nightcap I'd had in mind after all. Good thing I enjoyed the company of everyone in the group.

"Not me, darlin," answered Sam. "This lone cowboy's going to pine away up here and snore away in no time!"

"Me either," said Gary. "I'm going to our room, Nick. Keep it quiet when you come in, night owl."

Nick laughed. "Kind of a surprise that I'd be the one of us staying out late, with a pretty lady no less."

Carlotta didn't even blush. Her smile broadened a little at the compliment, though. "We'll meet you down there, guys," she said. "Darla and I need to run to the room first."

"Okay, we'll see you downstairs in a few minutes. Don't be late," Doug said. He locked his eyes on mine. Unlike Carlotta, I did blush. Been too long since anyone flirted with me, I thought. I'm not handling it too well.

We went back to our room, hugging Gary and Sam good night on our way out. Nick and Doug would get their hugs later. I brushed my teeth and repaired my makeup. I bent double at the waist and brushed my hair thoroughly from the roots out then straightened up and pushed it into place, securing it with hairspray. I hadn't danced any tonight, so I hadn't gotten sweaty and didn't need to change clothes. I'd picked a full gathered skirt and vest set with a matching tee shirt for the dance that evening. It was extremely comfortable and had the advantage of doubling as street clothes.

It didn't take me long to do my few things, but Carlotta had completely transformed by the time I finished. She'd changed into jeans and a tee shirt, but where my tee was a conservative, solid-color long-sleeved one, hers was pulled tight across her chest and accented with glitter. It went with her red hair, springing out in random tufts as usual. She'd changed shoes and now wore party-girl high heels. She'd added glitter to her eye shadow, too, and I began to feel a little dowdy next to her.

"We better go before you get any more dressed up," I told her. "I'm feeling like a schoolmarm already."

"Oh, nonsense, Darla. You look great. I get so sweaty at these dances I lose all my makeup and my hair reverts to its native state. I have to add the glitter as a distraction!" She laughed. "Come on, let's go!"

"Okay, okay, I'm ready. Although I'm thinking it's a little crazy to be heading out for a drink at this time of night. I should be heading to bed instead," I said.

"Oh live a little, Darla! I know you're working this weekend and I'm not on the clock, but it'll do you good to be a little crazy. Besides, how long has it been since you've been on a double date?" Her eyes sparkled more than the glitter on her shirt.

"Why, Carlotta, whatever do you mean?" I asked with an expression of mock shock. "I'm certainly not on a date. I'm all work, didn't you know?"

"Not on a date, my foot!" she laughed. "I saw the look Doug gave you. Believe me, you're on a date. Accept it." Her voice got more serious as she continued, "But I don't know about me, Darla. I mean, yes, I'm on a date as much as you are. That much is clear. But I'm less clear about who I'm on a date with. I'm having fun with Nick, but I really haven't learned much about him. He's not very talkative. You hear so many scary stories today about getting involved with strangers." The twinkle in her eye came back as she continued, "And he certainly seems to be involved in something strange. He's either undercover, a criminal, or really really unlucky. None of those are selling point to me. How about you?"

I didn't want to let on how much snooping I'd done into Nick's past, so I hedged. "Well, one way to find out more is to keep asking him. I'll chip in and help the cause by interrogating him subtly while we visit. You know I've always got a million questions in my head," I said. "Now come one, we're really going to be late meeting up with the guys."

We caught an elevator with no wait and were down in the bar in less time than we'd expected. I glanced at my watch and was surprised to see it was just 11:30. I thought we'd stayed in Sam and Doug's room longer than that. I did a quick calculation and figured I could get a solid five hours sleep if I was in bed by 2:30, which meant I had another couple of hours to play.

As we walked into the bar, I saw that the three guys had been joined by a fourth. They were now involved in an intense discussion, heads close together. Carlotta looked over at me and I nodded an answer. Her eyes widened and she looked back at the group.

We had apparently beaten the guys to the bar, so we staked out a table and went ahead and ordered drinks for four. The crowd had picked up significantly since I'd been here earlier with Doug and I couldn't hear the conversation at the bar.

"Let's go talk to them," Carlotta said, eyes sparkling with mischief. Carlotta might be an advertising executive, but deep down she longed to be in theatre. I got the feeling we were about to go on stage!

"Are you crazy? What on earth would we say and why? I'm ready to wind down with a little quiet time, forget our 'assignment' for a while."

"Oh, come on, Darla. What could it hurt? The guys will be down in a few minutes and we'll call it quits then. But this is such an opportunity. Let's just go talk to them about their shirts, just like we did everyone else at the dance. That was the plan. Your plan, remember?"

She was right. That was what we had planned. The plan I had offered. Who was I to back out on her now? I sighed and Carlotta let out a whispered "Yippee!" She was up before I could change my mind. She knew me too well.

She had no reservations about interrupting their conversation.

"Hi. I don't think we met at the dance. I'm Carlotta." She stuck her hand out to the man nearest her. Automatically he shook it, but he stumbled over his words. "Uh, nice to meet you. Uh…" He didn't introduce himself and none of the others offered anything. I stepped into the silence.

"And I'm Darla," I offered my hand to the man who hadn't been at the bar earlier. "I'm one of the callers for the Winter Solstice dance. Where you men from?"

There seemed to be a hesitation, but I wasn't sure. It could just have been a redirection of their attention from their earlier discussion to us.

"Nice to meet you. Darla, you say? Caller, huh? How'd you get into that line of work?" the man asked.

I gave my standard explanation and our conversation struggled along for several minutes. Carlotta and I were doing all the work. I was wishing more every minute that Nick and Doug would arrive and we could give it up. Not Carlotta, apparently. She forged ahead.

"We've been taking a sort of survey tonight," she explained. "We're asking about club outfits and what the pattern means and what club it goes with. That sort of thing. I notice you're all wearing a club shirt. Which club are you with?" I swear Carlotta could look innocent as a schoolgirl, glitter and all.

One of the men seemed to be ahead of the others on alcohol consumed. He turned to look at Carlotta and wavered on his stool. "Uh…" he began, but couldn't get past the start. The other two men looked at the one I'd introduced myself to. I was beginning to think of him as the leader of the group. Sure enough, he was the one to respond.

"We're from a little town out in west Texas. I'm sure you've never heard of it. Waxmoor. The club's just called the Waxmoor Square Dancers. Nice to meet you ladies, but I'm afraid we were just leaving." He gave a nod and the other three started fumbling for their wallets.

"I got it," he said, and put a bill on the bar. It was a hundred. The bartender came over to pick it up and the man signaled to him to keep the bill. I had no idea what their tab was, but judging by the look on the barkeep's face, I'd say he got a hefty tip. The man was obviously in a hurry to leave. The whole conversation had taken less than five minutes.

The waitress brought over our drinks as soon as Carlotta and I sat down at the table. I figured she'd probably waited until we came back so she'd be sure to get her money. I paid for the round and told Carlotta she could get the next one.

We sat in silence and sipped our drinks, making a comment to each other every once in a while. After several minutes, the guys still hadn't shown. I realized the day was catching up to me and I'd never make it through a couple of hours.

"Carlotta, I know I'm the one that suggested we come down here, and I hate to be so fickle, but I'm fading fast. Why don't we just call the guys and wimp out? We'll try for tomorrow night," I suggested, trying not to whine too much.

"You're probably right, Darla. I run on high energy until I run myself out. I'm willing to stay, and I'd probably keep going till the wee hours, but then I wouldn't be worth a whit tomorrow. Keep me on track, girlfriend!"

"Thanks, Carlotta. Hate to squash your good times. I'll wait with you till the guys get here if you want to stay," I offered.

"No. I'll go with you. They've got a house phone at the end of the bar. I have no idea what's keeping them, but we'll just call and let the guys know we're flaking out on them, then we can head upstairs. Actually, now that I think about it, a tub and bed do sound pretty good about now," she mused. We made the call from the bar and Doug apparently was similarly feeling tired – in fact, had he had fallen asleep according to Sam. In the other room, Gary said Nick was showering. I guess he was planning on a very intense nightcap. Gary promised to give him the message.

It occurred to me that it was usually the guys who were complaining about how long we took to get ready, and here we had them beat. Well, their dawdling ended up meaning more sleep for all of us.

Chapter 13

Now that I'd admitted how tired I was, my body and brain gave up all pretense. I was exhausted, and my mind seemed to be working several paces behind normal. Carlotta and I walked into the elevator and I just stood, waiting for the elevator car to whisk me to my room and sleep. Carlotta gave me a quick look, then reached across me to press the button for the 8th floor. With a sheepish smile, I mumbled "oops, sorry."

Two security guards got on just before the doors slid shut and pressed the button for 7. I looked up to make eye contact with them. Confusion set in when I recognized the face of the solo square dancer I'd talked to earlier. The two had put on zipped-up khaki uniform jackets that matched their pants, along with khaki caps, and the combination conveyed the image of security guards if you didn't look too closely.

Something in their faces set off little alarm bells in my head despite my slow reaction time. I instinctively glanced at the readout above the elevator door and saw we had only reached the second floor. I angled my hand toward the control panel to press 3 and get us off the car as soon as possible. One of the men grabbed my arm and twisted it powerfully behind my back. My shoulder and elbow spasmed. I guessed a yelp escaped because he leaned into my ear and growled, "Not a word."

I could feel the tip of a knife press into the back of my ribcage and I had no doubt the man knew how to use it. I shut up. Carlotta, on the other hand, let go with a bloodcurdling scream that jolted me and I knocked the back of my head into my captor. The knife pricked my skin through my vest and shirt. Her scream lasted only a split second and then I saw a quick movement out of the corner of my eye and I saw her crumble to the floor. I instinctively started to turn toward her to see if she was okay, but the man tightened his grip on me and I got his message. The ride was agonizingly slow.

I purposely held my voice low, hoping to avoid punishment, but I had to ask. "What do you want with us?"

"No, little Miss Caller, the question is: What do you want with us? You and your amateur gang of detectives." The term was filled with derision. "At first we thought that Tricot fella wanted a piece of our action. We tried to warn him off, get him out of the picture. Then we realized he was with you, just an amateur out to get us. Not a wise idea, you know. We're professionals. No match for the likes of you."

The elevator dinged and the door slid open at 7. A third member of the gang stood lounging against the far wall across from the elevators.

"Well, about time you got here."

"Shut up, Harry, and help us get them downstairs."

My captor, who I had begun to call The Leader in my mind, pushed me forward into the hallway, looking down the hall to make sure no one else was around. The man he called Harry entered the elevator car and helped the other man lug Carlotta out next to us.

"Let me see if she's okay," I said.

"Get moving," was the only response I got. That and a nudge with the knifetip. I moved. Number Two lifted Carlotta and swung her over his shoulder like a sack of cement. Our little parade started toward the stairway door. Harry held the door open while Number Two and Carlotta went first, then The Leader pushed me into the stairwell. Harry came in last, checking that no one had noticed our activities and then pulling the door closed behind him. We made slow progress down the stairs. After about three flights, I was relieved to see Carlotta's fingers instinctively begin grabbing for the man carrying her. She was alive.

My relief was immediately replaced by the fear that she would start screaming again and provoke a bloody fight – our blood. I wondered whether I should caution her or if words would just earn me a sliced ribcage. She began struggling, but fortunately remained silent. Number Two stopped and stooped down far enough to slide her feet onto the carpeted floor. She slid down and stumbled, then righted herself and looked around. I shook my head as she opened her mouth. She shut it again without a sound. Number Two efficiently whirled her around and got her in a chokehold and we resumed our march.

When we reached the bottom floor, Harry circled around and went ahead to open the exit door. He peered out and then nodded to The Leader. I felt his grip tighten but we didn't move.

"You ladies realize the need for silence?" he asked.

I looked at Carlotta. She was being held in the same position as I was and I assumed she had a knife blade or gun in her back as well. Her eyes were large and she nodded. I said yes and we moved in pairs toward the door Harry held open.

An armored truck was parked in the loading zone just outside the door with the engine running and the fourth member of the gang at the wheel. The Leader hustled me around back and Number Two followed with Carlotta. The back end of the truck was open and a loading ramp led from the pavement to the interior. Harry ignored the ramp and jumped up into the truck's open space ahead of us. We walked, faster this time, up the ramp and into the truck. I finally felt the pressure release and I stood up straight to ease my complaining muscles.

Before I realized what was happening, my legs buckled out from under me and I sat hard on the truckbed floor. As if it was a timed rodeo event, Harry hog-tied my ankles and brought my hands together in front of me and tied them together. Something went around my head and pushed my mouth open as he tied a gag tightly into place.

Carlotta gasped and Number Two mashed his hand against her mouth. Then he pushed her away from him and she stumbled in her high heels. I was almost prone by this time and struggled to a sitting position. Another tie cord materialized from thin air and Harry tied her ankles and hands like mine. The gag, which I assumed was the same as mine, was a bandanna. I could only guess where it had been before my mouth.

Without a word, The Leader and Number Two worked as a team to bring up the ramp and secure it in its place on the side of the truck wall. One hopped down to the pavement while the other reached up to grab the overhead door and start it down. He ducked under and left us. I heard the door lock into place. Darkness descended as I heard Harry moving past me toward the cab. With a click a dim light came on. A utility light hanging from the ceiling of the truck fought against the night. It didn't give out a lot of light, but enough to see each other and a little of our surroundings. Its heavy orange extension cord snaked through the window into the cab, where I assumed it was plugged into the car's battery power. I don't like being in small or dark places. I really don't, and this was one of those places. I focused on breathing evenly so I wouldn't hyperventilate. Now was not the time to pass out.

"Don't worry about them, ladies. I'll be your flight attendant for this trip," smirked Harry. He pulled a small gun from under his khaki jacket and placed it in his waistband, then reached up to grab a strap loop that hung from the front of the truck. "If I was you, I'd lie down. You're liable to get thrown around pretty good in this big open area." He heard the gears grind into place and he tightened his hold on the strap.

The truck took off with a jolt. I rolled over to one side and saw Carlotta do the same. My skirt tangled around my legs but I had no way to get it straight. I wiggled to get it out from between my thighs, but Harry warned, "Settle down there, Miss Caller. I want you both nice and quiet." He patted the gun at his waist. "I'd hate to use this on two such pretty women, but I will if I need to." I didn't doubt it for a minute, remembering the article about the security guard they killed.

The route wasn't straight and we rolled around on the floor of the truck at each turn. But the ride was relatively smooth and I could tell we were on city streets. I searched my mind for a way out. I didn't expect one if the gang had an opportunity to carry out its plan. I had to come up with something before we reached our destination. I had to get out of the back of this truck. I knew what was probably waiting for Carlotta and me if we didn't, but the confined space was driving me crazy in the meantime, making it hard to think.

A turn in the road threw me against the wall of the truck and I noticed long rolls of canvas. I had no idea what they were for, but I immediately put my mind to the task of finding any way I could use them to help us. They appeared to be almost the full length of the truck, maybe 15 feet, rolled tightly and stacked along the wall. There didn't appear to be any sharp edges or loose pieces I could take advantage of. I looked around the rest of the truck. There was a small sliding window above Harry's head. It apparently opened into the cab of the truck, but it was closed now and probably locked. I remembered that the truck appeared to be an armored truck, so there was probably plenty of security between the cab and the storage area. On the other hand, if the guys weren't using it like an armored truck, they might have gotten sloppy. I couldn't see any way the window did me any good.

Another curve rolled me from one hip to another and I felt my cell phone dig into my hip through the fabric of my skirt. My phone! Surely I could use it to help. I looked at Harry, who was watching both of us with amusement on his face. He had nothing else to draw his attention, and I had no reason to expect any privacy when I could use the phone. I kept thinking. Who was the last person I called? Doug! On the way to the hotel! If I could get to the phone and press the redial button, it would call Doug's cell phone. It was a long shot. First, could I even get to the redial button without Harry's eagle eye seeing me and, second, would Doug have his cell phone on and be near it? Carlotta and I rolled across the truck floor on yet another turn and I struggled to come up with a better plan. None came.

Using the tips of my fingers, I worked the elastic of my skirt sideways around my waist. With the gag in place, I couldn't let Carlotta know what I was doing or ask her to distract Harry. I kept an eye on him, but hated to watch him directly. I was afraid I would attract his attention. Despite the fact that my full skirt was riding up, giving him a good view of my hips, he seemed to prefer looking at Carlotta. That was a break for me and I rolled as far away from her as I could while

I continued to work the folds of my skirt around. Finally I could feel the weight of the phone fall between my legs. I shot another look at Harry and took the opportunity of a sharp curve to throw myself face-first against the truck wall.

Bracing my legs against the floor so I wouldn't roll away before I completed my mission, I worked my hands partially into my skirt pocket. I felt the phone. I had turned it off when I started calling and, as far as I could remember, I had never turned it back on. I managed to get the clamshell case open and I felt for the pattern of keys at the bottom of the dial. Picturing the keypad in my mind, I pressed what I thought was the 'ON' button. A familiar beep heralded the onset of power. I didn't risk looking at Harry. I figured if he heard it I'd know soon enough. The phone settled down and I knew it was blinking its happy message to me, waiting for my command.

This time I did sneak a look at Harry. Something, maybe the beep, had drawn his attention away from either one of us and he was absorbed in something in his jacket pocket. I looked over at Carlotta on the other side of the truck. She was looking at me, but apparently had not noticed I was doing anything different. Her eyes were frightened but, bless her, not defeated. I tried to telegraph encouragement to her. I rolled to face the wall.

I waited for cover, for some noise to mask the beeping of the phone. I knew that when I punched the redial button, the series of beeps would be louder than the few beeps that sounded while the phone powered up. I had no idea how long it would be before we arrived wherever they were taking us, and I felt pressure to hurry up. At the same time, it would do no good if I hurried and was discovered.

My hands where they rubbed together were sticky and I could tell they were sweating. In the distance, I heard an angelic sound…a train whistle. If it would only come toward us, I thought, it would mask the phone sounds. I waited for the next blast. Thank God, it was louder. The third was louder still and I wondered fleetingly if we would stop at a train track or if the driver would try to race the train. As if in answer to my thoughts, I heard the engine rev into a higher rpm. Oh, good, we had a chance to get killed by a train and by a gang of thugs. This was my lucky day.

I punched the redial button, I hoped, before the next blast, trying to time it so that the blast would cover the dialing following my action. I timed it right. I felt the rumble of the train tracks as they passed under the truck at the same time a train blast sounded like it was directly on top of us. Then it was behind us, so loud that I couldn't tell if the phone had made its connection or not. All I could do was pray that I pressed the right button, that the phone made its connection, that Doug answered his phone, and that the sounds we made were enough to alert him to trouble and not just have him hang up on what he thought was an incomplete call. Lots of maybes, but all I had to go on.

To help Doug out, I began to holler through the gag and bang my feet on the truck wall. That got Harry's attention. He let go of his security strap and shuffled over to me. I flashed as much hate as possible through my eyes and lunged toward him, making as much noise as possible, hoping Doug would get the message.

"Hold it down, Miss Caller. You got nowhere to go and I'd say you weren't in any position to help yourself. You might even hurt yourself and then where would you be?" He seemed to have particularly amused himself with a good joke. He drew back his hand to hit me and I cringed as far as possible away from him and scrunched my eyes closed.

Suddenly I heard a whump and cursing. I opened my eyes. Apparently Carlotta had inched herself up behind Harry while he was crouched over me and swung her legs into his knees, bringing him down hard on his rear. While I appreciated her enthusiasm, Harry was right. We were in no position to overpower him, and antagonizing him would only give him reason to make it worse. Still, I had to smile at Harry's wrath over being attacked by a couple of women trussed up like calves in a corral. He scooted on his behind to the front of the truck and stood up, brushing off his clothes and regaining his composure.

"You think you're hot stuff, don't you ladies? Well, you haven't seen hot stuff yet. You'll get yours sooner than you think." The smile left my face. I thought of my daughter Heather, pictured her in her dorm room studying English from a vampire who'd sucked the life out of a language. It was a small thing, sending her that book, but she'd counted on me to do it. She counted on me to be there for her, to help her make pies and turkey and look like she was in control of her kitchen. I had to be there for her no matter what she needed, large or small. I couldn't fail her in that. I had to figure some way out of this.

Chapter 14

I noticed after we crossed the railroad tracks the time between curves became longer and the road noise changed into an even hum. Ignoring my claustrophobic brain block, I interpreted that to mean we had moved to highway driving. I wondered where were going. Carlotta and I had quieted down and Harry squatted against the front wall of the truck. I went into sort of a trance from exhaustion and, I suppose, fear.

Soon the sides of the truck were closing in on me. I had forgotten to breathe, and I was feeling a little dizzy. I jerked out of it when the truck slowed and made a sharp turn. I felt myself roll over on the phone and I thought I heard the clamshell snap closed. If so, the call was cut off, assuming there was a call to start with. There was nothing I could do about it now. The road immediately got rough, like it was unpaved. In a few minutes, we braked to a stop. The engine was still running when the back door slid up.

"Well, ladies, did you enjoy your ride?" Sarcasm was thick in The Leader's voice. "You'll pardon us while we confer, I'm sure. You didn't give us much time to make a plan back at the hotel. Harry, get out here."

As soon as they were gone, I scooted over to Carlotta. I was amazed how much we could communicate with the gags in place: You okay? Yes, you? Yes. What do we do now?

Good question. I wished I knew the answer. I'd watched enough detective stories on television to know we should try to untie each other. I nodded to her hands, made motions with my fingers, then brought my hands up to hers. She immediately understood and began working with the knots. She'd seen the same shows. I had no idea how long the gang would discuss our fate, but we had to try something. To my surprise, I felt the ropes around my wrists give slightly. I mmppppheed approval to Carlotta. The ropes came loose.

I immediately pulled the gag down over my chin, then went to work on Carlotta's wrists. She jerked them away.

"What?" I asked. "We've got to get out of here." She pulled away again, shaking her head and mmmmpppphing to beat the band. I pulled her gag out of the way.

"What the heck?" I asked.

"Leave me alone. It's better that one of us is completely free than both of us partly. Get your ropes off your feet first, then you can work on me if there's time. We don't know how long we have!"

She was right. I went to work on my own ropes, the slick sweat on my hands making it rough going. But I got them loose, thinking madly all the while what good it would do, how to take advantage of our freedom. When I was free, I went to work on Carlotta's ropes.

"Carlotta, we need a diversion. Can you fake a convulsion?"

"The best convulsion of my life. Why?"

"I'm gonna wrap my ropes back around my hands and legs like they're still tied and pull up my gag, although I'm gonna loosen it up a little. I nearly gagged for real when he tied it on. When the guys come back in, you go into a convulsion and I'll start making all the noise I can. My guess is that they'll come to me first if I'm making the most noise. If they let me talk, I'll tell them you have traumatic convulsions and need water. Of course, they probably won't care, but it will give them something to think about and divert their attention. If I get the chance, I'll run out the back, or through that window up there, and get into the cab of the truck. These things can't be that hard to drive, can they?"

"Sheesh, Darla, you think you can just hop into the driver's seat and take off? If you've never driven one of these things, you won't know the first thing about getting it going. Not to mention, I don't think 'the guys' will be happy to let you have the wheel."

"You got a better idea? I'm all ears."

"Well, no. I guess we can't duke it out, can we?" She didn't expect an answer to that one and I just grimaced.

"Okay, convulsion it is," she said. "We'll just have to play it by ear. Good luck. Been nice knowin' ya."

"No negativity, Carlotta. I'm gonna retie your ankles, but I'll make them as loose as I can and still look legit. I hope you can shuck out of them. Here, tuck the ends of the ropes around your wrists into your hands and hold them tight so they look like they're tied. Okay, anything else before I put your gag back?"

"No. Think we'll get out of this?" I put the gag in place.

"Sure we will. Think positive." She knew I was bluffing.

I rolled to the other side of the truck and lay facing into the center. I just had time to finish faking my own ropes when we heard footsteps coming around the side of the truck. Carlotta looked at me and I nodded. She went into her convulsion…it was a good one. So good I hoped she didn't injure herself. I went into my yelling and kicking routine. Number Two looked into the truck, took in the situation, and luckily come over to me first.

"Problems?" A mean smile played across his face.

"MMMMpphh!"

"I don't know what you two are playing at, but it's not working." Yes, it was. He was having to follow our script instead of his. A good start, at least.

"MMMMMMMphhh!"

"You think you got something to say?" He kept his oily smile in place, but he leaned down to pull the gag away from my mouth. I struggled like it was really tight. Carlotta continued her convulsion. We ought to get more than an academy award for this one. I spit and coughed.

"She has convulsions sometimes. Noise, lights, stress. We don't know why. Let me go hold her so she won't hurt herself, " I explained.

"She's tied up. She's got a gag in her mouth that will keep her from swallowing her tongue. So she bangs herself up a little. It won't hurt her," he sneered in response.

Carlotta played it just right. She slumped momentarily to the floor and Number Two looked over to her.

"See? She's finished with her little spell. Now we can get on with it." The sneer was gone and a look of distaste had replaced it. I worried how bad it was going to get if it was distasteful to this cold man. Carlotta started back up in earnest.

"Please? Let me get up? Do you have any water?" I pleaded.

The Leader walked up to the truck's open door. He took in the situation, immediately angry.

"Dammit. What the hell did you do? Get that gag back in place. I told you to check on them, not make friends with them! No talking, you idiot! We've got a job to do. Get out here," he barked.

Number Two's filthy fingers placed the gag back into place and the smile played around his lips again. His eyes were as empty as cateye marbles. "Back in a few, ma'am."

When they were gone, I took a couple of seconds to decide. Running out the door and around the truck to the driver's seat would be the easiest route, but longer and more likely to be exposed to our captors. On the other hand, the window might be locked, in which case I didn't have any choice. It was high enough and small enough I wasn't sure I could get through it. I sure didn't want to get my hips stuck in it just when the gang came back for us. I made the choice, unwound my ropes, and pulled down the gag again.

"See if you can get out of those ropes, Carlotta. I'm making a break for it."

I slipped the ropes off my ankles, then stood up. And immediately sat.

"Shit. No circulation." I rubbed my legs and tried again. Wobbly, but okay. I moved to the window. It slid open when I squeezed the latch. I peered through it and saw the bench seat of the truck cab. Man, those gears were huge. I shot a quick glance over my shoulder, didn't see anyone coming after me, and lunged. My head and shoulders made it through on the first attempt and I rocked back and forth on my ribcage. I squirmed enough to get my hips into place and panicked. They wouldn't fit. Yes, they will, I ordered myself. I kept squirming. The cell phone caught on the window frame and the elastic waist of my skirt gave. It slid down past my hips to my knees, giving me a little buffer between me and the metal frame. It tangled around my feet and I kicked it away. It felt like I was ripping the skin off my hips, but they finally made it through. My body throbbing with pain and exertion, I rolled onto the seat and righted myself behind the wheel. Carlotta snaked through the window like it was a waterslide.

"I thought you'd never get through, Darla. What was the problem?"

Given her tiny body, she really didn't know. There wasn't time to explain the laws of physics or space and time. The engine was running, so all I had to do was put it in the right gear and gun it. Was the brake on? Probably, but where was it? Shit.

I've driven standard transmissions most of my life and prefer them to automatic, so I knew the basic routine. I pushed in the clutch, surprised at the pressure it required. I had to sit forward on the edge of the seat to reach it. I pushed the gearshift into what I hoped was first gear. I looked around for the brake and located a likely candidate.

"Carlotta? This look like it?"

"Man, I don't know Darla. Give it a try."

I twisted the knob and air whooshed out of the airbrakes. No turning back now, they would have heard that sound and be on their way over here in no time.

"Carlotta! The doors! Figure out how to lock them!" I couldn't believe we'd forgotten them. Carlotta figured it out quickly and locked her door, then crawled behind me in the seat to reach mine and lock it. The truck rolled forward and the engine coughed, but didn't die. I jammed the gas pedal. I expected a spurt of speed, but got only a sluggish forward motion.

Out of the corner of my eye, I saw two faces at Carlotta's window. They were banging on the window and truck door. Only two. Where were the other two?

"Oh, shit! And the window. Does it have a lock?"

Carlotta scrambled up to the window behind us just as a face appeared in it. She slammed it shut, but couldn't find the lock. She held it closed.

"I can't find the lock, Darla! I've got it for now, but I don't think I can keep it closed. You think it's bulletproof?"

"I hope so. If this is really an armored truck instead of a regular truck faked up to look like one, it should be. Keep holding. I'm speeding up."

The road was gravel. Apparently we'd turned off down an entry road to an oil well. I could see the chainlink fence and equipment off to the side of us. I barreled ahead, hoping this was a field where they'd built a u-turn road rather than expecting the driver to turn the oil trucks when they came for service. I was in luck. The road had a turnout at the end, but in the midst of my joy I realized that if I took the road back, it was possible that The Leader would be waiting to ambush us. Not a problem if the truck really was bulletproof. Big problem if it wasn't. I could cut off across the pasture, but I didn't know where it would take me and I might get penned in. I still hadn't gained much speed, and I opted for the u-turn.

"Steady yourself, Carlotta. I'm going to take the u-turn fast so maybe I can shake off our passengers and give you a little relief at the window."

"Ready."

I pumped the gas pedal and made sure it was all the way to the floor, then heaved the wheel to the left. The faces disappeared from the side door and I heard a dreadful scream. I heard a thump in the rear of the truck but I didn't doubt he'd be back as soon as he gained his feet.

We made it to the straightaway and I let up on the steering wheel. By now the gas was reaching the motor and the truck was picking up speed. As I feared, The Leader was standing in the middle of the gravel road with his gun aimed directly at the windshield. I started weaving and bobbing my head side to side, but I held my hands steady on the wheel.

"You might want to get down behind the seat if there's any room there, Carlotta. Looks like we're going to find out if this is a bulletproof windshield."

"Remind me why we're here again, Darla?" Carlotta said as she finagled her way as far down behind the seat as she could without letting go of the window.

I saw The Leader's hands jerk as he fired and the bullet hit at the top of the windshield. Splinters of glass flew out, but the windshield held. Another bullet hit dead center in front of my face and more splinters flew. Instinctively I ducked, but again the glass stayed intact. I kept steady pressure on the gas and moved inexorably toward him. At the last minute, I saw him fling himself out of my headlights to the side of the path.

I had no idea what I would do when we reached the highway and prayed for little traffic. As if in response, I saw headlights ahead in the dark and knew we weren't far from the road. Which road, I had no idea. Any road looked good right now.

"Carlotta, you still got a parasite back there?"

"I don't know. There's no pressure on the window right now, but….yikes! Yes, he's still there!"

I saw the highway ahead and looked to see if I needed to slow for traffic. I decided not to. I was in an armored truck, after all, how bad could it be? Okay, it could turn over, I could injure or kill innocent people, it might...I jerked my mind to the task at hand.

"We're going onto the road at full speed, Carlotta. Brace yourself."

I wrenched the wheel to the right and the truck jumped up onto the pavement. Carlotta screamed and landed on the passenger door. I heard a thump in the rear of the truck and hit the brakes hard. Another reassuring thump. Carlotta hit the dash.

"Shit, Darla. Do you think you could avoid killing us while you're saving our lives?"

"Sorry, I'm doing my best."

"Yeah, sure." She picked herself up and climbed back to the window. I saw her zip the window open and closed again. "I couldn't see him. Either you lost him out the back or he's too far forward for me to see."

"Probably the latter. When I slammed the brakes, he should have slid forward, not back. I don't think I can get enough pickup in this thing to slide him out the back. Maybe he's disoriented or, better yet, out cold." I looked down at my lap. Pettipants, no skirt. "Carlotta, can you find my skirt? My phone's in the pocket. Call 911."

"Darla, I hate to break it to you, but your skirt's in the back with our parasite. I could ask him, but I don't think he'll make the call for us." It was an attempt at humor, and I was glad to hear her offer humor in spite of our situation. It spoke well of her attitude.

I had settled into the routine of the highway, but I hadn't shifted yet. The engine whined in complaint, and I couldn't get the speed up. I studied the gears again and made a choice. I ground the gearshift into place and the truck jumped. If I could just get it going fast enough, I could hope for a patrolman to stop us for speeding. I kept the pedal to the floor and jerked the wheel in random motions left and right. After a few minutes, Carlotta spoke up.

"Okay, I give up. What the hell are you doing? You think it's easy balancing and here holding this window closed not knowing what's on the other side? What's with the swerving?"

"I'm trying to attract attention. I figure if we can't make the call, maybe one of the other drivers will call for us if they think we're having engine trouble…or drunk. Again, I'm open to suggestion," I explained.

"No. Good idea. I'm just glad I'm in good shape or I'd never be able to keep at this," she answered.

Apparently something worked. I saw flashing red-and-blues coming from both directions, one in my windshield and one in my side rearviews. I drove until I saw the lights of a shopping center ahead and gratefully pulled into the parking lot. Even after I pulled to a stop, my hands were frozen on the wheel and I couldn't move them. In a fog, I saw uniforms surrounding the truck, some with guns drawn and held steady. I sat without moving as Carlotta continued to hold the window in place. I was shocked to feel tears running down my cheeks as the adrenaline seeped from my system.

Chapter 15

Somewhere amid the flashing lights, sirens, and shouts to get out of the cab with our hands up, the realization hit me that they didn't know we were the good guys. I tried to let go of the steering wheel, and couldn't. I saw with a shock I was missing my skirt, not exactly dressed to impress. Even in shock, I was thankful that I had decided to wear my pettipants under my long skirt. With all the confusion, my tears turned to uncontrollable shakes, and flashbacks to the night Clint was killed. Once again, I thought how it was ironic that I became a caller to get away from just this kind of excitement.

Carlotta was the first to find her voice. "I'm coming out, don't shoot!" she hollered. Then, "We need a little help here!"

One of the police officers climbed into the cab and wrapped a blanket around me, helped me down, and escorted me to a cruiser. I glanced over to look for Carlotta and they were taking her to a different cruiser, to question us separately, I supposed.

"Darla!" I heard my name and turned to see Doug and Sam and Nick being held at a distance. The officer kept hold of my arm and turned me toward the car. I bent my head in response to his firm hand so I wouldn't hit my head getting into the back of the cruiser. The door closed and I watched the action outside almost as if I was watching a movie. I could tell there were at least two different sets of law enforcement uniforms rushing around at the rear of the van, local and state, probably. A circle of officers seemed to be trying to figure out what to do next. Finally, I saw one signal another to go into the back of the truck. He must have given an "all clear" because there was a sudden rush of activity and the paramedics were running toward the open truck door.

"Ma'am." I jumped as an officer opened the door behind me and started talking. "We need to ask you some questions, but this paramedic is here to check and make sure you are not injured first." He withdrew and a woman in white pants and shirt slipped into the seat beside me. She started to check my pulse and yelled to her partner for sterile solution. I hadn't realized my face and wrists were bruised and covered with dried blood until she started washing them to see the damages.

When she swabbed my forehead, I jerked back with a painful reflex and she frowned at what she saw. By the time she worked her way down to check my legs, I realized my hose were in shreds and there were scrapes on my ankles. She finished her assessment and gave me reassuring words to let me know I was in one piece. She gave my hand a pat before she exited the cruiser, making sure the door closed securely.

As I looked out the window after her, I saw a stretcher with someone on it being carried from the back of the van. I strained to tell if he was completely covered, indicating he was dead, or if he showed signs of life. A figure stepped in front of the window and blocked my view. The door opened again, and there was good old Harbinville. Where had he come from? And where the heck was my skirt? I pulled the blanket over my lap.

"Ms. King? You're looking charming this evening." He smirked in the dim light. "I've explained to the local and state authorities that you are not a suspect, but they still need to talk to you and your friends. It shouldn't be too much longer."

"Paul, what are you doing here?" I asked somewhat annoyed that he was seeing me in this condition, though it really shouldn't matter.

"You have some very determined friends, Ms. King. You should thank them when you have a chance." He turned to go.

"Wait! Paul! What's happening?"

He hesitated, then just shrugged and closed the door, leaving me in silence again.

When I had a chance, he'd said. It appeared that would be awhile. Now that I was safely in the arms of the law, and not a suspect, I was getting my second wind. Good thing, too. It appeared no one was in a hurry to let me go.

Even though I was locked into a small space, which would normally drive me crazy, the patrol car had plenty of window area so it didn't feel too bad. I peered out the window, trying to follow the activity. I thought at first someone had pulled a second truck up between the squad car and the truck I'd driven. It took me a minute to realize I was looking at the same truck. Instead of glistening white metal, the sides and back of the truckbed were made of laced, rather worn canvas. Together with the mud splatters on the cab from the wild ride we'd taken on the gravel road, and the pockmarked windshield from bullets I remembered way too clearly, the canvas truckbed gave the impression of a shabby farm truck. It would have blended in well with any truck carrying feed, hay, or agricultural supplies.

I remembered the rolled canvas inside the truck. A synapse fired in my overloaded brain. So that was how they managed to blend in and not be spotted. The van had its own camouflage! I was so excited, I tried to open the door and jump out. I had to tell someone! Of course, that wasn't possible. The doors had no handles. I fidgeted in my makeshift prison, impatient to tell someone my revelation. Eventually, the driver's door opened and a policeman slid behind the wheel. I blurted out, "I have to talk to someone about that canvas! I know why they used it. I know what they did!"

"Yes, ma'am." His calm voice burst my balloon of importance. "You'll have plenty of time to tell them down at the station."

I saw a clock when we walked into the station. Five a.m. About five hours since we were spirited out of the hotel. Seemed like a lifetime ago. I was still huddled in the scratchy blanket the officer had wrapped around me and I pulled it into a sort of sarong as I followed the driver into a room at the back of the building.

"Want some coffee?" he asked as I settled into a battered wooden chair.

"Sounds like heaven," I answered. "Make it half milk."

He returned in a few minutes and set the coffee on the table in front of me without a word, nodded to me, and left, shutting the door. I could see through the large glass pane of the door, but my angle of vision kept me from seeing much. I raised the cup to my mouth and sipped the coffee and choked on it. I looked down. Globs of powdered whitener floated on coffee the color of tar. Here and there clouds of whitener dissolved into the tar, turning it a suspicious shade of gray. I tried again. This time it didn't taste so bad. I sipped periodically while I awaited my inquisition.

Three different officers questioned me. The second one brought my skirt with her, but offered no privacy for changing so I waited until she left to slip it on, happy to shed the harsh blanket, though I had to hold the skirt in place due to its busted elastic. I had no idea what time it was. After the third one left, I folded my arms on the table to form a pillow for my head. At first I dropped my head straight down onto them, but the pain in my forehead made me quickly reposition it. I ended up with my head turned sideways and my cheek resting on my arms. My eyes closed of their own volition and I drifted into uneasy blackness. I jerked awake at the sound of the door opening yet again.

"You're free to go, Ms. King. I'll take you to the debriefing room. Mr. Harbinville wants to talk to you before you leave."

Harbinville. No one had yet identified which federal agency he was associated with and he seemed to enjoy the "silent" and "mysterious" façade he was projecting. Although at some level, the mystery was exciting and sexy, I was beginning to get a little peeved with his lack of communication and his omnipresence. As the same time, I was beginning to see why feds might be in on this. Since I'd seen the canvas on the truck my mind had been churning, and I'd worked out a possible scenario. If I was right, it would attract attention at federal level, all right.

"Is it safe for Carlotta and me to leave, officer?" I asked. "Are we still targets for the men who kidnapped us?"

"Mr. Harbinville will tell you more, ma'am. I can tell you you're safe. That's one of the reasons we've held you so long. We wanted to bring in the other men before we let you go. We've got them all in custody now," he offered reassuringly.

I was a bit surprised, and curious, but I bit my tongue and followed the officer into the debriefing room. I expected to see Carlotta, but I was surprised to see a weary Doug, Nick, and Sam as well. My eyes slid to the clock on the wall. Eight thirty. Saturday morning, I certainly hoped, but at this point I wouldn't swear to it.

"None of you are suspects at this point," began Harbinville. "You are free to go. We have all four suspects in custody." Even though I already knew this tidbit, I could tell it was news to the rest. "However, I do ask that you not discuss the recent events with anyone. There are points of this case that require confidentiality. I want you to know that we are keeping what happened last night under wraps. We'd appreciate it if you would help with that. We expect that we may be able to wind this up, but not if there are any leaks. I'm sure you understand and will cooperate." He looked directly at me. "Do you each agree not to discuss anything regarding this case?" I nodded. I think I said yes. He stared at each face in the room in turn and each nodded or grunted assent. He surveyed the group.

"You would be wise not to interfere any further with this official investigation...or any other," he said gruffly.

"Now wait a cotton-pickin' minute. We didn't…" Sam jumped in, but quickly realized he wouldn't make a dent in Harbinville's attitude. Sam shrugged and turned toward the door, visibly controlling his temper. Doug stepped in.

"Is that all?" he asked.

"That's it," said Harbinville. "Just remember your agreement."

We filed out of the room silently, Sam and Nick in the lead. Carlotta and Doug waited for me and each one slipped an arm around my waist. I couldn't wait to get out of the place. By the time we got to the parking lot, Sam's sense of humor had returned.

"Well, Darla darlin'! You look like you have seen better days!" he teased.

"I'm tired, I'm hungry, I want to know all that you know, and somewhere in between I vaguely recall that I am supposed to be calling a square dance workshop today – in a few hours as a matter of fact," I replied expressing my exasperation with the whole mess.

"Not to worry, Darla darlin.' Doug has already called Tom, and the rest of the callers will cover for you during the day. But we told 'em to count on you for tonight. And as for food, I think we could all use something to eat. I am kinda disappointed they found your skirt and let ya have it back though," he chuckled.

"Yeah, yeah. I'm so tired I don't even have a comeback for you, Sam," was all I could come up with.

"Darla, are you really alright? I was so worried about you!" said Carlotta.

"Yeah, I'm ok, I guess. How are you doing Carlotta?" I asked.

"I am never gonna suggest we try to figure out a mystery again! I am hungry and tired, and…" she looked at the guys, "…I want to know how all the police and you guys found us!"

"Just hold your horses, Carlotta! Once we all get out of here, we'll find someplace to eat and debrief. No point in repeating ourselves." Sam chimed in.

"Yeah, let's get out of here!" pleaded Nick as he gave Carlotta a hug. "I need a change of setting and some food and some answers!"

"Y'all go ahead. I thought I was hungrier than I was tired, but it's not true. I'm tireder than I am hungry. If I don't sleep soon I'm going to pass out," I said.

"Darla, how can you? I'm wired to the max!" responded Carlotta. Her eyes sparkled and her small frame vibrated with energy. It made me feel even more tired to look at her.

"Just catch me up tomorrow. I'll take a cab back to the hotel." I said.

"Nothing doing, darlin.' You're not going back there by yourself, nevermind what that guy told us. We'll all just head back to the hotel," offered Sam. Carlotta and Nick shot him a look I couldn't miss.

"I won't let you do that, Sam. Really, I can take a cab. You guys go on ahead." I tried for a light tone to convince them. "I feel bad enough as it is; I don't want Carlotta keeping me up for hours while she winds down." My joke fell flat, but they did decide to go on to a nearby restaurant. Doug handed his keys to Sam and stayed behind to ride with me.

"I'm not fooled. You guys just want to be alone," ribbed Sam.

"Sam," I sighed, "I'm so exhausted I can't even remember what you mean by that." I had enough energy to give him a smile. When Doug and I went back into the station to call a cab, one of the patrol officers volunteered to run us to the hotel. Despite my exhaustion, I felt a quick shudder go through me when I had to get back into the back seat of a squad car.

Chapter 16

I suppose I still had my room key. Or else we got one from the front desk. I suppose we rode the elevator to the room. Or maybe we flew. I suppose Carlotta came in sometime later. But you couldn't prove any of it by me. It was early afternoon when the phone in our room started ringing, ringing way too loud in fact. I answered groggily.

"Hi Darla. Are you gals getting hungry at all? Nick just called, and Sam and I are getting dressed now. We're planning on meeting downstairs and grabbing lunch in about 30 minutes. Want to join us?" Doug asked.

"Hold on, Doug." I looked over at Carlotta, who already had apparently showered and seemed wide awake, and I shared Doug's comments and question.

"Sure, I could eat, and we could check out what's happening at the dance as well!" Her enthusiasm was sickening.

"Okay, Doug, we'll meet you down there in about 30." I hung up, crawled out of bed, and headed for the shower, my belly so empty it hurt. The shower stung my face and I checked it in the mirror when I got out. Ugh! The bump on my forehead had leaked down into my eyes and I had dark circles under both of them. I did the best I could to cover them with the makeup I had in my bag, but I was moving slow and it ended up taking me a little longer than 30 minutes to get ready.

I considered calling Heather to let her know I was okay, then realized there wasn't any reason she'd think I wasn't. As far as I knew, no one had called her. I wanted to hear her voice, but I didn't know what to tell her. I just hoped she didn't pick today to stop by the dance! I put off calling her, but I did take time to call my sister Julia. I wanted to hear her voice, too, and knew she'd manage to lighten my mood with her latest romantic antics. As usual, it didn't seem odd that I didn't' do any of the talking. By the time we finished our conversation, I was feeling better. Carlotta and I, dressed in jeans and casual tops, walked through the lobby and into the hotel restaurant.

"Carlotta, we're over here!" called out Nick with an affectionate smile for Carlotta. We sat down and ordered. I was surprised to see Tom come into the restaurant. He headed our way.

"You on break?" I asked.

"I'm not scheduled for this session," he answered. His forehead creased when he saw my face. "Darla, how are you doing? You sure you want to call tonight?" Tom asked in a concerned tone.

"Yeah, Tom, I'll be ok. Thanks for taking care of the daytime workshops for me."

"Not a problem. Your friend Paul called early this morning, even before Doug did, and said you'd been in some kind of accident. It's the least we could do. Is your car totaled?" he asked.

"My car? Uh, no. That is, I wasn't driving. I mean, I was driving, but not my car…" My voice trailed off. I was at a loss how to describe my "accident" without discussing what had actually happened. So that was the story Harbinville was putting out. Why a cover story, I wondered.

Tom laughed. "Okay, whatever you say. But you better cook up a better response than that because with that face you're gonna get a lot of questions! I gotta run." With that Tom walked away, while I sat there with my mouth open.

"Did he say 'Paul said'?" Doug whispered. "I guess the 'cover story' this time is an 'accident.' Interesting."

Other square dancers we knew were eating in the restaurant, and several came over to say hello. Even the ones who didn't ask about my appearance looked questioningly at my face. I managed to give vague, apparently acceptable, answers to any that asked.

"We can't talk here, there's too many ears," I said. "I assume Carlotta gave you guys a rundown on the evening. Doug, did you get the story?"

"Yes, Darla, I did. After I got you safely settled in your room, I knew you'd be out for the count. I was dying to know what happened, so I called Sam to check where they'd gone." He looked a little sheepish. "Of course, then I remembered my car was with them. I called a taxi to take me to the restaurant. Carlotta caught us up on your…part in the evening."

He looked around to make sure no one was close enough to hear him. "You had a really close call, Darla. I…we could have lost you...uh, you and Carlotta, both of you." His arm went around my shoulders protectively.

"Okay, then it's my turn," I said. "Come up to the room and give me the full story. How the heck did you guys show up at the scene so quick?"

We paid our tab and went up to the room. When we got there, the story unfolded. It turned out my call to Doug had its intended outcome. Doug had gotten the call from my cell phone and realized I was in some sort of trouble. He and Nick had actually gone down to the bar to meet us. Apparently our messages never got past their respective roommates. The call came while they were waiting for us to show. When he realized what was happening, Doug told Nick to call the police. Doug kept his phone glued to his ear while he ran up to our hotel room and banged on the door to my room, where he assumed I was in danger. By the time Nick caught up with him and there was still no answer at my door, Nick called the police again and asked them to trace the call.

"I didn't know you could trace cell calls," I said. "I was just hoping you'd realize I was in trouble and call out the cavalry. I'm not sure what I thought you could do, I just couldn't think of anything else to try."

"You can, but not easily," broke in Nick. "Not to mention that the police took forever to take me seriously and start the trace. You did a good job of keeping the line open long enough for them to get a general idea of the direction it was coming from. But then the call cut off and they were ready to quit. They didn't believe there was a real danger."

"We called the state police, county sheriff, and everyone we could think of, but all we got were stonewalls and delays," added Doug.

"That's when they roused me," put in Sam. "They figured three heads were better'n two, I reckon. I told 'em we oughta just get in the car and head out, so that's what we did. Lord knows how I thought we were gonna find you, but you know me. I'm one for taking some kind of action even if it turns out it's pointless."

"There's nothing pointless about you, Sam," I assured him. "You always come through."

Nick picked up the story. "Before we left though, Doug thought of calling Harbinville."

"I still don't know how he fits into the picture," said Doug. "But he seems to be everywhere we are and know more about this thing than anyone. I called Sheriff Lorys in Clearton. Woke up him and his wife and told him what was going on. Asked him to call Harbinville. To his credit, he didn't hesitate. Called him as soon as I hung up, I guess, because Harbinville called me back within five minutes."

Doug tilted his chin down and looked over at me from underneath raised eyebrows. "When I told him you were in trouble, it's the first time I've heard him get excited," he said. "He took what little information I could give him, then put the wheels in motion. Is there something going on between you and him?" I made a face in response.

"So anyway, we took off outa here." Sam jumped in for his share of the attention. "We started driving in patterns around the area. We did that for some time, getting more and more frustrated, I can tell you. When the sirens and all the cruisers headed one direction, they pinpointed your location for us. That's how we found you. We just followed a police escort!"

They had watched as the state and local forces surrounded the van, and as we got out and were taken to separate cruisers. They all agreed that Harbinville just appeared miraculously out of nowhere at about the same time, but he hadn't talked to them at all. They had watched the stretcher carried out of the back of the truck. Apparently, all my swerving and crazy driving had been a little more than our parasite could handle.

"Well, thank the Lord it's over, is all I can say. I guess I owe Harbinville a thank you," I said.

"You don't owe that starched suit a damn thing. If he'd been more forthcoming about this whole deal, you and Carlotta probably never would have had to go through this ordeal. Thank him! I think you ought to sue him!" I couldn't figure out why Doug was so upset about Harbinville. After all, he had apparently saved my life. I was a tad grateful, but I let the subject drop.

"So now can we get back to life as normal?" asked Carlotta. "Forget the mysteries, robberies, and PI work and just dance?"

"Well, I might keep on with the survey about the club outfits," said Nick. "I'm kind of enjoying finding out the history. I might just write that article we've been talking about."

"No doubt about it. I'm bowing out of the PI business," I said. "In fact, right now I'm bowing out, period. If I'm gonna be calling tonight, I'll need more energy than I've got right now. You guys gotta take off. I'm gonna catch another 40 Zs. Carlotta, would you be sure I'm up by 6 so I'll have plenty of time to make the dance by 7:30? You know, the show must go on!"

"Sure thing. I think I'll take a quick snooze too. My unflagging energy is flagging on me," she answered with a yawn.

After a way-too-short nap, Carlotta shook me awake. We got dressed in our square dance duds and went down to meet the men. The day had been filled and there wasn't time for dinner so we walked on in to the ballroom. Compared to the previous night, it was pretty uneventful. But then, compared to the previous night, a Cajun Mardi Gras would have been uneventful.

For the Saturday night dance everyone had been encouraged to wear their club colors, and I caught myself scanning the room for men dressed in soft hues or khaki-colored clothes a couple of times. I had to remind myself that the criminals were safely locked up. I was calling with Tom again, and he realized at about 9:00 that I was fading fast. He told me to just sit tight and look pretty. I could definitely do the former, but I wasn't too sure about the latter. But I did know there was one more call I wanted to do.

"Thanks, Tom, I'll take you up on that right after my next tip. There's a new singing call I've been working on lately, and I just think I want to sing it after all that's gone on. I'll do this one and then the rest are yours, okay?" I took the mic for my turn and faced the dancers. "This is a new one for me, folks, so be patient. But it's one I hope will become one of your favorites, as it is mine. It's called 'Love Will Find Its Way to You.' And here we go!

I mixed the calls in with the lyrics, repeating the chorus. It went surprisingly well, especially given it was a debut call and I was fading. I don't remember much after that. I know I ate some of the refreshments and drank coffee, and finally made it to our room and to sleep.

Sunday morning, and we were closing out the Winter Solstice. It had been pretty successful, other than our Friday night escapade. We had apparently succeeded in keeping that from the rest of the attendees. The event had collected lots of gifts and donations for the less fortunate, in addition to providing lots of fun and friendship for those in attendance, present company excepted.

Thinking of these things helped to warm my heart as we finished the morning dance. I was still looking pretty rough, but most people evidently thought it kinder or more polite not to mention it. After we said our goodbyes, our somewhat weathered group went up to the rooms to pack and head out from the eventful weekend. I thought about calling Heather, and stopping by, but decided that probably wouldn't be a good idea given my bruised face.

In the room, I flipped on the TV for background noise while we packed. The news broadcast caught my attention when I heard the name Harbinville. "…sources indicate that the gang is believed to be responsible for multiple heists and burglaries in Texas and possibly other states. The man believed to be the mastermind of the operation, Sal Cochinski, was apprehended by federal agents at the docks in Galveston late last night. The three others were apparently taken into custody on Friday night just outside Austin. Agent Harbinville and other officials stated that they had been investigating multiple unsolved crimes and their investigations had led them to the men, who were responsible for breaking into the Natural History Museum and stealing multiple, priceless artifacts and books. The investigation eventually led to Galveston and to Cochinski, who was apparently set to receive the stolen goods. In other late breaking news...."

Carlotta was shouting at me, "Did you see that? They caught someone else! You mean those guys got loose and were out the whole time we were dancing last night? Do you think we will have to testify? Who's Sal Cochinski?"

Brrrrinnnng. I picked up the phone and before I could even say hello, Doug was asking the same questions.

"Yes," I said. "We were just watching the news here too. I have no idea what happened. We'll just have to stay up with the news for a few days."

"That's incredible! I heard about the theft at the Natural History Museum, but I didn't think it was part of our little mess."

"Me either. Doug, I've got to go. We have to check out before noon and we're not finished packing yet. We'll meet you in the lobby and say goodbye. Maybe we've heard the last of this little escapade this time. I just hope all the excitement will die down and we can have a little time to relax. Talk to you later."

Even before I hung up, I saw Carlotta staring at me open-mouthed. When the handset hit the cradle, she exploded.

"What do you mean die down? What do you mean 'stay up with the news for a few days'? We're entitled to the inside track. We're not just anybody, you know. We're the reason Paul-the-Snob Harbinville captured that gang in the first place. And, you'll notice, he didn't bother to act like it was any big deal. A kingpin who was receiving stolen goods at the Galveston docks sounds like a very big deal to me. You gotta call Harbinville and weasel the whole story out of him."

"I doubt there's any chance of that, Carlotta. I don't think anybody weasels anything out of Paul Harbinville."

"You could. Didn't you notice he's sweet on you? Why do you think Doug's been on his case? You could get the story if you wanted to." I'd swear Carlotta was sulking.

I took a few minutes to call Heather. Coming in to the dance, I had hoped she would stop by and now, as I looked at myself, I was really glad she hadn't. I didn't catch her at her apartment, but I left a reassuring message that everything was fine. I still didn't have any idea if she had a reason to think it wouldn't be, but after the news broadcast I thought there was a chance. And I had to admit, I wanted to talk to her for my own peace of mind more than hers. After my near-death experience, I was feeling the need to hold my baby in my arms. I just better not let her hear me thinking of her as "my baby." She'd flip out on that one.

Carlotta rode with me part of the way home. She worked on me the whole way. By the time I handed her off to the guys in Lincoln, she had talked me into meeting with Harbinville. I had to contact Sheriff Lorys and spin him a yarn. He still wouldn't give me Harbinville's number, but he took mine along with a request that he call me.

Chapter 17

"I was flattered to get your call," Paul commented.

I sat with Paul Harbinville in a small Italian restaurant in Houston. He had returned my message pretty quickly, and we had set a date for dinner the same week. Unfortunately, this 'date' didn't hold any of the promise that a real date with a hunk like him should generate. It just seemed so deceptive. I couldn't look him in the eyes so I looked down at my plate instead, nervously smoothing the tablecloth on both sides of it. He reached across the table and took my hands, his fingers closing around them so his fingers pressed my palms. I went rigid and jerked my eyes to his face.

"Look, Paul…"

"Don't worry, Darla. I know you didn't invite me out to dinner because you're interested in me." He smirked at me again and I realized that his smirk might simply be the way his face looked when he smiled. As far as I knew, he hadn't had much practice smiling, so maybe his face just didn't know how to do it.

"But I was so pleased to get an invitation from an attractive, interesting woman such as yourself that I was willing to accept on whatever grounds you had in mind. I can guess what they are," he continued.

He let go of my hands and I slipped them into my lap out of reach. I took a breath, sighed, and squared my shoulders. Despite the circumstances, I could see he actually did have some charm to go with his good looks.

"As long as we're being honest, then, Paul, I'll come clean. I did ask you to dinner to pump information from you. How in the heck did you foil a heist that shouldn't even have taken place?" I just about hissed across the table, trying not to yell.

An eyebrow shot up at my melodramatic choice of words. "A 'heist'?"

I held my ground. He shrugged.

"Okay, a heist. Well, you know I can't give you details. I'll just say that we convinced the gentlemen in our custody to move forward with their planned activities, to not deviate from the original plan, and to include us in the plan," he explained with another shrug.

"You wired them?" I asked.

He hesitated, then shrugged again. "Between the gentlemen themselves and their vehicle, you could say we had a significant investment in electronic monitoring equipment. I've been involved in this case for quite a while, and I knew this was a chance to advance it."

For a moment he almost lost his egotistical veneer. "Although I know there's always a bigger fish out there than the one you catch. We're nowhere near the top of the food chain," he added with some sense of frustration.

"But then again, Sal Cochinski is no minnow. You better thank that man of yours for having the sense to bring me into it," he said. Yup, the egotistical veneer was back, solidly in place.

This time it really was a sincere smile as he continued, though. "Although evidently I was backup insurance. You managed to alert the law enforcement community quite well all on your own. You had six patrol cars on you before we pulled you into that parking lot. It was how we finally located you." He shook his head and chuckled. I was obviously not the only one missing a few pieces of the information on our rescue.

"Who are the men who kidnapped me?" I asked.

"The men we caught that night – and I include you in that 'we' Miss PI – were the worker bees. Cochinski assigned them the targets and worked out the plan. They'd follow through and then meet him with the merchandise afterward," he explained.

"To do what with it? It's seldom that a fence can handle such diverse types of items, not to mention one-of-a-kind collector's items that come from museums and collections," I offered.

"Be careful, your background is showing. Aren't you a square dance caller these days?" After another chuckle, and a sip of his coffee, he added, "He's not a fence in the common definition of the word. We're still investigating, but we think he loaded special items on a boat and took them overseas to countries that make a market in American goods and especially American relics," he replied.

"Where would that be these days? America isn't the worldwide icon it used to be," I noted.

"True," he agreed. "But you'd be surprised at the wealthy individuals who want to boast of unique American possessions."

"So, how did square dancing ever enter the picture?" I asked, curious how that had gotten Doug, Nick, and the rest of us involved in the first place.

"According to our interviews with one of the men who kidnapped you, they encountered a square dance convention on one of their first jobs. They noticed how easily everyone came and went at the hotel, how accepted they were by the staff, and how easy it was to blend into the crowd if you wore the right clothes. So they suggested to Cochinski that it might be a good cover. They tried it a couple of times and it went so smoothly that he regularly chose targets in towns with square dances scheduled. It gave the workers a reason to be in town in case they were questioned about the crimes – which they hadn't been until we captured them," he explained. He continued, "You square dancers advertise your events well in advance, so it was easy enough for them to check a 'community calendar' and go from there."

"So I helped you make a breakthrough" I gloated.

"You helped, yes. We already had most of the information in hand, but you did connect some of the dots. At first you were an annoyance," he stated with some disdain. "Then I began to admire your determination and inventiveness. After the other night, I certainly respect your composure and resourcefulness under pressure." He was having a hell of a time being gracious about my help.

"So you'll remember that if I need a favor from you," I asked with a smile, not sure what kind of favor I might come up with.

"Are you expecting to need a favor from me?" he asked, raising his eyebrow ever so slightly again.

"Not a chance. I'm giving up the PI business. But it never hurts to have an ace in the hole," I replied.

"You are welcome to contact me anytime, Darla. But I'd rather it be personal than professional" he answered. His voice held soft, warm tones that surprised me but got his underlying message across. He reached across and took my hand again, slipping a business card into it. I didn't look at it.

I didn't say anything. I don't think he expected me to. I certainly was having enough trouble progressing on the relationship with Doug, nevermind starting up with someone like Harbinville. He had sex appeal, granted, and his hand was warm on mine, but his cool detachment would be more of a challenge than I could handle for now. Plus, his involvement in law enforcement at whatever level was too reminiscent of Clint.

"Now, what shall we have to eat?" he asked, changing the subject as I put my hand back in my lap.

"That's it? That's all you're going to tell me about the case?" I asked, sounding like a petulant child even to myself.

"The rest of it is just details, Darla. I think you're creative enough to fill them in yourself. Now, shall I order for you or would you prefer to order yourself?"

#####

When I got home after my dinner with Paul, I put off calling Doug or the rest of the crew. I felt guilty keeping my new knowledge to myself, but I couldn't quite face the ribbing I'd take for getting it the way I did. I don't know why I let Carlotta talk me into the idea of a date with Paul. But then I hadn't seemed to need too much persuading. Before the dinner, I had convinced myself that I was going only as an operative to gather information. But I have to admit that after

I got there I'd enjoyed myself a little more than I thought I would. Paul's shell didn't exactly crumble, but I think I saw a crack here and there.

So instead of facing a grilling by the Clearton Caper Squad, I called Heather. I actually talked to the real person, not her voicemail, and I made arrangements to visit her the next morning. So now I was on my way to meet up with her, and I still hadn't called Carlotta or Doug or Sam or Nick. .

I was familiar with the route to Austin, and I rounded a bend in the road to see the roadside café that served as my halfway landmark. When I started driving back and forth to Austin a little over a year ago to visit Heather, it had been a small building with only a couple of rooms. Every time I'd driven by, there were cars in the gravel parking lot. It was apparently doing quite a business, and every time I passed by now there was something new to see.

I enjoyed watching it prosper. Today, framing was going up on the side of the original building, signaling an expanded serving area. Despite the construction, there were plenty of cars in the parking lot and it was clear they were conducting business as usual. Either the food or the service, or both, must be pretty good and I made a mental note to allow time to stop there and eat on one of my trips over to see Heather. Not today though. Today I just wanted to see my little girl.

As I moved on down the highway, I wished them well, appreciating the many ways that people make their livings and support each other. Then I took a deep breath and began sorting through the things I needed to do and what order I ought to do them. I really had to call Carlotta. She'd been the one to talk me into grilling Paul and I owed her some kind of report. I glanced at the dashboard clock. It was 10:30 on a Tuesday morning. Perfect. Carlotta would be at work and I could safely call her home phone and leave a message without facing questions. I reached into the console and disconnected my phone from its umbilical charger line and, as I held it in my hand, I realized I probably owed my life to that little piece of technology.

I punched in the series of buttons that took me to my stored numbers and found Carlotta's home number. As I listened to it ring, I prepared my message in my head. I waited for the familiar click that signaled her answering machine had picked up.

"Hello?" Oops. My mind shifted into a different gear. Not an answering machine.

"Carlotta? It's Darla. What are you doing home? You okay?" I asked.

"Hey, Darla. Yeah, I'm okay," she said. But she sounded frazzled.

"What's up, Carlotta?" I asked. "I expected your machine. What are you doing home this morning?"

"Well, I'm okay but my washing machine has seen better days. It refused to drain this weekend, and then yesterday when I got home it had decided to drain – all over my kitchen floor! So I have a repairman out this morning figuring out whether it's worth saving. Hold on a minute, will ya?" I heard her voice far away from the phone answering a question, then she said, "So what were you going to tell my answering machine?"

"Nothing much. Just going to let you know I met with…" was as far as I got.

"Hold it, Darla," she interrupted. I heard a few disjointed comments about water and some choice words emphasizing that yes, she knew how to work the machine, then she was back.

"Sorry, Darla. He thinks I'm an idiot." She raised her voice ever so slightly before adding for the repairman's benefit, "and I'm sure he is!" There was a pause, then she started in a normal tone of voice again, "So you met with Paul and…?" she prompted.

"And I'll tell you all about it in greater detail tonight at the square dance. I was just going to leave you a message letting you know…."

"Hold it, Darla," she said again. I could tell she was getting more irritated with the repairman, and this time I heard her end of the conversation clearly. So did the repairman, I imagine.

"Sorry, Darla, I gotta go. My floor just flooded again. I'm gonna have the cleanest floor in the county after I – make that we – mop it up again. Call me later and give me the scoop. Bye." She was already talking to the repairman before she hung up the phone. I pitied the man, but knew she'd manage to get his best work in the end and probably with a new friend in the bargain if I knew Carlotta.

With a reprieve of sorts, I reconnected the phone's charger and dropped it into the console. The gray December clouds weren't providing any warmth and my feet were getting chilly, so I fiddled with the heater and directed its fan to the floor. The last half of the trip went smoothly, and I walked up to Heather's apartment door about noon. I knocked and the door flew inward before I had time to drop my hand. She had worry lines between her eyes.

"Mom! Are you okay? I've been getting more worried about you ever since you called. Is everything all right? I know something must be wrong. I was already planning to come home for Christmas break in a few days and you would have seen me then. You didn't need to drive over here unless you have bad news. What's wrong?" she fired at me in rapid succession.

"Whoa, honey, calm down. Everything's okay, really." Her anxiety level surprised me. She certainly hadn't sounded worried when I talked to her last night about driving over to see her today. I had been so proud of myself for sounding unconcerned when I called, and just saying I thought I'd come over to get a load of anything she wanted to bring home for the holidays. She'd sounded surprised at the time, but not worried. I gave her a long hug and reassured her.

"I didn't mean to worry you, Heather," I said. "I just wanted to see you, okay? How are finals going?" I could tell she wasn't completely convinced. I needed to get better acting skills.

"Fine." Her voice was tentative as she continued, "but you didn't need to come over. I told you I'm just bringing a couple of suitcases home for Christmas. There's nothing you need to pick up."

She was still sounding a little too concerned about my being here, and I began to think it wasn't over my health. I smiled, put my hands on her shoulders, and stood at arm's length looking directly into her eyes. "Some reason you don't want me to be here?" I asked. I could tell by her expression I'd hit the nail on the head.

"Well no, of course not, Mom. I just didn't want you to go to any unnecessary trouble…"

Her voice trailed off and her eyes looked toward her feet, a sure sign that she was evading the truth. I wanted to know what was going on with her but, on the other hand, I didn't. Should I push her on it or not? I decided not. I opted for my ignorance and her reassurance. Sometimes the mom in me just doesn't want to know.

"Honey, it's never any trouble to come see you. You're my favorite daughter, didn't you know?" I said.

She smiled at our long-standing joke and I saw her relax a little. The door was still standing open, and I reached behind her to push it closed. I linked my elbow through hers and turned us toward the kitchen.

"Now," I said, "let's fix a cup of Earl Grey tea and sit down. I've got a little story to tell you."

#####

I made it home with plenty of time to take a nap and head into Clearton. I didn't need to pump my favorite waitress for information, but I decided to stop for a cup of coffee on the way. I think I was just avoiding facing Doug once he found about my dinner with Harbinville. I walked into the café and Sadie waved. I took a seat and she came over, ready with coffee and my order for anything else.

"Howdy! Haven't seen you around in a coupla weeks. Did the square dancers stop dancing or something?" she asked with a smile.

"No, Sadie, nothing like that. Just been a little busy, and didn't have time before the dances for a few weeks there. I missed your coffee though!" I answered and saluted her with my coffee cup. "Anything exciting happening around here?" I asked, really just to make conversation.

"Well, now, the board met last night, and there will be excitement for sure. They approved that camp Doug Weathers was working with. Even Mr. Butard over there," she said as she pointed to a man across the way," voted for the camp. Seems like everyone's happy now." She looked over again to the older, somewhat scruffy looking man, and he tipped his hat and smiled.

"Sadie, that's wonderful! I hadn't heard. Thanks for letting me know. I'll be seeing Doug when I leave here and I'll be sure to congratulate him!" I was smiling and very excited for Doug. I finished my coffee and smiled all the way to the square dance.

As soon as I saw Doug, I ran up to him. Excitement showed in his eyes. He gave me a hug and then kept talking to some of the other square dancers about the plans and the approval from the night before. Before long, it was time for me to break up the discussion, and give the usual, "Square 'em up folks!" It was the graduation dance for new dancers, so I reviewed all the basic and mainstream calls to put them through their paces before I sent them off with no training wheels. At some point, Carlotta and Nick came in, and joined a square. Then midway through the scheduled dance, the club had a 'graduation' ceremony to officially welcome the new dancers to the club.

During the longer than usual break after graduation, Carlotta got Nick, Sam, and Doug, and came over to talk to me. I was going to wait until after the dance to tell Doug about my dinner with Harbinville, but Carlotta piped up.

"So, Doug, what do you think about our sleuthing now?" she asked Doug.

"What do you mean? Did you find out something?" he asked.

Carlotta looked at me. "You haven't told him yet?" she asked.

"Yes, I found out a few of the details," I said. "I can tell you about them after the dance."

Nick and Sam said they couldn't wait to find out, but Doug wasn't a happy camper. I felt bad to have spoiled his good mood and excitement over the camp.

"How did you find out?" he asked.

"I asked Paul Harbinville. I met with him to ask him about everything," I said.

"You did what? Where did you see him?" he asked.

"Oh, give it up, Darla!" Carlotta said to me. She turned to Doug and continued, "She took him to dinner and pumped him for info. And she got it."

"What? You invited Harbinville out to dinner? What on earth possessed you to do that?" he spouted, seeming a bit jealous to me.

"Give it a rest, Doug," laughed Carlotta. "I talked her into it. How else were we going to get the inside scoop?"

"I could have researched it. I don't want any of us to be in his debt," Doug argued.

"We're not in his debt," I bristled. "In fact, he said he owed us a favor. Now, do you want to hear the details or not?" Although mild jealousy might be flattering, his attitude seemed a little over the top.

"Well, if you've already done it, you might as well share what came out," he conceded.

I quickly filled them in with as much information as Harbinville had seen fit to divulge. Everyone but Doug listened avidly, and eventually even he was drawn in and gave up his disgruntled attitude. I answered as many questions as I had time for and then went to the front of the room to call the last tip for the night. After the final tip, as I often do following a graduation, I ended by having everyone form a circle, alternating men and women, much as I do when we start the lessons. It was no surprise when I called a Grand Right and Left Grand.

After the thank you's, I packed everything up, and the gang came by and chatted some more about our great adventure. Doug seemed to be his usual relaxed self, and he helped with the process. I again congratulated him on the camp, and he indicated he would be pretty busy getting that going in the next few months. Doug and I lingered behind at our cars when the others left the parking lot.

"With all this behind us, and the holidays coming up fast and furious, can we find some time for just the two of us? I'm beginning to feel like we don't know each other anymore. I miss you, Darla" he said. "This incident really made it clear to me how much I care about you."

"Sounds good to me. What did you have in mind?" I asked.

His response was to take me in his arms, his firm hands massaging my back while his tongue worked my mouth. I felt myself melting into him and responding for a change.

"That's what I have in mind, at least for a start. I'll give it some thought and see what else I can come up with. I promise we'll talk more about it soon. For now, just say it'll happen," he promised as he broke off the embrace, a little breathy and heavy lidded.

"One way or the other. I'm sorry we haven't had any time together, too. Good night, Doug," I answered softly, licking my lips.

"'Night, Darla, drive careful," was his parting comment. His goodnight kiss promised me that we would indeed find some time to spend together. My reaction to the kiss told me it better be soon. The kiss stayed with me as I drove home and I had no trouble thinking of the various ways and places we could get together.

Little did I know as we drove off in our separate directions that before too long our square of friends would be relaxing on board a cruise ship. Well, I would be working, not relaxing, but we would be ringing in a New Year of excitement!

www.ingramcontent.com/pod-product-compliance
Lightning Source LLC
LaVergne TN
LVHW020711110826
845149LV00012B/2207

9780985012922